Praise for *The Baseball Widow*

"Kamata's prose is direct and elegant ... three characters navigate love, baseball, and the cultural space between the United States and Japan ... sections are particularly engrossing, as they explore the everyday life of an immigrant in Japan with a Japanese family and the experience of raising a disabled child with little help from an absent spouse ... depiction of the world of Japanese baseball will be fun for those who are unfamiliar."

—*Kirkus Reviews*

"In *The Baseball Widow*, Suzanne Kamata deftly offers both an insider's and an outsider's view of Japan. Through a diverse group of characters brought together by Japan's passion for baseball, she explores identity, the loss of idealism, and the ragged beauties to be found in that loss."

—**Annabel Lyon**, Author of *Consent*

"Suzanne Kamata's *The Baseball Widow* embeds her readers in the thorny lives of Japanese high-school baseball coaches and bicultural families with even-handed compassion and insight. Kamata is a dazzling, deeply empathetic writer."

—**Kevin Chong**, Author of *The Plague*
and *My Year of the Racehorse*

"Suzanne Kamata has penned yet another compelling page-turner about life and love in Japan, telling it like it is, with details and background I can vouch for as a fellow ex-pat."

—**Wendy Jones Nakanishi**, a.k.a. Lea O'Harra,
Author of *Lady First (An Inspector Inoue Mystery)*

THE
BASEBALL
WIDOW

THE BASEBALL WIDOW

a novel

SUZANNE KAMATA

Wyatt-MacKenzie Publishing
DEADWOOD, OREGON

The Baseball Widow

Suzanne Kamata

ISBN: 978-1-954332-07-2
Library of Congress Control Number: 2021944483

Watercolor Artwork © Giorgio Gosti.

Epigraph 1, Lemmon, Amy. "Saint Nobody." Saint Nobody. Red Hen Press, 2009.
Reprinted with permission of the publisher.

Wyatt-MacKenzie Publishing
DEADWOOD, OREGON

Wyatt-MacKenzie Publishing, Inc.
Deadwood, Oregon
www.WyattMacKenzie.com

This book is dedicated to the members of AFWJ.

"Lately the pain is sharpest where my wings would be."

AMY LEMMON
"Saint Nobody"

under a faraway sky
the people of America
began baseball
I can watch it
forever

—Masaoka Shiki (1867-1902)

PART ONE

Late July, 2005

When she comes to, she finds herself on the floor, her cheek pressed to hardwood. Through eyes slit barely open, she sees light all around, as if she has been sleeping in a bed of diamonds. There is so much sparkle, so much shine, that she wonders for a second if she is among stars. Or maybe she is dead? In heaven? But when she tries to move her arm, her entire body answers with the kind of immense pain only the living can feel. Something is not right. Something is broken. Her nostrils fill with the coppery scent of blood. The smell of shrimp. She listens. A clock is ticking loudly. She can hear a swooshing sound, the low murmur of a TV. She is listening for something else. *My children! Where are my children?*

1990
CHRISTINE

At one time, Christine had believed herself to be a good person. She had gone to Thailand to help Cambodian refugees, leaving Hideki behind. *This will be a test,* she'd told herself as she boarded the Thai Airways jet. She glanced back, hoping, ridiculously, that Hideki might be running after her, that he might beg her to stay. But no. He'd promised to write, and then he turned away. In his place, there was only a steady stream of Japanese businessmen, and young families gearing up for a holiday in Phuket or wherever. She found her window seat, unloaded her backpack and stuffed it in the overhead bin. She buckled up, overcome by a sudden weariness.

I am going to do something important, she reminded herself. In Japan, where she had lived for the past two years, no one had needed her. She'd been like a doll on display. A talking doll. An amusing diversion between the business of grammar and spelling. None of the students at the high schools where she'd taught had truly wanted or needed to learn to speak English. Why should they? Japan, as everyone knew, was set to take over the world. Those girls, with their Chanel watches and Louis Vuitton bags, those boys who shaved their eyebrows and grew out their fingernails, only cared about appearances. Christine had tried to interest them in the AIDS crisis and poverty and the devastation of wars in nearby countries, but their eyes had glazed over; sometimes, they'd even fallen asleep. At the end of her tenure, Christine had begun to dislike them a little for their lack of concern, for the pampered lives they assumed to be their birthright.

Once, hoping to inspire them, she'd brought a newspaper photo of a starving child. One girl—an impossibly thin girl herself—had turned to her friends and said, "*Ii, na.* If I was like that, I wouldn't ever have to diet." As if that wasn't bad enough, the head teacher had admonished Christine after class. "It's better to talk about fun things," she'd said. "It's against the rules to be political." As if talking about the problems of the world was political. Christine had read somewhere that Japan had the highest rate of anorexia nervosa in the world. It was as if, in peaceful, prosperous Japan, there weren't enough problems, so they had to be created.

Of course, things were much more complicated. At the night school, where Hideki taught, the students were underprivileged and disenfranchised: children of sex workers, destitute single mothers, prisoners. Maybe she could have had an impact in a posting like that, but the Board of Education would never have assigned her to the night school.

At the Cambodian refugee camp where Christine had volunteered to work for six months, everything would be different. Her days would be filled with purpose. She fantasized about starving brown children plumping before her eyes, their mouths filling with protein bars and English, their futures as doctors and lawyers and teachers, the thank you notes she would get years later. In the meantime, she was heartsick, already composing in her head the first letter she would write to her lover.

She brooded until the plane took off, then shook off her gloom. If she and Hideki had something precious and true between them, it would last. If not, he would go along with the arranged meetings that his mother was trying to pressure him into and find a suitable bride. Christine imagined someone bland and kind. And she, well, maybe she would never marry at all. She'd keep going around the world, to India and then on to Africa, and then maybe to some war-torn Eastern European country like Bosnia. At some point, she might adopt an orphan.

When food service came around, she ate a plate of noodles

in peanut sauce, and then braced herself for the landing. There was supposed to be someone waiting for her at the gate. Another volunteer named Sven. He would help her get to the refugee camp. She'd heard there were close to 150,000 refugees.

From the cool of the plane, she could see the heat waves rising from the tarmac. Japan had been steamy, but the weather in this place looked brutal. She quickly slathered sunscreen on her face and arms then grabbed her backpack and deplaned.

There he was, that scrawny blond guy holding a sign with her name written on it in bold black strokes. Sven. She waved and caught his eye. He grinned. "Welcome to Thailand." They shook hands. His fingers were moist.

"Got a lot of stuff?"

"No, just this." She'd sent a crate of clothes and souvenirs back to the States the week before. She was ready to live like a monk.

The jeep bumped through the jungle, throwing up dirt behind. They passed a man leading a water buffalo; there were palm trees, rice paddies. Christine saw some children playing by the side of the road. They were dressed in mismatched T-shirts and shorts, probably from some missionary grab bag. One little girl waved a stump as they went past, her good hand hanging at her side.

Sven caught her eye. "Landmines," he said. "You'd better get used to it. You'll see people like that everywhere."

She nodded and tried to compose herself. She thought of the picture books she'd tucked into her duffel bag: Curious George and Amelia Bedelia and Clifford the Big Red Dog. She looked down at her own two hands, the Swatch watch encircling her wrist. Suddenly she felt ashamed.

Sven drove her around the camp. Long houses were arranged like barracks. The whole place was surrounded by barbed wire fences. Lush green mountains rose in the background. They arrived at a recently constructed wooden hut. "This is where you'll be staying," he said with a sweeping gesture.

It was simple and clean. She inhaled deeply. The wood was fragrant, like sawdust.

"You can get water at the pump between six and seven in the morning. And be warned, there are a lot of blackouts. Make sure you have fresh batteries in your flashlight."

She wrote a letter to Hideki, then went to bed early. She wanted to be alert for her first day as English teacher at the Site Two refugee camp, but the noise and sticky heat and nerves kept her awake. Some of the other volunteers had gathered a couple of huts down. Sven was among them. He'd invited her to join them for a beer, but she'd declined.

"Well, whenever you're ready," he'd said, and she wasn't sure if he meant later that night or sometime in the not-too-distant future when she would need release from the sorrow and hardship of living among people who had nothing left to lose.

On the long drive from Bangkok, Sven had rattled off facts and figures: two million Cambodians dead between 1975 and 1979 due to torture, execution, starvation, and disease; 38,000 intellectuals slaughtered; ninety percent of artists killed; ninety percent of all books destroyed. There were no more teachers among them. The Khmer Rouge had used the National Library grounds to raise pigs.

"Don't expect too much," Sven had said. "Most of these people are starting from zero."

She lay there in her bunk, eyes wide open, listening to tinny Thai pop music and laughter from a few yards away. She heard voices—a man's and a woman's—outside her window, and then a wet, smacking sound, heavy breathing. Even in this place, there was desire.

She thought of Hideki. What was he doing right at this moment? Was his mind full of her? She pictured him sleeping, his arm flung over his head, his mouth half open. It had only been two days, but her longing for him was an agony. Her thoughts skittered over all the things they'd done together over the past two years, and then, somehow, she drifted off; and then a harsh light was blazing through the flimsy curtains, and Sven was banging on her door.

"C'mon, wake up! Time to get water! The pump's only open an hour a day."

She grunted her reply. There was no time to eat breakfast or mess with her hair. She quickly pulled on some shorts and a T-shirt, splashed water on her face, and grabbed her jerry can.

Sven was waiting outside, next to two rickety bikes. "You can have the blue one," he said. He lashed her water can to the bike and pushed the handlebars toward her.

"Thanks," she said. She knew that the next day she would be expected to do everything by herself. As far as she could tell, the other volunteers had already gone on ahead.

"Sleep well?"

"Mm." She scratched at her neck. Her legs were blistered with mosquito bites. Must remember to check the net before I go to sleep, she told herself.

Sven took off in a cloud of dust and she pedaled furiously after him, determined to keep up.

Two hours later she was at the camp, standing at the center of a patch of dirt, surrounded by about fifty Cambodians of various ages. A young mother swathed in scarves rocked her baby, her gaze latched on Christine's face. A trio of boys sat off to her left. Even through their shirts she could see the outline of their ribs. They'd brought long sticks, and they were already sketching in the dirt. There were no notebooks, no sheets of ruled paper, no number two pencils in this place. She would have to make do. She wondered if the boys would consider breaking their sticks into smaller pieces so that others would be able to write as well. And then she wondered if the man missing both arms would be able to write with his toes.

They watched and waited. In Japan, classes were regimented.

The students stood in unison, bowed to their teacher, then sat down. Here, on this patch of dirt, Christine wasn't sure of how to begin. She looked around at the sea of worn, solemn faces—even the children had a world-weary look about them—and took a deep breath. "Good morning," she said. She pointed to her chest, then to her nose, as the Japanese did. "My name is Christine."

They stared. Flies buzzed around her head, as loud as helicopters. She smiled and patted her chest. "Christine." Then she pointed to a boy sitting in front of her. "What's your name?" He dropped his eyes, embarrassed or ashamed. Christine repeated the gesture, the question, gently and persistently. He finally opened his mouth and whispered, "Kong."

Over the next few weeks, she met them at the same spot. She asked their names and drilled them with flashcards: "apple," "dog," "car." There were no apples in that place. She doubted that any of them had ever had a car. And yet she kept going. She drew letters in the dirt with her fingers or with sticks. She sang the alphabet song over and over, and sometimes they chimed in. But then one day the boys with the sticks stopped coming. And then she lost Kong, and also the man with no arms.

Christine popped open a can of beer and took a long swallow. The brew was lukewarm, but she didn't care. She just wanted a buzz. She'd been at the camp for almost four months, and she'd yet to get a letter from Hideki. The only person who'd written was her mother: *My roses are blooming. Your cousin had a baby! When are you coming home?*

Sven watched her from across the room. He unfolded his long legs and moved to sit beside her. "That bad, huh?"

She attempted a smile. "I don't know what I'm doing here. English is so beside the point for these people. They don't need me. Or maybe I'm just bad at teaching. They keep dropping out of my class."

"Well, think about what they do need, then." He brushed a strand of hair from her face. "And try to lighten up a bit. If you don't pace yourself, you'll burn out by the end of the month."

Compassion fatigue. She'd read those words in a novel once. She hadn't truly understood their meaning until now. She hadn't known that one could go numb from helping others, and for just a moment, she wanted to have Sven inside of her, in order to feel something, anything. But she wouldn't do that to Hideki.

"I don't have enough empathy," she said, "for all of these people."

Sven shrugged, his arm brushing hers. "Then just pick one."

She flashed on Kong, his grim, gaunt face, his feminine hands. Then, the ones with the missing limbs, the giggling girls, the boys with sticks. The mother with the baby. She would choose her. The mother, Chanira, had lost her husband. He'd had his head blown off right in front of her eyes, so that every night she dreamed of a crimson explosion. Chanira had survived. Every day, she came to Christine's class with a smile on her face. In that smile, there was hope for the future.

In the afternoons, Christine tried to help out at other stations. She went where she was needed, sometimes dishing out spicy soup in the dining hall, sometimes rolling bandages at the infirmary, like a nurse in a Hemingway novel. In spite of her lack of artistic ability, she helped to design posters warning against the dangers of unprotected sex. At the end of the day, she was exhausted, too tired for recreation. But then one evening, Sven rapped on her door and said, "C'mon. There's a puppet play in the south quarter. Let's go watch."

She couldn't help thinking of Japan. In Naruto, Christine had visited the site of a World War I POW camp where German soldiers had been held. There, in the green hills, among monkeys and dragonflies, the men had managed to produce plays, publish books, and put on concerts. Nothing, it seemed, could truly quell the creative spirit. She splashed some water on her face, then, revitalized, went out to join Sven.

They picked their way through the camp, past children playing some complicated game with stones, past windows seeping incense, past a man sitting on a mat selling cigarettes.

"American brand," he said, holding up a single cigarette. "Cheap, cheap. You want?"

His face was shaded in the dusk, but there was something familiar about him. Christine leaned closer. "Kong!"

"Hello, Miss Christine," he said. "You want?"

She waved her hand. "No, I don't smoke. Why don't you come back to English class?"

He didn't answer, and she didn't really expect him to. Clearly, he had all the English he needed for commerce in this place. What did he need with "apple" and "dog"? What did any of them need with "apples"?

As she sat watching the shadows of puppets dancing against a backlit sheet, she gave in to exhaustion. She let go of her ambitions. When a letter from Hideki finally arrived—*I miss you, I want to marry with you*—a mixture of relief and shame washed over her. Kong would never go to Harvard. She would have to find another way to save the world.

April 2005
HIDEKI

Hideki stood at home plate, forty boys at attention before him. It was a perfect spring day, an in-between afternoon of sun and breeze, blue-winged dragonflies, and cherry blossoms swirling as if stirred by ghosts. It was the kind of afternoon, just after the chill of late March and before the damp discomfort of the rainy season, that his wife, Christine, would while away sitting on the verandah in a floaty print dress, sipping sweetened ice tea and reading a book. He imagined his children learning how to hold pencils and sit still, eager for the bell that would signal their release. In Japan, this was a season of beginnings: the first shoots of rice poking up through the flooded paddies, newly minted workers showing up for their first days on the job, the start of a new school year, and a new baseball team.

Here they were, his boys, in all of their pimple-faced, gangly-limbed glory, gathered hopefully on the red dirt infield. They wore their Tokushima Kita High School uniforms: white shirts, green jackets, neckties, pants with a subtle plaid; but by next week, they'd be in baseball practice uniforms, unless he scared them off today. He took a long look at them, these boys in all shapes and sizes. There were one or two slouchers, a couple still carrying pouches of fat in their cheeks and guts, but he'd whip them into shape. Give him a few months, and they'd be as sharp as cut glass. And courteous. His boys were as polite as Citadel cadets, Christine had said.

"Good afternoon." His voice boomed all the way to the cherry trees at the edge of school property. The boys responded and bowed in unison.

Hideki nodded in approval. Manners were important. "If

you are here today, that must mean that you want to play baseball. If you come back tomorrow, when we hold our first official practice, then I will take it to mean that you love baseball." He paused for a moment to look them over again, to absorb their unwavering gazes. "And I hope you love it more than sleeping in on weekend mornings, more than playing games at the video arcade, more than making out with your girlfriend."

At this last part, Toshiya Miki, his assistant coach, snickered behind him.

Miki wasn't a teacher at Kita High. He and Hideki had gone to different high schools. Although Hideki had been the better ball player, Miki's team had made it to the national high school baseball tournament at Koshien. Hideki had never been there. Later, they'd played on the same team at university, although Miki had been a year ahead. After graduating, Miki had taken over his father's trucking business, helping out with his son's Pee Wee team in his free time. Hideki had gone on to get a degree in education. They hadn't kept in contact all that much in the intervening years, but when Hideki had become a coach, Miki had volunteered his services and Hideki'd been happy to take him up on it. Miki had been a big help, especially in the days of Christine's difficult second pregnancy, and later, when his daughter always seemed to be in and out of the ICU. However, they didn't always agree on how to get things done. And Miki was sometimes disrespectful in front of the players.

Annoyed, Hideki went on. "You must be prepared to *devote* yourself to this game." Hell if he was going to put up with slackers, after all the work that had gone into making this team. He turned to the blackboard set up on an easel at his side. This was where he wrote out the practice schedules. Today he grabbed a piece of chalk and wrote in English: "Dream big. Work hard." An image of his wife Christine flashed through his mind. These were her words, after all, now printed up on the team towels as their slogan.

"I want to tell you a little story. Six years ago, there was another boy standing here. A boy who had sat on the bench throughout most of his junior high school baseball career."

Just then, he felt a humming, as if his pocket were full of bees. *Damn.* He'd forgotten to turn off his phone. He angled away from them, and reached into his pocket, fumbling for the button that would turn it off. A few heads turned. "He wasn't very big," Hideki went on, louder than before, "but he had a big dream, and he was willing to work hard. He went from being a second-string shortstop in junior high school to an ace pitcher on this very team. He's the one who helped bring us to the quarterfinals for the first time. And now that kid is playing for the Tokushima Indigo Socks."

The Indigo Socks were a minor league team, part of the recently formed Shikoku League. An upstart organization, a little bit desperate: The Kochi Fighting Dogs were recruiting in Burundi, of all places. Also, the pay was low; in the off season, Takehara, the boy he'd mentioned, worked as a fire fighter, and he lived with his parents, so he didn't have to pay rent. Still, to be able to play baseball and get paid for it was a dream come true, and Takehara's rise made for a good story. It gave him street cred, showed that he knew what he was doing. If they followed his advice, they could grab onto bright shiny futures.

"Of course, he didn't win all of those games all by himself," Hideki said. "This is a team, and we will all work together to reach our dream."

It went without saying that the dream was to win the prefectural championship and participate in the national tournament at Koshien. This had been Hideki's dream since he was a small boy. It had been his father's dream before that. And it was the dream of every kid in Japan who'd ever tucked his hand into a baseball glove. Koshien was a special place, more cathedral than stadium. All the greats had played there: Sadaharu Oh, Masumi Kuwata, winning pitcher in the high school tournament *twice*; Ichiro Suzuki, Daisuke Matsuzaka—even Babe Ruth on his visit to Japan, and Eiji Sawamura, who struck him out. And any high school graduate who could boast of having helped his team get to Koshien, was pretty much assured a job in the company of his choice, even if he wasn't pro material. Everyone knew the kind of effort required to get that far.

"You are all equals." An electronic melody beeped out of his pants pocket, the theme to "Rocky." A few kids ducked their heads and snickered. *Damn.* He thought he'd turned it off. He pulled it out and silenced it, then continued with his spiel, even louder than before. "You will help each other out. And I am your coach. Remember that I know more about baseball than you do. You will do what I tell you to, or you won't play. Got that?"

"*Hai.*"

He introduced Assistant Coach Miki, and the three girls who'd signed up as managers. They stepped forward and bowed.

"All right, then. See you tomorrow. Same time, same place."

As he watched them at ease, milling about, he felt a surge of hope. What a different feeling that was from six years ago when he'd founded this team. He'd started out with three aluminum bats, ten dozen balls, and eleven kids. Six of them were new to baseball, hadn't even played on their junior high teams. Most of them were college-bound. The ones who live for the sport went to Tokushima Commercial: a.k.a. Tokusho, or Seiko, or Naruto Tech. Maybe they were aces in the classroom, but they were a sorry bunch out on the field. Ground balls went bouncing through their outspread legs. They batted at air, never connecting with the red-seamed ball; at first, a simple dash to first base left most of them winded.

Hideki had thrown himself into the job, determined to whip them into shape. He gave them intensive tutorials in batting and fielding, video-taped them and conducted team critiques. He spent hours on the phone with former teammates-turned-high-school-coaches, begging for practice games, in which his boys were routinely humiliated. Massacred. Every week he had to come up with a new pep talk, and he spent half of his time trying to talk wannabe quitters into sticking with him. He no longer had time for golf or fishing or going to movies with his wife. There were no more romantic excursions to Singapore or Phuket. There was only baseball. He and his players had slogged through six years of trials and errors, but finally, all of that hard work was about to pay off. Hideki had snared himself a pitcher.

He remembered the first time he'd seen Kikawa throw, as a junior high school student. The kid had grown up in a fishing village outside of Naruto, a city famous for its huge natural whirlpools and tasty *wakame*. Hideki could smell the sea from the baseball diamond, could almost hear the water lapping against the pilings. The kid was quiet, polite. Simple. Hideki could picture him threading a worm onto a hook or hauling in nets full of seaweed with his dad, hanging the *wakame* out to dry in the sun. But he was meant for more than that. This kid had pure, raw talent, and already he was better than just about any high school pitcher in the prefecture.

He sidled up to the kid's coach. "You clocked him?"

The Coach grinned. "His fastball's about 142 kilometers an hour."

Hideki nodded slightly. He was trying to play it cool, but he could hardly keep still. His mind was racing. What could he promise this kid? How would he convince him to choose Kita High School over all the other schools that were no doubt after him? He wondered what kinds of gifts were being lavished on the family. Bribes were against the rules, of course, but that didn't stop some coaches from being a little generous.

When the kid came off the field, he took off his cap and wiped his forehead with his sleeve. A girl in school uniform rushed up to him with a tray and offered a cup of cold, barley tea.

He was a good-looking boy, with big eyes and broad shoulders, the kind that girls liked. Hideki expected to see arrogance but, no, Kikawa looked the girl in the eyes, smiled shyly, and took the cup with a slight bow. He downed the tea in a couple of gulps and bowed again when he returned the cup to the tray.

"Kikawa," the junior high school coach shouted. "Come here."

The boy bounded over, his face blank.

"This is Coach Yamada from Tokushima Kita High School."

"*Hajimemashite.*" He doffed his cap.

"I'd like you to think about coming to our high school to play baseball," he said.

Was it his imagination, or did the kid's face brighten a watt or two?

"Thank you, sir."

"We'd love to have you." And that was it.

He followed up a couple weeks later with a visit to the boy's house.

He'd knelt at a low table with the kid's parents. His father's face was nut-brown and creased with wrinkles from all those days and months and years out on the sea. His mother, who wore a spotless white apron over a dun-colored house dress, brought out dishes of rice crackers and poured cup after cup of green tea.

"Those other coaches were all talking nasty about each other," the father said. He lit a cigarette and watched the plumes of smoke rise to the stained ceiling. "They said some rude things about you, as well."

Hideki grunted. He felt a flicker of annoyance but tried not to show it. He knew how some of his colleagues operated. Ichihara, the coach of Naruto Tech, for one, was relentless. His wife had divorced him a few years ago, and now he had nothing but baseball. He could be cutthroat.

"Our son is a good boy. He studies hard."

"Well," Hideki said, gearing up for his pitch. "Our school has a reputation for helping students get into some of the best universities in the country."

The man nodded. "Last year, one of yours went on to Todai. I heard about that."

Hideki was surprised that the fisherman knew about the student who'd been accepted to Tokyo University, let alone cared. He'd thought this man might want to keep his son close to home to work on the boat. He'd thought he'd have to argue about the benefits of traveling a few extra kilometers to go to an academic high school. After all, Naruto High School was within cycling distance of home.

"We want him to go to a good college," the man went on, "and you seem like a gentleman. We'd like our son to go to your school."

And then they'd called Kikawa himself into the room, and he'd entered, head bowed, and Hideki was suddenly so happy that he almost cried. He looked at the boy and thought, "With the proper training, this kid can take us all the way to Koshien."

Way back in the beginning, when Hideki had been unsure of whether Christine would stay in Japan or not, when he'd still been thinking of her as a flight risk, he'd brought her to the baseball stadium at Koshien. It was a test, of sorts. She already knew that he'd been the star of his high school and college teams, that he'd been almost good enough to play professionally, that he'd become a high school teacher in order to be a baseball coach. And if he became a baseball coach and his team won the prefectural championship, they would be able to participate in the national tournament on this very field. Koshien. It wasn't just any baseball stadium. It wasn't just the home of the Hanshin Tigers. This place was hallowed. After each game in the spring and summer tournaments, the losing players would drop to their knees and scoop up dirt to take home with them, dirt that they would enshrine and keep forever as a memory of fleeting youth and dreams attained or thwarted. And Hideki wanted to make sure that Christine understood all that before things went any further.

At the time, Hideki had been teaching at a night school, one of those hardcore assignments that were given to young, freshly licensed teachers in the public school system or to veterans who turned out to be oddballs, those who didn't quite fit in. His students were often at risk. Some of them had fathers in prison, mothers who worked late at night in hostess bars. One girl had dropped out of day school to have a baby.

Christine had a job as an assistant English teacher up the coast in Naruto, on a one-year government program. She could renew her contract a couple of times if she wanted to, but she seemed restless. She talked about going to Thailand to teach English in a Cambodian refugee camp. Or traveling through India with a backpack, and maybe helping out Mother Theresa for a few months.

"I don't feel like anyone really needs me here in Japan," she said. Back then, people were talking about how the U.S. was in decline, how Japan was set to conquer the world. Hawaii, MGM, the Rockefeller Center: all of it belonged to them now. The students that Christine taught were, she said, slightly contemptuous of the United States. What did they need her for?

I need you, Hideki had wanted to say. But he wasn't given to pouring out his heart. *I love you. Please stay.*

He invited her to go with him to the opening game of the summer tournament at Koshien. They arrived at the stadium early enough to get seats behind home base. The bleachers quickly filled, over 57,000 spectators in all, there to cheer on their hometown heroes. The nervous energy radiating through the stands was contagious. Hideki's stomach was awhirl. Beside him, Christine sat with her back perfectly straight, her fingers knotted together. She could feel it, too.

They watched as teams from as far away as Hokkaido and Okinawa marched in lockstep once around the field, then to the center where they lined up in rows. During the opening ceremony they remained statue-still in spite of the blazing sun and the sweat dribbling down their faces. When they spotted the team from Tokushima, they clapped harder. They'd beat out thirty-two other teams in the prefecture to make it to the national level. Only one team from Tokushima had ever won the national championship: that had been Ikeda High School back in 1980; but just getting to Koshien was an accomplishment worth celebrating. For the rest of their lives, they would be honored and anointed by their time on the field. On a more practical level, it looked good on a college application or a resume.

Hideki translated for Christine while the captain from the previous year's winning team issued remarks, and then the Crown Prince delivered his greeting from high up—the highest!—in the bleachers, reminiscing about past games. They watched the teams file off the grounds with military precision, and then the two teams matched up in the first game took to the field for preliminary practice. Finally, a brand new baseball was dropped from a helicopter and the starting pitcher stepped up to the mound.

As they sat in the bleachers, Hideki watched Christine in profile. Her lightly freckled face was shaded by a straw boater and her hair, gathered into a French braid and hanging down her back, glimmered in the sun like spun gold. Whenever a player stepped up to bat, she leaned forward on the bench, biting down so hard on her lower lip that he worried she'd split the skin.

"Someday I'm coming back here with my team," Hideki said.

Christine turned to him and smiled. They both knew that he didn't have a team—not yet—and that schools with winning teams did their best to hold on to their coaches for as long as possible. There weren't many openings for new coaches, and when there were, they were usually at the schools with the worst teams. If his wish were granted, if he were made baseball coach at a high school in Tokushima, he would have a lot of work to do.

"It's good to have a dream," she said.

They heard the ping of struck aluminum and turned back to the game in time to see the ball flying over the fence. Home run.

"Dream big," Christine said.

Watching these boys, his new team, he was barely conscious of the rumble of an engine somewhere behind him, the opening and slamming of car doors, the whimper of a little kid. He didn't turn until one of the new boys said, "Who is *that*?" and then he saw them. A woman in sweatpants—sweatpants!—with frizzy brown hair pulled into a ponytail. A five-year-old boy with a huge purple stain covering one eye. A black eye? How the hell did he wind up with a shiner? And a little girl in a wheelchair. His shoulders and jaw tensed. They were coming toward him. His family.

CHRISTINE

Christine loved Trina's oak table. She loved this kitchen with its American-sized refrigerator decorated with animal magnets and children's art, its scent of baked bread, and the cross-stitch samplers on the wall. She loved Trina's dishes, painted with blue Chinese landscapes, like the ones that she had eaten from at her grandmother's house when she was a child. She remembered that once her oyster casserole or Thanksgiving sweet potatoes were cleared away, she'd wondered about the pagoda on her plate, wondered what it would be like to visit such a place. And then finally she had. She'd been to China, Thailand, Singapore, Malaysia, and of course, Japan, where she now lived. Ironically, although Christine had fled America in search of the exotic and adventurous, Trina's Blue Willow patterned dishes, this room itself, now filled her with yearning for all that she had left behind.

"How was the send-off?" Elizabeth asked from across the table, snapping Christine out of her daydream. Elizabeth looked great, as usual. Even though she'd given birth just a little over a month ago, she managed to keep her bottle-blonde hair touched up, and her poplin blouses ironed and unstained. Right now, the baby slept nestled in her arms.

Christine smiled. "It was fine. Nobody cried. Not even me." She'd thought that sending her son off on his first day of elementary school—on foot no less, since the children were required to walk to school in groups—would have been more wrenching, but what she'd felt was mostly relief. For the first four years of her life, her daughter Emma had been in and out of hospitals, and then there was that one terrifying week when both kids were in the ICU at the same time with pneumonia. But now they were

21

healthy and sturdy and ready to be out in the world. Plus, it was nice to finally have some time for herself.

Trina gently tapped a spoon against her "Support Our Troops" mug. "I hereby call this meeting of the American Wives' Club to order," she said.

Christine raised her coffee cup to Trina in a toast. "The American Wives' Club," AWC for short, wasn't an official organization. There was no club secretary, no president. They got enough of protocol with the Japanese PTA and *Kodomo Kai* and other Japanese mothers' groups. In reality, the AWC was composed of the three of them: Christine, Elizabeth, and Trina, wife of a Japanese professor, whose two chestnut-haired children, not yet school-aged, were now under the table clawing at knees. Elizabeth's eldest child, a daughter, was in the second grade at a private academy with an English immersion program.

Although coffee was enough of an excuse for a gathering, on this morning they'd gotten together to give Elizabeth a baby shower. According to Miss Manners, a baby shower was supposed to be held in the eighth month of pregnancy, but etiquette be damned; the members of the AWC put enough time and energy into keeping track of and adhering to Japanese customs (exactly how much to spend on a summer gift for one's boss, where to stand in an elevator, which days were inauspicious for hospital visits, etc.). Sometimes a little anarchy was just the right thing. The belated celebration was also out of deference to Christine, whose daughter had been born fourteen weeks ahead of schedule, during Christine's seventh month of pregnancy. For days, weeks, months, Emma had struggled in an incubator at the university hospital, and they had all learned not to take a baby's easy delivery and good health for granted.

The doorbell rang then, and Trina jumped up. "Oh, I forgot to tell you all. I met a woman at the library the other day. I thought she might like to join us. She's Canadian, but I think we can make an exception. We can be the North American Wives."

"Yes, of course," Elizabeth said. "The more, the merrier."

Trina went to open the door, and the others moved their chairs to make room for another guest. Their heads turned when a slender, pale woman with strawberry blonde hair stepped into the room. She held a little boy of about three by the hand. Christine could tell by his eyes and brownish hair that he was biracial ("hafu" as the Japanese said) just as all of their children were.

"Hi, I'm Sophia Lang," she said. She extended her hand to Christine, and then to Elizabeth.

"Sophia has just signed on as an adjunct at Tokushima University," Trina said. "Her husband is a scientist at Otsuka." Christine nodded. They were all familiar with the pharmaceutical company, one of the area's largest employers, and maker of that ubiquitous, ridiculously named sports drink, Pocari Sweat. Elizabeth's husband worked there, too. "They just moved here from ... where was it?"

"Maryland," Sophia said. "My husband is originally from Tokushima. We thought it'd be nice for Kai, here, to get to know his father's family better. And also, work on his Japanese language skills. My husband asked for a transfer, and here we are!"

She had that fresh-off-the-plane look about her. Christine had read somewhere about the stages of culture shock; she'd experienced them herself. First, was the euphoric falling-in-love stage, where everything was new and exciting. Pretty soon the shine would wear off, and irritation would set in. She'd get sick of having little kids point at her hair, and of people asking if she could use chopsticks. She'd discover that the bank machines closed early, at nine p.m., and that if she didn't have her laundry out by eight in the morning (so late!), the neighbors would chat about her.

"Have a seat," Trina said, ushering Sophia into a chair. "And Kai, maybe you'd like to go play with Nana and Kenta. Kids! Out from under the table! Show this nice little boy your toys!"

Trina's two- and three-year-olds emerged, giggling, and ran out of the room. Kai looked up at his mother for confirmation before scrambling after them.

"Ah, peace at last," Trina said, pouring coffee for Sophia into a University of Virginia mug.

They went around the table and introduced themselves.

"I'm Elizabeth Tanigawa, from Kentucky. I'm doing some research about expatriates in Tokushima," she drawled. "I'm planning on writing a book or an essay or something." She was always immersed in some project. For a while, it had been indigo dyeing, and before that pottery, and even longer ago, she'd been obsessed with local folklore. During the latter phase, she'd compiled dozens of stories about trickster raccoon dogs, but she'd never tried to publish them. It was just something to keep her busy.

"Well, that sounds interesting," Sophia said politely. "I didn't know there were enough expats here for a book."

It's true that there were hardly any foreigners in Tokushima Prefecture. Christine had gone days without seeing another non-Japanese in the capital city; weeks, even. Although bridges now linked the island of Shikoku via sparsely populated Awaji Island with Honshu, there were no high-speed bullet trains zipping across the island. There were few jobs for foreign women outside of teaching English or pouring drinks in hostess bars, and tourists from abroad rarely added the island to their agenda.

"Oh, but there have been lots," Elizabeth said, and here, she nodded at Christine. "Missionaries from South Carolina, an entire camp of German Prisoners of War, and there was also a Portuguese sailor who settled here and married the little Japanese girl who was his housemaid. Kinda like Madame Butterfly. There's a museum about his life up on top of Mount Bizan."

"A *girl*?"

"She was quite a bit younger," Christine put in. "But she was an adult. I'm sure she knew what she was doing." In truth, Christine thought the sailor, who appeared in photos with a long white beard, was way too old for his bride, but she suddenly felt perversely defensive of all things Tokushima. It was her home now, after all.

When it was her turn, she said, "I'm originally from Michigan, most recently from South Carolina. I've been living here for ten years. My husband is a high school baseball coach."

"We call him the 'imaginary husband,'" Trina said, "because no one has ever seen them together."

Christine forced herself to join in the laughter, even though she was the one who'd first come up with the moniker.

"She's a baseball widow," Elizabeth explained to the bemused Sophia, who hadn't been in Japan long enough to understand how demanding high school sports could be. There was no such thing as a baseball season. Once students joined the club, they were busy practicing and playing all year round. The only days off were during the ten days of winter vacation. The rest of the time, even during the "off-season," from the end of October till about the beginning of February, they had training sessions every day after school and on weekends. Hideki was almost never home.

"I saw your husband on television," Elizabeth said. "Just a couple of weeks ago. His team made it to the quarter-finals, didn't it?"

Christine nodded. "Yeah, I was there. Up in the bleachers." Before the kids had come along, she'd gone to all of his games, but they were too young to enjoy baseball. The one time she'd brought Emma to the stadium, she was dismayed to find that there was no wheelchair access, even though the arena was relatively new. She'd had to ask a couple of high school boys to help carry Emma and her wheels up the concrete steps, into the stands. And then of course, after glimpsing Daddy at the sidelines and waving furiously with no response, both Emma and Koji had grown quickly bored. Now Christine mostly watched the games on TV. Once the number of teams was whittled down to eight, the games were broadcast on the local NHK station, or at least public access TV. It was hard to concentrate, though, when Koji and Emma were grabbing at the remote control, pushing for cartoons. The other day, Christine had asked her mother-in-law to babysit so that she could watch Hideki's team live. Even though they'd lost, she'd felt emotionally involved in the game. Being there made her feel closer to Hideki, almost as if they were in it together.

"Do you have any children?" Sophia asked, bringing her cup to her lips. Christine saw that her fingernails had been manicured. A diamond glinted off her ring finger. In a couple of months, she won't be wearing that, Christine thought. She'd figure out that it was way too gaudy for rural Japan.

"Yes, two. A boy and a girl."

"Do they go to school?" Sophia asked.

"Koji's at Aizumi West. He just started first grade today."

"And your daughter? You said you have a little girl?"

Christine nodded. "Her name is Emma, after Queen Emma of Hawaii." Christine and Hideki had gotten married at a plantation on Oahu. Afterwards, they'd done some sightseeing around the islands, and Christine had become captivated by the biography of Queen Emma, who was both Anglo and Hawaiian: a multicultural woman who did good deeds, a mixed-race royal. The perfect role model and namesake, Christine thought. "My daughter goes to the kindergarten at the School for the Deaf."

"Oh!" Surprise and pity flashed across Sophia's face. By now, Christine was used to apologies and embarrassment at the revelation of her daughter's disabilities. She forced a smile to show that it was no big deal, that there was no need to feel sorry for them. *Everything was fine!*

"Have you thought about taking her to the States?" Sophia asked. "My husband and I had a little scare after an ultrasound, and we decided that if our child had any handicap, we would stay in the U.S. Japan is a couple decades behind in that area, isn't it?"

Christine felt the blood rush to her face. "We're keeping our options open," she murmured, though that wasn't exactly true. Hideki was passionate about his job and she would never ask him to quit. He had become something of a local celebrity. People respected him, just as they seemed to respect her for being married to him. Whenever she dropped by the baseball field, say, to bring Hideki his forgotten cell phone, or drop off Koji to "help out" with Saturday afternoon practice sessions, the players doffed their caps and bowed to her, the coach's wife. It made her feel like a First Lady. More importantly, as a public-school teacher, Hideki was assured lifetime employment, and he also had good health insurance. With a kid like Emma, you had to have ample coverage. Christine suspected that with all of her pre-existing conditions, Emma was uninsurable in the States. And last, but not least, as the only and eldest son of his widowed mother, Hideki was expected to look after her and act, when necessary, as head of the family, representing the Yamada clan at weddings and funerals that his mother didn't want to attend. He had responsibilities.

Not every family had the resources, or desire, to up and move across the world every time circumstances changed. And yet, Christine had often wondered if Japan was the best place for their daughter. Or for their son, for that matter. At times, she thought they'd be better off in Sweden, where parents were required by law to teach their deaf children sign language. (Here in Japan, Hideki was too busy to study anything but baseball stats, and Christine often had to interpret between father and daughter.) Other times she fantasized about moving to Hawaii, where multicultural was the norm.

"Well, then, ladies," Trina said, clapping her hands together. "I think it's time for some games."

Pick up at Emma's school wasn't until four, so Christine had enough time to stop by the grocery store after the baby shower. She did her shopping, hurried home, changed out of the dress she'd worn to Trina's into a pair of sweat pants and a baggy T-shirt, took down the laundry, and scrubbed the toilets and sinks. She thought about changing back into the dress before going to fetch her daughter, but then decided not to. It would be her act of "kokusaika": internationalization. The government was always coming up with terms and goals to make Japan more global-minded, more open. Americans were practical. What was wrong with that? Sweats were more comfortable than dresses. It was hard to push Emma's wheelchair in high heels, anyhow.

She picked up Emma. When they got home, she looked into the back seat to find that she was sleeping. She decided to leave her alone for a bit, and sat down on the front porch, waiting for Koji to come home. Pretty soon she heard children's voices, and then caught a glimpse of yellow hats and black satchels, and then there Koji was, in front of her, head bowed.

"Hey," Christine said softly. "How was your first day of school?"

He shrugged the black leather backpack off of his shoulders and let it fall to the ground. Christine winced. That thing had cost nearly fifty-thousand yen, close to five hundred dollars. Day one, and it probably already had a scuff mark. But when he finally looked up at her and she saw his bruised face, the backpack was forgotten. She sucked in her breath and pulled him close. "Wh-what happened?" She immediately thought of her own foreign face, and Emma in the car. Had the other kids picked on him because he was only half-Japanese? Or because they knew that his sister was disabled?

He wouldn't tell her anything, so she packed him into the car and sped off toward the school. Thankfully, when they pulled into the parking lot, Emma was still sleeping. Christine wouldn't have to deal with the wheelchair; she'd just let her nap. She cracked the car windows, locked the car, and hurried into the school and towards Koji's classroom, pulling him along. She stepped up her pace, until, out of breath, she came face to face Koji's new teacher, the fiftyish Mrs. Kan. Koji covered his eye with one hand.

"Can I help you?" the woman asked.

"This," Christine said in Japanese. She peeled away Koji's

hand and tilted his chin so that she could get a good look. "Can you tell me about this?"

Mrs. Kan's eyes widened in surprise. "I don't know anything about it. Perhaps he got into a fight on the way home?"

"A fight?" He wasn't a fighter. She knew that much about him. Even when Emma had tantrums and threw toys at his head, he kept calm, ducking out of the way.

"Oh, you know how boys are," the teacher said in Japanese. "They're not good at communicating at this age anyway. But I suggest that you speak Japanese with your son at home. It'll help him learn faster."

Christine was stunned. Did this woman think that just because she was American her son, born and raised in Japan, couldn't speak the language? He'd spent three years at an all-Japanese pre-school, and many hours in the care of his Japanese grandmother while she'd been tending Emma at the hospital. His Japanese was fine. And didn't this woman, this *educator*, know that language experts agreed that it was best for a mother to speak to her child in her native tongue? Was Mrs. Kan suggesting that Christine bring up Koji with less vocabulary than she herself was capable of? With her awkward syntax and grammatical errors?

Koji staring at the floor again, tugged on her hand. "*Iko.*" Let's go. In Japanese.

Christine's thoughts were bubbling like hot lava. Her boy had been attacked by another kid on his first day at this school, and the teacher was insinuating that it was her fault because she had raised him in English. Was it possible that the teacher was condescending to her because she was a foreigner? Because she had appeared in sweatpants and a ponytail? She needed back-up. She needed Hideki, with his bulk and his deep, thunderous voice, to deal with the situation. She uttered a crisp, "Arigato," before yanking her tortured son in the direction of the car.

DAISUKE

This necktie is choking me. And these pants, they're what—polyester?
Jamal and Rico would be laughing if they saw him now. But they
were in Atlanta, on the other side of the world. No more jeans
and sweatshirts for him, at least not on a school day. No more
polo shirts and khakis. Here at Tokushima Kita High School, in
the Boondocks, Japan, he had to wear *a jacket* to school.

He'd been born in Japan. He knew the drill. When he was in
the elementary school here, he'd had to dress like a little Prussian
soldier. But for the past three years, while his father was on overseas assignment, things had been pretty relaxed. He and his sister
went to American schools. In seventh, eighth, and ninth grade,
he could wear whatever he wanted. Now they were back in their
hometown, among the rice paddies and sweet potato fields.

The walls of his American school were always covered with
bright posters and student artwork, but these walls were totally
plain. He counted forty desks, all in rows; twice as many as in his
classroom the year before. A chalkboard dominated the front
wall. The only thing that might pass for decoration was a banner
pinned to the bulletin board that said "Boys, be ambitious." It
was a famous quote, but he couldn't remember who'd said it.
This place was all business.

One guy sitting over by the window looked familiar. His eyebrows had been razored into thin lines. His hair was kind of long,
curled up at the ends. *Hey, I know him,* Daisuke thought, his mind
clicking. *That's Shintaro Nakamoto.* He was a lot taller than he was
the last time Daisuke had seen him. They'd played on the same
baseball team in elementary school. They weren't exactly friends,
though. Shintaro's father owned a nightclub and had some sort

of connection to *yakuza*—Japanese mobsters—so as kids, everyone was always a little afraid of him. Daisuke wasn't scared now, but he looked away before he caught Shintaro's eye.

There was another kid he remembered from before: Junji. They used to go fishing together once in a while, when they weren't playing catch. Now he had a *bozu*, a shaven head like a Buddhist priest or an American army recruit, so Daisuke knew he was on the baseball team. He was still kind of small, though.

A group of girls huddled at the back of the room. They all looked alike with black bobbed hair and plain, unmade-up faces. They were showing each other photos on their cell phones. And then one of them glanced toward the door, leaned forward and whispered something to the others. They all turned at the same time and glared.

Daisuke looked in the direction of their gazes and saw another girl had just walked in. She had these huge brown eyes and this little cupid mouth. Pale, smooth skin. She could be a model or a pop star. Maybe was, for all he knew. Her skirt had been hemmed just above her knees, and her hair was streaked with magenta.

The girl glanced around the room, then lowered her head. She didn't seem to know anyone, or at least she didn't seem to want to talk to anyone in the room. She took the empty seat in front of Daisuke's (*yes!*) and let out a sigh. Her long hair was damp. He leaned forward and inhaled the scent of shampoo, something floral and fresh.

While he was sitting there trying to think of something to say, the rest of the seats filled up. The room was buzzing with chatter and laughter; that is, until the second bell rang and the teacher walked in. Then, silence.

The guy looked to be in his forties, about Daisuke's father's age.

"I am Tanaka-sensei," he said. He wrote the ideograms for his name on the blackboard: the kanji for "field" and "in." Mr. "In the Field," Daisuke translated.

Mr. Tanaka told them that he would be their homeroom

teacher *and* their English teacher, and then he laid down the rules about cell phones (not allowed during class!) and tardiness (punishable by extra homework!) and hair color (only black!).

He took roll, starting with the boys' names.

"Asano Junji?"

"*Hai!*"

Daisuke looked out the window, thinking about how he couldn't wait to tear up the clay with his cleats. He wanted to be running bases, throwing balls, not stuck here in this room ....

"Uchida Daisuke?"

He was startled by the sound of his name. "Here!" he said, automatically in English.

The other students start to laugh.

Mr. Tanaka frowned.

Great. Now everyone thought he was a show off. "Sorry, sir. I mean, *hai!*" he said, trying to correct himself.

But it was too late. The group of girls across the room cut their eyes at him and whispered to one another. They giggled until Mr. Tanaka told them all to be quiet.

Daisuke tried not to let his mind wander. He listened to the names and made an attempt to memorize them. Especially Takai Nana, the name of the girl sitting in front of him.

At the end of homeroom, Mr. Tanaka went off to teach a class somewhere else, or maybe to hang out in the teacher's room. A woman with glasses came in to teach them math, and then they sat through fifty minutes of social studies with yet another teacher.

Third period, Mr. Tanaka came back for English.

He greeted them again. "Good morning." Except it sounded like *Good-o moaning-goo.*

Ew. Is that what he sounded like when he first got to America? He suddenly understood why the kids made fun of his accent back then.

Mr. Tanaka took a long look at Daisuke, turned, and wrote a

sentence in Japanese on the board. There were a couple of unfamiliar kanji. "Okay, Mr. Returnee," he said, looking back at Daisuke. "Stand up. Show me what you learned in America."

He pushed back his chair and stood.

"Please translate this sentence into English."

Everyone was staring at him, except Nana, with her hair that smelled like flowers, who seemed to be studying the gouges on her desk. His heart went *buh-Boom, buh-Boom* and he could feel the blood rushing to his face, moisture gathering at his armpits and hairline. He cleared his throat.

"Uh, 'In the spring ....'"

His mind flipped through all those kanji workbooks his parents had made him do while he was in the States, but the pages were a blur. Did he actually learn this character? Or was it something that would come up later in the semester, something that his classmates learned in extra-curricular cram schools during spring vacation? Maybe it was something really easy, and everyone was thinking that he couldn't have possibly passed the entrance exam for this school, and that his father must have given the principal some kind of, uh, *gift* to get him admitted. To be honest, that's what he was thinking himself. He didn't belong there.

"I'm sorry, sir." The air suddenly felt heavy, like a pile of bricks on his shoulders. "I don't know."

There were a few titters. Mr. Tanaka sneered. "So you're not such a big hot shot after all, huh?"

What? He'd never said he was. He was just trying to make it through the day.

"Sit down," Mr. Tanaka ordered.

Daisuke crumpled into his seat, defeated.

"Can anyone else translate this sentence?"

Immediately, seven hands shot up.

Luckily, Mr. Tanaka didn't call on him for the rest of the period.

Lunch was in the classroom, but they could sit wherever they wanted. At noon, everybody started moving their desks around. The five girls who were showing each other photos earlier nudged their desks together to form a pentagon. Shintaro dragged his over towards a couple of kids Daisuke didn't know. Junji looked over his shoulder. Their eyes met and Junji motioned him over. Well, he wouldn't have to eat by himself. That was good. Only Nana stayed put, her desk still facing forward. She unwrapped her lunch box and arranged her chopsticks and then started eating, her eyes downcast.

Junji tore the plastic wrap off a couple of store-bought rice balls.

"That's your lunch?" Daisuke asked.

He shrugged. "Since my dad was transferred to Tokyo, my mom stopped making an effort."

He nodded. His dad was in Tokyo, too, but his mom was still pretty diligent. He guessed they were lucky to have been able to stay together when his father was sent to Atlanta. If he'd been shipped off to another prefecture for two or three years, they probably would have seen him only on occasional weekends, like now. He and his sister would have stayed behind in the house where they'd always lived and kept going to the same schools. He couldn't believe it when he heard about Americans who sold their houses and moved their families to a new city every few years.

He unwrapped his bento and took his chopsticks out of their case. Junji just about drooled when he lifted the lid. The box was packed with rice sprinkled with black sesame seeds, fried chicken, a rolled omelet, little cherry tomatoes, sprigs of broccoli, and sweetened black beans.

"You going out for baseball?" Junji asked.

"Yeah," Daisuke said. "You?" He already knew the answer, of course. He could tell by his hair, or lack of it. Junji played first base when they were in elementary school. He was really good back then, hardly ever made an error.

He nodded and stuffed half a rice ball into his mouth.

"Did you play in America?" Junji asked.

Daisuke nodded again. On his team in Atlanta, he had been a star. He'd had the highest batting average of anyone: .412. And he'd caught every fly that came his way, even if he'd had to jump or dive or do a somersault. They'd called him Little Ichiro. His coach had invited him to live with him so he could stay in America and play baseball. He'd had this idea that Daisuke could get a college scholarship in a few years. He'd even told his father that the scout for a Major League team had handed over his business card and asked him to keep in touch after seeing Daisuke play, but his father said he couldn't remain behind. "We are a family," he'd said. "We stay together." He didn't tell Junji this, though. He didn't think he'd want to hear him brag.

Instead, Daisuke jutted his chin toward Shintaro. "What about him?" he asked in a low voice. "Do you think he'll join?"

Junji leaned closer and whispered. "I heard a rumor that he was recruited. He didn't do so well on the entrance exam, but the coach was impressed by his pitching. They let him in."

"Huh." Daisuke's scores hadn't been that great either. He and his mother had flown back to Japan for the entrance exams. Tokushima Kita High School was famous for its baseball team, but it was also well known for its students. Kids from this school were always in the newspaper for winning calligraphy prizes or drawing pictures that got painted on commercial airplanes or winning classical music competitions. Daisuke hadn't done so well on the kanji part of the test, but he'd aced the English and scraped by on the math. Exams were another thing he didn't really want to talk about, so he looked around the room, trying to think of a different topic. And then his eyes fell on Nana, eating alone.

"Hey, do you know that girl?" He asked, trying to appear nonchalant.

"Nana? No, not really." He lowered his voice to a whisper. "But I heard that she doesn't have a dad, and her mom works in a bar. I also heard that she goes out on dates with older men for money."

Whoa. He must have heard wrong. "Like a hooker?" He thought of the heavily made-up woman in very short shorts he had once seen on a street corner in Atlanta.

Junji shrugged. "Yeah, I guess."

The thought of Nana out in a restaurant with some guy his dad's age made his stomach turn. He tried to hide his disappointment.

NAHOKO

After Daisuke and Momoe had wheeled off to school on their bikes, Nahoko untied her apron, poured herself another cup of coffee, and slipped a CD into the stereo. She waited for the first strains of Karen Carpenter's voice, waited to be carried to the days of her youth. Sometimes Karen's sweet voice was the soundtrack as she went about her housework, wiping dust from the shelves, pushing a mop across the floor. Other times, like this morning, she just listened.

Years ago, she'd had all of the Carpenters' records. Now she just had the one CD, *The Carpenters' Greatest Hits,* which included "Please, Mr. Postman" and "On Top of the World," the two songs that Nahoko had practiced for karaoke.

Of course, she didn't go to karaoke clubs these days, but back when she'd been single, an office lady who made tea and photocopied memos, she'd gone singing with her friends once or twice a week. They'd rented a small booth equipped with a microphone and karaoke machine, drunk some beer or pink cocktails, and belted out their favorite songs. Nahoko had excelled at English. She'd gone to English conversation school all through junior and senior high school, and she'd passed level one of the STEP test. She liked to show off a bit by singing in English.

She'd sung at office parties, too. It would have been bad form to have refused anyway, and the other workers, including her ordinarily gruff boss, had praised her voice and her command of English.

"You are just like a songbird," Jun Uchida had once told her. "A lark."

This had been at the annual Party of Forgetting, the end of

the year fete when everyone was supposed to expunge every unpleasant thing that had occurred in the past twelve months. Jun, who was handsome and single and brilliant, a rising star in Research and Development, had never spoken to her before, although she had definitely noticed him. A lark, she thought. On top of everything else, he is a poet. No matter that he was wasted on sake and *shochu*.

The next time she saw him, at the water cooler, he nodded and blushed. He's shy, she thought. She took the initiative and invited him to join her and a group of friends one night after work. He said yes.

After they'd been dating for a month or two, she began imagining their future together. How many children would they have? Would she get along with his mother? Would he mind if she quit her job? And what were the possibilities of a posting in a foreign country? The company had several branches in the States and Europe. It was more than likely that Jun would be expected to do a stint abroad, and she knew that with her English-speaking abilities, she'd be an asset to him.

Three months into their relationship, he asked her to marry him. A year later, she was pregnant with Daisuke.

Nahoko remembered those delicious days of anticipation. She'd had an easy pregnancy. There'd been no morning sickness, no complications. She'd given up coffee and beer, but otherwise gone along as usual, meeting friends for lunch, attending yoga classes, sometimes swimming at the health club. She scrubbed the bathroom more than usual, following her mother's advice that cleaning the toilet would ensure a beautiful baby. And she went to the shrine of the dog god to pray for an easy delivery.

Daisuke had been born after seven hours of labor on a *daian*, an auspicious day on the calendar. Although she hadn't had much control over his exact birthdate, she felt proud of herself for the timing. Both her mother and mother-in-law had complimented her on this.

Daisuke was the first grandson on both sides of the family.

He was a beautiful baby with plump limbs and a full head of soft, black hair that stood up like a cockscomb. Nahoko had made everyone proud.

It would be another twelve years before they would live in Atlanta. By that time, Nahoko's English had gone rusty, but she could still remember the words to "Please Mr. Postman," could still imbue the song with feeling.

She sat on the sofa, coffee cup in hand, and closed her eyes. She had a sudden urge to abandon her housework and dash off to a karaoke box. Who could she get to join her? One of the baseball team members' mothers? Masami? She seemed sort of quirky and spontaneous. Then again, she worked at night. She'd probably be sleeping. And Jun might object to having his wife consort with a divorcee. He was in Tokyo, but word got around. He'd find out somehow. Keiko? They'd been friends when their kids went to elementary school together. They met up for lunch once in a while, but Keiko was pretty conservative. She'd probably find Nahoko's urge bizarre.

She wished that she had some foreign friends. An American friend, maybe, like her friend Delia in Atlanta. Delia had been a little bit wild (she'd confessed to smoking pot in college), but she'd been a lot of fun. They'd gone to Happy Hour once and let strangers buy them drinks. Nahoko had found the situation both thrilling and dangerous. They were both mothers! PTA members! They were wives!

She wondered what Daisuke's coach's wife was like. She'd heard that Coach Yamada had married an American, an English teacher. She'd never met the woman, but she'd heard that she was beautiful, if a little unkempt.

"She hardly ever wears makeup," one baseball player's mother had said. The woman lived a couple doors down from the Yamada family. "And she goes out in her pajamas to get the newspaper."

"One of their kids is a cripple," another woman had added. "She's always in the hospital."

Nahoko had the sense that the other mothers felt sorry for her, but didn't want to have anything to do with her. Sometimes it seemed as if they felt sorry for Coach Yamada most of all. If only he had married a Japanese woman, they sometimes implied, his life would be so much better. Nahoko wanted to meet her anyway.

The phone rang just as the last notes of "We've Only Just Begun" faded away, as if on cue. Nahoko sighed. *Back to the real world.* She knew exactly who was calling. Jun was in Tokyo now, but he only called in the evenings. It wasn't him. She picked up the receiver. "Yes, mother?"

HIDEKI

By the time Hideki stepped over the jumble of shoes in the entry-way, it was nine o'clock. *"Tadaima!"* he called out. "I'm home!" He toed aside Christine's overturned clogs and shucked off his sneakers before bending to line them up, toes pointing toward the door. A commotion erupted in the next room. The door opened, exhaling the aroma of grilled fish and steamed rice, and Koji rushed into his arms. The swelling around his eye had gone down a bit, but his skin was patched with blue and purple. Emma came crawling behind.

Although Christine sometimes grumbled that nine thirty was too late for a five- and a six-year-old to go to bed, she kept them up so that he could give them a bath. My, how she had changed. He remembered how she'd been startled by the newspaper pho-tos of fathers and daughters huddled together chin-deep in the bath. Americans, she said, would find them perverse. As if being naked was bad. As if all fathers were incestuous molesters. But after the birth of their children, she'd come around to Japanese ideas about child-rearing and intimacy. In this land of no hugging and kissing, bath-time offered a rare opportunity for "skinship." Now they had their own photos of naked Emma in his big hands, being lowered into a plastic tub when she was in the NICU. Naked Emma, who was so skinny and undeveloped that she didn't have a vulva. She looked like a frog. But then she'd fleshed out and grown and Hideki had continued to bathe her, as Japanese fathers did. Christine had started calling him "The Bath Guy."

She appeared just then, her eyes smudged by dark circles. She was still wearing those sweatpants. "Hey," she said. "Did you call the school?"

"Yes, I talked to his homeroom teacher. She said that every-thing was fine at school today. It must have happened later, on the walk home." He braced himself for the outburst that he knew would come. Christine had taken the kids to visit her family in America during spring vacation. She always came back dissatisfied with everything in Japan. He figured it was partly guilt about living so far from her parents, partly regret, partly thinking that the grass is always greener somewhere else. In any case, she would be hard to please for at least another couple of weeks. He wanted a drink.

"Go on to the bath, Koji," she said sweetly, shooing their son away. As soon as he was out of earshot, she started up in a loud whisper. "See? I knew this would happen. He's just a little kid. I'm not letting him walk to school any more even if those are the rules. And we need to find out who did this to him. He won't tell me. Maybe you can get it out of him."

"Christine ...."

"We need to get him out of there. We need to get him into Seiko, with Elizabeth's daughter, away from those—those horrible bullies."

Hideki sighed. For all of her views on social justice, she could be such a princess at times. "Seiko's expensive. We can't afford the tuition. If you went back to work full time ..." Emma grabbed onto his knees. He reached down and heaved her into his arms. He felt a tug in his back. She was getting heavy. They wouldn't be able to lift her for much longer.

"You know I can't do that." Her eyes darted around as if she were looking for an emergency exit before returning to his. "You could ask your mother for tuition money."

Hideki's jaw tightened. "You hate my mother."

"I don't hate her. I invited her over for dinner next week for her birthday, didn't I? I just don't want to live with her."

Never mind that if they moved in together as he'd suggested, as tradition dictated, they wouldn't have to worry about how to pay their bills. They'd be able to pool their expenses. Christine could stay home if she wanted, or she could get a job and his mother could cook their meals and babysit.

"Or maybe I should take Emma and Koji to the States ...."

"Go ahead." He was already tired of this conversation, but he knew that they would have it again and again.

Koji's voice came from down the hall. "Daddy, not yet?"

He shrugged, shifting Emma on his hip. "Gotta go."

As he left Christine standing there, he felt a twinge of guilt. It was hard for her, raising these kids by herself in a foreign country and she deserved to have a little more help from him, but that was the nature of the job. He worked up to ten hours a day, seven days a week, all for the love and honor of his family.

His stomach growled, like a bear gnawing on his insides, but he knew the drill. He carried Emma to the bathroom down the hall where Christine had already filled the tub with orange-scented water and laid out fluffed-up towels.

Emma poked his cheek with her finger. "Papa," she said, the one word that she could pronounce.

In the early days, they'd spoken only English around the kids. Christine had propped them against her bent knees and said, "I'm Mommy. That's Daddy."

Once, Emma had mustered a string of da's, and for a long time, Christine took that as proof that she could hear. But "daddy," as it turned out, was too difficult to say. Emma couldn't see the word on the lips, the movement of the tongue. When Emma was about three, Christine had switched to "papa." Emma picked that up right away, but she had some trouble mastering the "m" sound. She couldn't even sign "mama" very well, since it involved brushing the index finger along one cheek, then extending the pinky. Those small movements that others took for granted required concentration and control. Emma had neither.

Hideki had shown her how to hold a pencil, and then, with her fist enclosed in his, he guided her hand, wrote the word "mama." He pointed to Christine, who was at the sink washing dishes, lost in some daydream, then to the word on the page.

Emma's eyes widened. She smiled and gripped the pencil, then wrote the word again, by herself. "Baba," she said softly. In Japanese, those two syllables meant something like "old hag," but Christine always said, "There must be some language in the world in which 'baba' means mother."

Emma filled the white space with letters, then she called out again. "Baba!"

Christine looked up. "*Nani*?" She wagged her forefinger. "What?"

Emma held the paper up. "Baba!"

"Oh, honey!" Christine shook the soapsuds from her hands, wiped them on a towel, then enfolded Emma into a hug. "Thank you," she said.

Hideki had watched his two girls dance around the room and tried not to think about all the words that his daughter had yet to learn.

Now, he rubbed his whiskery cheek against hers before lowering her onto the bathroom floor.

Koji was already naked and shivering on the tiles. He seemed somehow punier than he had the day before. Hideki helped Emma undress, shucked his own clothes, then entered the bath stall with her. He dipped the scoop into the steaming bath water and sloshed it over his son.

"Do you want to tell me what happened?"

Koji's head moved, almost imperceptibly. *No.*

Hideki knew all about the casual cruelty of boys. He'd been one himself, had endured cockroaches dropped down his shirt and gym clothes dunked in the toilet while his buddies roiled with laughter. Boyhood was a long hazing of thoughtlessly perpetrated kicks, punches, jeers, and flicked towels that were just as quickly forgotten. If Koji could make it through the gauntlet, he'd be a man. It was better not to make a big deal out of this. No one liked a tattletale.

"You have to stand up for yourself," Hideki said, his voice

harsher than he'd intended. "Don't let the other kids push you around."

Koji nodded, his lower lip quivering. Hideki ignored the accumulation of tears, pretended they were drops of water from the bath. He ladled another scoop of water over Koji's scrawny limbs, then he held up his palms. "Here, show me what you've got."

Koji balled up his right hand and took a swing. To Hideki, it was like catching a gently lobbed tennis ball. Well, never mind. It was only the first day.

When the kids were bathed and tucked into bed, he finally sat down to his dinner. Christine dropped into the chair across from him, stifling a yawn. "So?"

"We had a talk," he said. "He'll be okay."

She nodded. The fight had gone out of her, at least temporarily. He could relax.

"How does your new team look?"

Hideki slurped from his bowl of miso soup and nodded. "Good. There's one kid, a returnee just back from Atlanta, who can really whack the ball."

"Atlanta, huh?"

"Yeah. Someone from your old neighborhood." Christine's parents and brother lived in South Carolina, the next state over. They'd all driven to Atlanta for a Braves game on one of Hideki's visits to the States, before he'd become a baseball coach himself. He remembered Atlanta as a hot, sticky city where all the streets were named after peach trees.

He'd have to ask Daisuke about it. Ask him if he ever had a hot dog at Nathan's, or visited the Coca Cola Museum, or Martin Luther King, Jr.'s childhood home. They might have a little something in common, Daisuke and Hideki. But for now, he was treating him like everyone else, watching from afar with muted awe as the kid blasted the ball during practice.

Kikawa was probably the best high school pitcher in the prefecture, but he needed back-up. Without good batting, it would be hard for them to win a tournament, and up until now he hadn't been impressed with his boys at the plate. But Daisuke ... that kid had it. That kid might be the answer to his prayers.

DAISUKE

To tell the truth, Tokushima Kita High School hadn't been Daisuke Uchida's first choice. When it came time to talk about high school, he told his parents that he'd decided on Tokushima Shogyo, a vocational high school that was renowned for its baseball team. Either that, or Naruto Tech, whose team had made it all the way to the final at Koshien the year before. But his father wouldn't even consider the idea.

"You're going to college," he said. "All those schools will prepare you for is a job on an assembly line, or as a garbage collector."

During their time in Atlanta a brand-new high school had opened back home in Tokushima. This school was planned as an academic school, a stepping stone to the best universities in Japan. Some of the top teachers in the school system had been transferred to the new school. Only students with scores in the upper fifth percentile on the entrance exam would be able to enroll.

"Does it have a baseball team?" Daisuke had asked.

"Of course. The coach played on Tsukuba University's team. There were a hundred players on the team, but he was a regular."

Tsukuba, Daisuke knew from his father, was a leader in the sciences. They were always coming up with new inventions, like the robot suit that allowed disabled people to walk. It was pretty cool. He was impressed by the coach's credentials. Even so, he didn't have high hopes for the baseball team. How good could they possibly be? They'd only been around for a few years, and the first team had been composed entirely of first year students: at best, kids who'd been second stringers in junior high school.

On the other hand, he couldn't help but shine among a ragtag crew like that. He could be team captain! A star! He and his mother had flown back to Japan for the entrance exams.

Now that he was here at Kita High, he was glad. Coach Yamada was strict, but fair. He was big on manners. He didn't cuff the boys like some other coaches did, and there was no enforced hierarchy on the team. In most clubs, first year students were relegated to washing their elders' uniforms and cleaning up after practice. The older players could boss the younger ones around as much as they liked. When the great Ichiro Suzuki had been a first-year high school student, he hadn't been allowed to practice at all. Only after a long, grueling apprenticeship were aspiring players allowed to touch the ball.

Kita High wasn't like that at all. The very first team members hadn't had anyone to serve. The following year, there were so few students that they bonded quickly, working together, trying to create a pleasant environment so no one would quit. The democratic atmosphere had continued. During the practice games, first-year students mixed it up with second- and third-year students. There was mutual respect all around.

On Saturday morning, Daisuke Uchida was surprised to see a little boy running around the bases. His hair was brown, and as he rounded third base and headed for home, Daisuke saw that his eyes were big and round. When the boy caught sight of him, he slowed and stumbled, then hurried to the office.

He came out again later when the team was warming up, clinging to Coach Yamada's leg.

"This is my son, Koji," Coach announced. "He'll be helping out today."

That explained the brown hair and saucer-shaped eyes. Daisuke knew that the coach's wife was American, and that he had two kids. There was something wrong with the other one, the girl, and she spent a lot of time in the hospital. Maybe she was sick now, and that's why Coach had brought his son along, but he knew better than to ask.

"Go talk English to him," another player said, nudging Daisuke toward the boy.

"I bet he speaks Japanese," Daisuke countered. "He lives in Japan, right?"

Daisuke hadn't used his English in a while, not outside of English class where he was careful to mimic the accents of the others. Even though he knew he was fluent and could speak with a native's rhythm and speed, it was best not to rub it in. Occasionally, however, he wished he could use his English with someone who spoke the language. When he got up close to the boy, he said, in a low voice, "Hey, Koji. Do you like baseball?"

The kid was silent for a long time. He dropped his eyes and started scuffing at the clay. He'd probably rather be with his mom and sister or sitting in front of the TV. Or maybe he didn't understand. Finally, he looked up and shrugged. "Sometimes."

So he spoke English after all.

Coach came over then and ruffled the boy's hair. One of the managers trailed behind him. "Tomomi will play with you," Coach said. "She'll get you some juice."

Daisuke felt a twinge of jealousy. He couldn't remember his own father ever speaking to him with such gentleness. And when did he ever touch him like that?

"You're lucky, kid," he wanted to say. But he turned away and headed back onto the field.

After half an hour of calisthenics, ten laps around the field, and a hundred swings of the bat, Daisuke was tired. And hungry. He sank back on his haunches and lifted the plastic lid of his lunch box. He broke a pair of disposable chopsticks apart and started digging in. As he popped the wiener into his mouth, he thought of his mom standing at the stove at five a.m. When he had dragged himself into the kitchen that morning, he heard the sausages sizzling in the pan, smelled the coffee that his mom drank, black, from a big mug as she put together his lunch.

When he was little, she'd cut the wieners into shapes, octopus and crabs, for the special lunches he'd taken on field trips. She'd tucked in apples cut to look like rabbits, carrots in the shape of flowers. Now, she didn't bother with the cute stuff, but she made his lunch. Every day.

He scooped the sesame-sprinkled rice, now cold, into his mouth. Then a big bite of grilled salmon. Up until last year, she'd made lunch for his dad, too. But now he was working at the Tokyo branch office and only came home on weekends. Sometimes, not even that.

Daisuke dipped his chopsticks into the box again and pulled out a chunk of simmered pumpkin left over from dinner the night before. He'd eaten alone, as usual. On weekdays, baseball practice didn't finish till almost nine. His sister and mom ate earlier. They were always mad at each other. He imagined their cold, silent meals. Maybe it was better to eat by himself, in peace. He wolfed down the rest of the rice, a boiled taro, a bit of bamboo shoot. Lastly, for dessert, there was one perfect strawberry.

At the end of practice, as Daisuke was shoving his gear back into his bag, Coach tapped him on the shoulder.

"That was some nice batting," he said.

Daisuke nodded, suppressing a smile. He was used to hearing this kind of praise, had heard it all the time from his coach and teammates in Atlanta, but he was glad that Coach Yamada had finally recognized his ability.

"But you need to work on your bunting," Coach added.

Daisuke felt a blush rising. "Yes, sir."

In the States, no one cared about the bunt. There had been a few guys on his team who excelled at laying the ball into the dirt—not him—but it wasn't a necessary skill. It was far better to be able to blast the ball out of the park, which was something he *could* do. But he knew enough about Japanese baseball to understand that humility, embodied by the sacrifice bunt, was valued here. And having an outsized personality did nothing to endear you to your teammates. He wanted the respect of his peers. He vowed then and there to master the bunt.

He was hungry again by the time practice finished. Dinner was probably on the table, but he needed something to tide him over. On his way home he stopped by Lawson's for chocolate and to look at the comics. It was pretty nice to have his freedom back. In America, "Land of the Free," he and his friends weren't allowed to go anywhere on their own. But here, his parents weren't worried that he'd get knifed or something on the way home from school. Midway between home and school there was a *koban*, an outpost of the police station, but the officers who worked there usually didn't have much to do except help out people who needed directions, or answer inquiries about stolen bicycles. A bunch of bikes were parked in front of the convenience store. He squeezed through them, pushed through the glass doors, and there she was, Nana Takai, standing behind the counter.

She was ringing up another customer's bento, so she didn't see him at first. He watched her fingers fly over the keys. She seemed so professional. Daisuke was relieved to find her there. If she was working a minimum wage job, then there's no way she would be into compensated dating. Why bother if you could make ten times as much money and not have to wear the Lawson's smock? Clearly, the story about her being a junior call girl was just some nasty rumor.

He grabbed a Ghana chocolate bar and a copy of *Jump*, stepped up to the cash register, and took a deep breath. "Hey, Nana. How's it going?"

She stared blankly at him at first, as if she didn't recognize him. As if he didn't sit right behind her in home room. *Strike one.*

"Do you work here?" he asked. His voice cracked a little.

"Obviously." She rolled her eyes and reached for the chocolate. *Strike two.*

"Every day?"

She glared at him. Her eyelashes were heavy with mascara, which she must have applied after school. It made her look older. Intimidating. "What's it to you?" *Not a hit, exactly, but she* did *speak to him.*

He shrugged. "Just making conversation."

She was silent for a moment as she pecked at the cash register. "Five hundred fifty yen," she said.

Daisuke handed the money over, trying to think of something else to say, but his mind went blank. She didn't seem to want to talk to him anyway. Maybe she'd already decided that she didn't like him. "Well, see ya," he said, turning away. He was just about to push through the door when she called out to him.

"What?" Daisuke asked. *Yes!*, his inner voice shouted. *Still in the game.*

"You lived in America, didn't you?"

She *did* know who he was. "Yeah. For three years."

"What was it like?"

"Good," he said, thinking of his teammates chanting his name, hoisting him onto their shoulders after a big victory.

But then he remembered that time when he walked out of his ESL class and a big kid in chains and a backwards baseball cap slammed him against his locker.

"Hey, you speak-ee English-ee?" he had said, his spit showering Daisuke's face.

Luckily, Jamal came to his rescue. "Leave my friend alone," he said. "He's our homerun king."

"Sometimes it wasn't so good," he admitted to Nana.

"Kinda like here," she said. When she finally smiled, it felt like he'd hit a home run.

CHRISTINE

While Christine was setting the table for dinner, Hideki's car pulled into the driveway. It was odd for him to be home so early, but she felt a little leap of pleasure. For once, they'd be able to eat dinner as a family. She reached into the drawer for another pair of chopsticks. But no ...

"Sorry, Christine. I forgot to tell you. Tonight is the welcome party for new teachers." He stuck his head into the living/dining room for a moment, then disappeared down the hall. She heard the shower door open and close, the spray of water.

Christine sighed. Parties were the one thing she didn't miss about working in the public schools. Back when she'd been an assistant English teacher, she'd been more or less required to attend the end of the year parties, the parties at the beginning of the academic year and the end of each semester. There was always lots of beer and karaoke and then work the next morning. And of course, these get-togethers were only for co-workers, meant to promote harmony in the office. Spouses weren't invited.

"Where's Daddy going?" Koji asked. He'd spent most of the morning hanging out at the baseball diamond, but now he was sitting on the floor, building a castle with Legos. His sister was trying to help.

Christine mimed drinking from a glass, then rolled her eyes and staggered around. The kids laughed. It was mean, but she was feeling irritated. Why couldn't Hideki write this stuff down on the calendar, or something? More and more these days he seemed to take his family for granted. They were an afterthought.

He breezed into the room a few minutes later, shaven and suited up in a jacket and tie. When he bent down to her for a quick kiss, she caught a whiff of aftershave. And then he was off, till the early morning hours no doubt. Those P.E. teachers could drink, and they usually went on to a second and third party, ending up singing karaoke in some tiny hostess club where one of them kept a bottle of scotch. Christine would find the matchbooks in his pants pocket the next morning.

The mothers at the deaf school had parties, too, though not as often as the teachers. Christine had gone to one or two, but working out childcare was such a hassle, and she never had a good time. She'd stopped going after a while. She'd spent enough time with these women over the past few years anyhow.

It was Deaf School policy that the mothers of the three-to-five-year-olds hang around until their kids were ready to go home. "In case something happens," Nishioka-sensei, the head teacher, had explained. Most of the mothers whiled away the hours in the designated Mothers' Room where there was a coffee maker and a microwave and a long low table surrounded by cushions. Christine wasn't used to kneeling for hours at a time, and besides, she didn't want to sit around chatting when she could be doing something more useful. What did she have in common with the other mothers anyway, besides a deaf child?

Most of them were at least a decade younger than Christine. They'd all been born and raised in Tokushima. Only a couple of them had ever been abroad: one to Guam, on her honeymoon; another to Hawaii with her family the year before. Another woman's husband frequently traveled for business to Egypt, Saudi Arabia, and India, but she had never left the country herself.

A fourth of them had gotten married because "they'd had to," or maybe they'd just hurried the inevitable along. In the Mothers' Room, the youngest ones bragged about their youth. Once a week there was some conversation about sex (birth control, or maybe frequency of) and another about dieting, although they were mostly as slender as bamboo.

Christine had lived in Europe for a while before she came to Japan. She'd traveled in developing countries. She'd volunteered in a Cambodian refugee camp. Before that, she'd lived in four different states. She'd had a lot of boyfriends in her teens and twenties, a few tumultuous relationships she thought she'd never get over, but when she met Hideki, something had gone still at the center of her. She'd first been taken in by his untameable curls, his kind eyes, the lines that rayed out from them from so much smiling. Later, she'd been moved by his sense of social justice. Before he became a baseball coach, he'd volunteered with underprivileged kids in the next town over, the ones whose ancestors were butchers and tanners and undertakers, descendants of untouchables who still felt the sting of prejudice.

Christine's decision, after four years of knowing him, to marry and settle in Japan, had been careful and deliberate. They hadn't wanted kids right away, or at least she hadn't; Hideki had gently proposed starting a family as they downed a bottle of Dom Perignon on their first anniversary, but she'd wanted to travel a bit more and write a novel. When their son, and a year later, their daughter, had finally been born, they had been planned and wanted.

Christine's adult students had been eager to wring every possible bit of Native Speaker syntax and American culture out of her. They asked her opinions about Japan-U.S. trade friction, the bases in Okinawa, whale hunting, and they wrote down what she said. The mothers, though, did not seem at all interested in her point of view, and she avoided referring to her previous life in Michigan or South Carolina or France because she didn't want to appear pretentious.

She realized that she could have tried harder to fit in, but that she didn't really want to. When there weren't any meetings about the sports festival or the bazaar or the sleepover or whatever, Christine would sometimes slip away and go for a walk in the park, or even duck into a café and read a magazine. She always felt a little guilty when she returned. The mothers would look up in something like surprise when she pulled the door open. Sometimes she wondered if they talked about her when she wasn't there. They probably did.

Well, thank goodness for the American Wives' Club. And the internet. When supper was over and done with, the dishes washed and put away, and Emma and Koji were finally tucked into their futons, Christine poured herself a glass of red wine and turned on the computer to check her email. Several messages were waiting in her inbox. There were a few from the special needs listserv: a discussion about the pros and cons of Botox, a link to an article on deep brain stimulation, some raves about hippotherapy. There was one message from her parents, a couple from friends, and another from Andrew, a guy she knew from high school.

Actually, she hadn't known him all that well back then. Her dad had been transferred from Michigan to South Carolina just before her last year of senior high. Andrew, a white-blond guy with an acne-scarred face (now rugged in a Tommy Lee Jones kind of way) had been in her Western Civilization class.

Back in twelfth grade, she'd actually had a crush on him. It had never come to anything, of course, because he'd been dating one of those big-haired girls with the honeyed accents. Lisa Anne, or Lizzie Mae. Something like that. But she remembered how, when the other students in her class had laughed at her pronunciation of cement (presumably, it had sounded like "smut" to them), he'd remained sober and interpreted: "She means see-ment." She had always liked him for that. Even now, nearly fifteen years later. She'd seen him once after graduation, and even danced with him at the five-year class reunion. He'd been at the Citadel down in Charleston. He was about to be posted overseas, and she had already made plans to teach in Japan. On another evening with another glass of wine, when Hideki was off at a different work-related party, Christine had logged onto the internet and searched for childhood friends, former classmates, old crushes. She "reconnected" with Andrew. She wrote to him about how she had gotten married and started a family. He responded with the story of how he went to Iraq and was blown into pieces.

Christine clicked open his message: "Check out my new leg." He'd attached a photo of his prosthesis, a high-tech marvel of anthracite and silver. "Pretty cool, huh? It's computerized even. It comes with a remote control." She remembered the artificial limbs of the Cambodian refugees, the pieces of wood lashed onto stumps.

With this leg, Andrew wrote, he'd be able to do all of the things he had done before: walk, run, ski, jump. He would be able to sway on the dance floor with a woman pressed up against him. He might even go back to Iraq. Reading this, Christine felt a flash of jealousy. Even though he didn't have a leg, he would be able to get around on two feet while Emma was stuck in her chair. For a hideous moment, she thought: what if we chop off Emma's legs and fit her out with prosthetics? She shook the thought from her head—was she a monster or a mother?—and tried to think up a reply.

"Wow!" she typed in. "Very cool, indeed!" That wasn't enough. Maybe she could attach a photo of her own? One of Emma with her leg braces? She'd let Emma choose the color of the leather, and so they were bright orange, like traffic cones.

She scrolled through a bunch of photos and settled on one with her and Emma together. She knew she looked good in the photo. It had been taken during the entrance ceremony for the deaf school kindergarten so she was wearing makeup and a creamy jacquard suit, her hair swirled and pinned in a French twist. She attached the photo. Pressed send.

DAISUKE

After dinner, Daisuke checked his email. There was something from Rico. He clicked open the message:

The results of yesterday's game are in. Eagles—5 Bobcats – 1
Dude, we need you!

He remembered the Eagles. They weren't all that great: lots of errors, lots of wild pitches; his team, the Bobcats, had demolished them when they'd played them before. He felt a little bit sorry for his old teammates, but also glad that they missed him. And relieved that they still wanted him. In the back of his mind, he was keeping his options open. If things didn't work out with the baseball team here, he could always go back to Atlanta and sleep in Coach Harris's guest room. At his going-away party, the coach had clapped his hand on Daisuke's shoulder, looked him in the eyes, and said, "There will always be a place for you on this team. If you want to come back, my wife and I will treat you like a son."

There was a message from Jamal, too. He'd sent Daisuke, and about a million other friends, a picture of a cat sitting on a toilet.

In America, Jamal and Rico had tried to teach him about girls. "Tell them you like their clothes or say something nice about their hair," Rico had said. But Daisuke forgot how to string an English sentence together every time he came within three feet of a beautiful girl. American girls were kind of scary, to tell the truth. The ones at the middle school, and later the high school where he went for a few months before coming back to Japan, wore makeup and heels. They looked a lot older and more experienced than the girls he remembered from Japan. Plus, they were so confident, always walking in front of boys, never turning in their papers for them or refilling their drinks at lunch.

He could just imagine what Rico's girlfriend, Angela, would say if she knew that Japanese high school managers made *onigiri* for the baseball team: "Yo, you can make your damn rice balls by yourself!"

Of course, there were some quiet girls, like Lauren. She had been Daisuke's lab partner in ninth grade biology. She had long, red hair, and freckles all over her face and arms. He remembered how calmly she'd sliced into that fetal pig they were supposed to dissect. There wasn't any blood, but he'd hated the smell of formaldehyde, and he didn't like touching that rubbery skin. He'd thought he was going to throw up. Lauren, on the other hand, was totally unfazed.

"I'm going to be a doctor," she'd said. "When I'm in med school, I'll be cutting open dead people."

They got an A on the fetal pig, and everything else they did together. An A in science! His father was so proud. One kid complained that the Japanese exchange students were always warping the bell curve, but Daisuke knew that the good grade had nothing to do with him. He'd had to stay up with his English dictionary and biology textbook half the night, and even then, he didn't understand most of it. Now, riding his bike home, all those words jumped back into his head: mitochondria, nucleus, phylum. He still couldn't remember what they meant.

No, he didn't do all that great in his classes, but he'd starred on the baseball team. One morning, after a game in which he got a double and a single, Lauren had looked him straight in the eye and said, "You did good yesterday, Daisuke. I watched you."

People said stuff like that to him all the time, but when Lauren said it, he blushed. He didn't know what to say. He started stammering. "So y-you like baseball?"

She tilted her hand from side to side. *"Comme ci, comme ca."* They were in the same French class, too. "I heard rumors about you," she said. "I wanted to see if they were true."

At the next game he looked for her in the stands. He found her sitting alone at the top of the bleachers, a book in her hand. She didn't seem to have many friends. He knew how that was. When he'd first gotten to Atlanta, and couldn't speak English to save his life, he'd spent hours on the internet chatting with people back in Japan. He knew what it was like to be lonely. And yet, he could never get up the guts to sit by her at lunch or ask her to meet him at one of the Friday night school dances. What if he had been reading her wrong? What if she went to the game because she had a crush on another guy on the team?

The week before he left America to come back to Japan, Lauren showed up at his house on her bike. It was early March, still a little bit cold. She was wearing a green fleece pullover and jeans and an Atlanta Braves cap. "Hey," she said, stepping onto the porch.

Daisuke thought later that he should have invited her inside, but then his mother would have started serving tea and snacks and hovering over them like a mosquito. "Hey. What's up?"

"I brought this for you," she said, pulling the cap off. She reached up and tugged it onto his head. Her chest—her breasts!—brushed against him for an instant. He could hardly breathe. "Maybe someday you'll come back and play for the Braves," she said. Her voice was a little higher than usual, as if she were trying not to cry.

"Uh, thank you very much." He looked down at his shoes. "And thank you for helping me in biology. You were a very good partner."

He should have given her a gift, too. A folded fan, or an indigo dyed handkerchief. Or something else from that box of souvenirs that they'd brought over from Japan. But he was paralyzed. He couldn't move.

He thought of reaching out for a handshake, but then the most amazing thing happened. This strangely beautiful girl, with hair the color of marigolds, suddenly grabbed him by the shoulders and kissed him on the mouth. It happened in a heartbeat.

He was so surprised that he couldn't speak afterwards. Later, he wished that he'd wrapped his arms around her and kissed her back, or that he'd invited her to sip lemonade on the porch swing. Instead, he'd watched her run across the lawn to her bike and ride away. He hadn't even asked for her address.

NAHOKO

The phone rang in the middle of the night.

Nahoko stumbled out of bed and into the kitchen. Again, she knew who was calling. "Yes, mother?"

"Na-chan, I'm scared," came the tremulous voice. "Someone was touching my feet while I was sleeping."

"You were just imagining things," Nahoko said, suppressing a yawn. "It was only a dream."

Her mother whimpered on the other end of the line.

"Try to go back to sleep, okay? I'll be over in the morning."

When Nahoko went back to bed, she slept fitfully. She dreamed of a menacing presence at *her* window, a succubus crouched on *her* chest, someone touching *her* feet. In all that time in Atlanta, she'd never really felt scared, maybe because they'd had an alarm system in their rental house and policemen drove up and down the streets. Sometimes they'd heard sirens, but Jun was always there, sleeping beside her. Now that she was back in one of the safest countries in the world, she was suddenly infected by her mother's fears.

The next morning, as Nahoko and her mother sat at the kitchen table crunching rice crackers and sipping green tea, she noticed that Okaasan had framed a photo of Marilyn Monroe and put it on top of the television. How odd, especially since there weren't even any photos of grandchildren displayed in the room. But she knew what Marilyn meant to her mother. Whenever Nahoko had seen an image of Marilyn Monroe on a T-shirt or a poster or in a magazine in Atlanta, she'd thought of her mother.

As a child, she'd loved to hear Okaasan talk about Marilyn,

or Mon-chan, as she had been known in Japan, once the biggest foreign box office draw in the country. She'd flown into Narita for her honeymoon with Joe Dimaggio. Nahoko's mother had been a teenager then, and she'd been at the airport with her three best friends when the Pan American jet landed. The tarmac was mobbed with reporters and fans, the policemen on security duty just barely holding them back.

Nahoko's mother had managed to snap a photo of the honeymooners as they came off the plane: Marilyn beaming in her fur, Joe looking dour at her side. The photo was a tad blurry and a bit faded by now, but Nahoko figured it was worth some money. People were auctioning sales receipts and ashtrays left behind by famous people on eBay. If her mother wanted, she could make some cash. But the one time she'd suggested such a thing (as maybe a way to finance an apartment in the assisted living complex nearby), her mother had scoffed.

"This is my best memory," she'd said. "I'd never trade it for money."

A memory better than her own wedding day and honeymoon? Nahoko wondered. Better than the day she became a mother? Her faculties weren't holding up well. Although losing out to five minutes of Marilyn was wounding, Nahoko reminded herself that her mother was no longer as sensible and logical as she'd once been.

The elderly often remembered things that had happened in childhood better than they remembered the events of the day before, the nurse had said. So it wasn't altogether surprising that Nahoko's mother brought up Mon-chan even now.

"Right after I took that photo, those two got right back on the plane," she said. "There were so many people crowded around that they couldn't get through, so they slipped out the baggage hatch."

Nahoko nodded, feigning interest, although she'd memorized these facts long ago. "Joe bought her a string of Mikimoto pearls," she went on. "And they stayed at the Imperial Hotel."

As a girl, Nahoko's mother had saved newspaper and magazine photos of Marilyn and Joe strolling along the lawns of the Kawana Hotel, another photo of them dining at the Royal Host, a chain restaurant specializing in Hawaiian home cooking. The album also contained a clipping of Marilyn singing to the troops in Korea. It had been February, mid-winter, and there was snow in the air, but Marilyn had skipped out on her honeymoon to appear before 100,000 American soldiers in a flimsy purple sequined dress.

"She sang, 'Diamonds are a Girl's Best Friend.'" Nahoko's mother then proceeded to hum a few bars. At one time, she had known all the words, in English, no less, but her memory wasn't what it used to be.

"'The Honorable Buttocks-Swinging Actress,'" she quoted from a long ago news report, and giggled. "When she came back from Korea, she had a fever of 104 and a touch of pneumonia. Joe had to nurse her back to health before they could continue their honeymoon."

Nahoko had read that Joe Dimaggio had slapped Marilyn around, but for her mother, he remained saintly, a perfect gentleman. *He'd left roses on Marilyn's grave until he died!* Nahoko's father had never bothered to tend to his wife when she'd been in bed with the flu. It had always been Nahoko, or her older sister, Mariko.

According to tradition, Mariko was the one responsible for their mother now. Or Mariko's husband, rather. The plan was that Mariko would find a nice guy with a good job, get married, and he'd become the adopted eldest son. Their father had been adopted, changing his name when he entered the family. But Mariko wasn't all that interested in marriage. As soon as she'd finished high school, she'd fled to Tokyo. She'd studied design with hip city kids, shaking off all of her old-fashioned small-town values in four years. As she'd told Nahoko many times, she was never going back.

"But what about when Okaasan is old?" Nahoko had asked after their father died. "What if she can't take care of herself?" By this time, she had a family of her own. She'd made a point of marrying a second-born son so she wouldn't have to live with her in-laws.

"I don't think she'd be happy with me," Mariko said. "My apartment is so tiny." After college she'd gotten a job designing children's clothes. She liked to use images from pop art. She'd once sent a skirt for Momoe made of fabric printed with a motif from a painting by an American graffiti artist who'd died of AIDS. Another garment, coveralls for baby Daisuke, had featured the faux naïf art of a junkie who'd overdosed. Nahoko secretly thought that these clothes were inappropriate for children, and she wouldn't allow her son or daughter to wear them. If Mariko had kids of her own, she'd understand. Instead, she sketched while her Persian cat twined itself around her ankles, then sauntered into the bars of Roppongi with her young lovers.

"Did your husband take care of you when you were sick in America?" Okaasan asked now, memories of Joe DiMaggio somehow triggering thoughts of Jun.

Of course not! No matter where he was, he was too preoccupied to notice or care. But she didn't say this. "I never got sick in Atlanta," she lied.

No one took care of Nahoko, but someone was going to have to take care of her mother.

CHRISTINE

If Hideki wouldn't ask his mother to help them out, then she would. Christine knew that her mother-in-law would be horrified at the thought of her only grandson, the precious heir, being bitten and clawed by other children. She was coming over for her birthday dinner. Maybe Christine would be able to ask her then.

On her mother-in-law's birthday, Christine always baked a cake. She'd started this tradition when she'd married Hideki. Before then, his mother had never celebrated her birthday. Cakes and candles and wrapped presents were a Western custom, sometimes adopted for small children, but adults usually let the day pass by with little or no fanfare.

Christine liked to tell her kids that in America, people had birthday parties their whole lives. She'd been born on the same day as her great-grandfather, and they'd celebrated together until he died at the age of ninety-two. Birthday parties were one American custom that they embraced whole-heartedly.

This year, she'd made a Lady Baltimore cake from scratch, following the recipe in her tattered cookbook. Christine sent her mother-in-law off to play with the children while she put the last touches on her masterpiece. She hoped Hideki's mother, accustomed to airy cakes covered with whipped cream and fresh strawberries, with maybe a sprig of fresh parsley for color, would appreciate the butter cream rosettes. All afternoon she'd practiced squeezing homemade frosting from a tube. And hopefully, her mother-in-law would appreciate the children's hand-crafted gifts. She'd taken Emma shopping for beads: sparkly rhinestones, painted ceramic cylinders, round and octagonal beads, which she'd strung onto a silken cord all by herself.

Emma liked pretty things, and she liked stringing beads. Many little girls did. Once, in kindergarten, Emma's teacher had marveled at her concentration as she threaded wooden beads onto a string. When confronted with flashcards or worksheets, she had a tendency to squirm; what four-year-old wouldn't, Christine wondered. It was ridiculous to expect her to sit there and study at her age, and yet, the teacher had told Christine more than once that if she didn't force her daughter (her four-year-old!) to study, she could forget about college. That day in class, when Emma had strung nearly a meter of beads, her teacher had remarked, "She's good at this, isn't she? Maybe she can do this kind of work when she grows up."

Christine thought of the parking lot attendant at the YMCA where she used to swim. She could tell by his gait and his speech that he had cerebral palsy like Emma. He had gone to the same high school as Hideki, who'd told her that he'd had a hard time. And yet he had obviously learned quite a bit. He always directed her into the parking space in perfect English. What a waste, she thought, whenever she met him. He was obviously capable of so much more. And she would be damned if Emma did nothing but string beads when she was twenty-one.

Christine squeezed one last rosette, then loosely covered the cake with plastic wrap before sticking it back in the refrigerator.

Hideki breezed in with a platter of sushi from the Atom Boy restaurant down the road. Christine made it a policy of never attempting Japanese cuisine for her mother-in-law. And yet, for her birthday, she wanted to serve something that she would definitely like. She laid out plates for the sushi and little saucers for the soy sauce, ladled miso soup into lacquer bowls, and called everyone to the table.

Koji dashed out of the playroom and scrambled into his seat. Behind him, Hideki's mother held Emma up by her armpits and tried to make her walk.

"Honey, why don't you give your mother a hand," Christine

shouted. The woman had osteoporosis. She'd been warned by her doctor not to exert herself. If she injured her back, Christine would have two people with disabilities to take care of. That was the last thing she needed.

Emma could get to the table just fine on her hands and knees. She was agile and fast, and Christine kept the floor polished with Murphy's Oil Soap. But her mother-in-law hated to see her crawling around like an animal. She'd said as much, numerous times.

They'd barely begun to eat when the woman turned to her son and said, "I've learned of a masseuse in Ishii. He's helped people like Emma. I heard he helped a boy to walk."

Christine snorted. "What's his name? Jesus?" She'd been driving Emma to hospitals and various therapies and deaf school for years now. She was the one who coaxed Emma into leg braces every morning, who fitted the hearing aids into her ears, who drilled Emma in fingerspelling, who'd taught the little girl how to tie a bow.

Hideki ignored her. "Where is this masseuse, Okaasan? Did you get his business card?"

At that moment, she was irritated with both of them. Instead of trying to help Emma with what she had, those two were always looking for the magic bullet, the easy, instant solution, so they wouldn't have to be bothered to learn sign language or figure out how to get Emma up the stairs when she got too big to carry. Sure, she'd read up on the miracles at Lourdes and special therapies in Hungary. She had even gone to the Horinji Temple, one of the 88 on the Shikoku Temple Pilgrimage, to offer sandals woven from straw to the Buddha and pray for Emma to have strong, healthy legs. She didn't really expect anything to happen, though. She wasn't holding her breath.

"Emma-chan, you want to walk, don't you?" Hideki's mother said in a baby voice.

Christine sighed. She'd told her mother-in-law over and over that she needed to attract Emma's attention before speaking to her. Either the woman was ignoring her advice, or she was in deep denial. Probably the former. Oh, well. Christine had to stop directing communication. If the rest of the family wanted to converse with Emma, they'd have to find a way on their own.

Christine reached for the teapot and refilled her mother-in-law's cup.

Hideki devoured a piece of octopus sushi and started talking about some documentary he'd seen on TV. Apparently, there was a surgeon in Kyushu who'd successfully operated on patients with cerebral palsy. He cut a few tendons, and, after intensive therapy, the patients were able to walk. He'd already sent an email to this guy, asking if he could bring Emma for a consultation.

Christine bristled. She wasn't about to say, in her mother-in-law's presence, that this was the first time she'd heard about this plan. It would have been nice to have been consulted first, even if she was pretty sure she would have said "no." She didn't want any more knives going after her sweet baby girl.

When Emma was less than a year old, she'd developed a hernia. Christine remembered her shock at seeing the protrusion from her daughter's abdomen and the way that Emma had screamed when she touched it. It had been evening, so Hideki'd had to take her to the Emergency Room at the hospital while Christine stayed behind with Koji. The next time it happened, a couple of weeks later, this time in the afternoon, Christine had been the one to take her in. She'd dropped Koji off at his grandmother's and then later, stood by helplessly while the pediatrician eased Emma's intestines back into place. The third time, the doctor had recommended surgery. It was a simple, relatively non-invasive procedure, but it would require anesthesia and Emma was getting a cold. Back then, Emma's colds lasted for months, or else they came one on top of the other with no break in between. Hideki insisted that the doctor perform surgery right away, although the anesthesiologist warned that her cold increased the risk.

"Maybe we should wait," Christine had said. Maybe they

could wrap her abdomen so nothing would pop out. Or they could just bring her back if she had another hernia before her cold was cured. It wasn't worth risking her life.

But Hideki had looked at her with disbelief. "What are you talking about? I can't stand to see her in that kind of pain." The doctors, he said, were overly cautious.

And so she'd given in, although it went against her gut feeling. The operation went smoothly. Emma recovered and never had another hernia again. But Christine chalked the success of the surgery up to luck, not her husband's good judgment. It could have gone either way.

"More sushi?" Hideki asked his mother now. "You're the birthday lady. Eat up!"

She demurred, patting her flat stomach, though she'd eaten only a few bites. Perhaps she was just being polite. Christine passed the platter to her and pointed out that the rest of them had all had their share of the expensive tuna sushi, and the ikura sushi, the fish eggs that glistened like small orange jewels.

"Well, okay." Hideki's mother plucked up a couple more pieces and lowered them to her plate.

When the platter had been cleared of all but a couple of thin slices of pickled ginger, Christine went behind the counter to prepare the cake. She set out a stack of Wedgewood dessert plates and tiny forks, which Hideki dutifully distributed. Of course, she wasn't going to make the woman try to blow out sixty-one candles, but she did stab a few into the top of the cake just to be festive. She lit them with a lighter and instructed Koji to turn off the lights.

"Happy birthday to you," she sang, carrying the cake slowly to the table. Hideki and Koji warbled along, missing a word here and there. Christine set the cake in front of her mother-in-law. She knew that the Japanese didn't have the custom of making a wish before blowing out candles, so she made a wish herself: that Hideki's baseball team would make it to Koshien, that whoever had hurt her son would stop bullying him, that Emma would learn to walk. And then she realized she'd made too many wishes. She should have only made one.

Her mother-in-law drew in her breath and blew out the candles in one puff. Koji rushed to turn the lights back on. He was scared of the dark.

When the cake had been cut and plated, Christine waited anxiously for her mother-in-law to taste it.

She cut a dainty bite and lifted it to her mouth. Was that a grimace?

"Oh, Christine. This is much too sweet for me." She put down her fork, pushed her plate away, and cleansed her mouth with a swig of tea.

Christine filled her own mouth with cake to keep herself from saying anything. Yes, it was sweet. Yes, it was sinfully delicious and full of sugar and carbs and calories. It was cake! She had spent hours making it for this special occasion. She ate her entire piece in silence, not looking up once at the others. When she had finished, she noted with satisfaction that Emma, Koji, and Hideki had polished theirs off. She removed her mother-in-law's uneaten slice and covered it with plastic wrap to eat later herself.

Why couldn't the woman be gracious? Why couldn't she be kind? Christine felt like crying or screaming or throwing plates. Her irritation had to come out somehow. She felt, somewhat irrationally, that she needed reparation for how badly this evening had gone. Without thinking, she pushed the words out of her mouth. "Koji is being bullied. Would you loan us money so that we could put him into a private school?"

HIDEKI

So now Koji had a new teacher, a new uniform; this one with a red clip-on necktie and a dark gray jacket, as opposed to the mini-Prussian soldier outfit that the local public school required. It had a taken a bit of finesse and a lot of paperwork to get his son into the private school. Hideki had made phone calls. He knew the baseball coach, of course, and had gone to high school with one of the social studies teachers. Koji'd been subjected to the entrance exam, which included physical activities. Hideki had been embarrassed to find that his son was not good at jumping rope. He wondered briefly if Koji's supreme lack of coordination signaled some developmental disability, then shoved the idea aside. But there had been no doubt, not really, that he would be accepted. A decade or so ago, getting into the school had been highly competitive, but now with the declining population and the failing economy, enrollment had gone way down. Hideki knew that the school would be happy to take his mother's money, happy to add a bit of international flavor to the student body. He'd noticed that the Tanigawa kid, also a *hafu*, was featured prominently in the school's brochure. Koji would be a catch.

Although Hideki had feebly resisted his mother's offer to pay for tuition, he knew that once Christine got an idea in her head, she was like a dog with a bone. He didn't have the energy to go against her. He remembered how on their first date, Christine had talked about her dream of volunteering in a Third World country, helping Africans grow food, or teaching Southeast Asians about birth control. As the words flew out of her mouth, her hands fluttered like butterflies and her eyes were wide and bright.

Hideki had been impressed by her goodness then, her passion. When she left months later to teach English in a Cambodian refugee camp at the Thailand border, he hadn't even thought of stopping her. She was clearly a woman in need of a cause. Now she had another. She would rail against bullying just as she had been mobilized by Emma.

Emma's disability had actually animated her. It had given her something to fight for. Once, shortly after they'd learned that Emma was deaf, he came upon his wife cutting an article from the English-language newspaper she subscribed to. He tried to read the headline over her shoulder without being noticed, but she immediately swerved to him, her eyes filled with a manic light.

"There's an American woman in Tokyo who's opened a sign language school. She's here to help empower Japanese deaf people." She thrust the neatly clipped article at him and he was forced to take it. "She has a career," Christine went on. "She's traveled all over the world. This is the kind of role model that Emma should have."

Christine had been stockpiling books on Deaf culture. Already she was using sign language, not only with Emma, but with Koji, too. Hideki, however, had been reading about an operation that would help Emma to hear. Late one night he'd seen a documentary on TV featuring a little girl from Nagoya. She'd had this operation and now she was taking piano lessons and attending a normal school. Emma could have the same operation and there would be no need for hearing aids and sign language.

Around that time, one of his friends, a teacher at the School for the Disabled, called him on his cell phone to arrange a night out. Every six months or so they and two others who'd been in the same class in high school would make the rounds of bars and catch up on everything. Once they'd decided on a meeting place and time, the friend mentioned an art exhibition held the week before at the Culture Center.

"I saw your wife there," he said. "With your little girl."

He remembered then that Christine and Emma had gone on a field trip with the other toddlers in the early intervention program at the School for the Deaf.

He hadn't told any of his friends about Emma's deafness, or her inability to walk at the age of two. They didn't talk about things like that. Their conversations centered around work and the pennant race and world affairs.

"Yes," he said. "Christine likes stuff like that."

Maybe his friend had seen Emma's hearing aids, with the ridiculously pink ear molds that Christine had chosen. Maybe his wife had even gone over to his old friend and told him about all the times they'd been in and out of the hospital, the tests, Emma's disabilities. But he wouldn't discuss it now, just as he'd never questioned his friend about his wife's mental illness and the psychiatric treatments he'd alluded to.

That evening, after the children were tucked in, Christine was reading a book. Hideki was trying to watch the news, but she kept interrupting to read aloud passages.

"Get this," she said. "In Sweden parents are required by law to teach their deaf children sign language."

He grunted, then took a swig of beer. "So? Do you want to move to Sweden?"

She lowered the book to her lap and removed her reading glasses. "Is that such a bad idea? Japan isn't exactly the best place to raise a disabled child now, is it?"

"Things are changing," he said. "It takes time. Besides, if all the handicapped people in Japan left the country, how would everyone else learn to accept them?"

She put her reading glasses back on. "I wish you wouldn't use that word."

"What word?"

"Handicapped."

She was always insisting on a special vocabulary, always correcting his friends.

"I can't wait to see your baby," someone's wife had said when she was first pregnant. "*Hafu* babies are so cute."

"Double," Christine had corrected without a trace of humor. "'Half' is such a derogatory expression."

They meant well, his friends, but her belligerence had begun to offend them, so that now, instead of going out as couples, the wives stayed behind while the men drank together. He knew it was partly because his friends didn't know how to talk to Christine.

Then again, it wasn't as if he had time to get together with friends. He'd only seen his high school buddies during the New Year's holiday, and in summer, during Obon. They hadn't been able to dance Awa Odori together during the festival as they had in the past. All of their old traditions had been kicked aside. Baseball consumed him. He'd almost missed his daughter's birth because of baseball.

On that morning, when Hideki had arrived at his office at Kita High School, a rosy glow was just blooming on the horizon. He'd slept only a few hours the night before, having stayed at the hospital with Christine until midnight, after which he'd gone home and worried over his batting order for another couple of hours. Koji had been staying with his grandmother. He'd downed a can of hot coffee and the caffeine mixed with adrenaline was shooting through his veins. He was thinking about the game his team would play later that day. He was ready. In spite of the team's 0-19 win-loss history, he couldn't wait to gather up his players, all twelve of them, and get on that bus to Awaji Island. He'd booked a game with a school coached by one of his college teammates. They hadn't seen each other in years. He was looking forward to seeing his friend and rehashing those glory days, even if his players were sure to lose.

Through the window he could see some of his guys rolling in on their one-speed bicycles, their figures murky in the dawn. He felt a stab of tenderness for them. These were the boys who'd stuck by him week after week, month after month, while they lost to larger, more experienced teams. The diehards, who'd out-lasted the fifteen or twenty kids who'd almost immediately dropped out. The pioneers. Maybe their dads had told them how Coach Yamada had once been an ace pitcher himself. He'd been locally famous in high school, and then he'd gone on to Tsukuba University where he'd been named to the All-Star team. Coach Yamada knows baseball, they might tell their sons. Just give him a chance.

Before he'd been hired at this brand-new high school to put together a team from scratch, first year students only, Hideki had coached weightlifting. Although he'd become a high school teacher with the express goal of becoming a baseball coach, there weren't any openings when he was first employed. He'd been disappointed initially. Weightlifting was a minor sport; winning a meet didn't bring the same kind of glory as a soccer or a baseball victory. You'd never see the All-Shikoku weightlifting tournament on TV, whereas it seemed every television and radio in the nation was tuned in to the national high school baseball tournament at Koshien. Even so, he'd grown to love his job.

One day, this burly kid ambled into his weight room asking to join the team, and after a couple of years, Hideki had turned him into a national champion. They'd gotten newsprint. The kid had gone on to compete in China. He'd been awarded a full scholarship to college.

Coaching weightlifting had turned out to be immensely sat-isfying, so that when he'd been offered this new position, the first ever baseball coach at a newly opened high school, he'd hesitated at first. But he took the job. So now here he was, fumbling along, full of doubts. He no longer went to the movies with his wife, no longer had time for weekend junkets with her to nearby islands. He devoted himself to this fledgling team, while the parents complained his practice sessions were cutting into study time.

Even his wife grumbled.

"Why does baseball have to be so time-consuming?" Christine had asked several months earlier as he dragged in after dark. "In the United States, it's a summer sport, so why does it have to take up the whole year here?"

She'd left his supper on the table, covered in plastic wrap. Her own dirty dishes were in the sink.

"Your practice sessions and weekend games don't leave any time for family."

"My team is my family," he'd blurted.

She'd turned away, seeming to wilt a little, and he realized how much his words had wounded her.

He'd sat down at the table and peeled back the plastic to reveal cold gray meat edged by congealed fat. Normally, she would have warmed it up for him, but he decided to eat it cold as a kind of penance for what he'd said.

"I meant my *second* family," he amended, but it was too late.

Most of these kids would quit playing baseball after high school. Frankly, most of them had no talent. Once in a while he felt almost contemptuous of their clumsiness, their lack of motivation. When he'd played ball, the coach had practically dragged him off the field each day at the end of practice. He was always the last to leave. These kids were different. They didn't love the game the way he did. The ones who lived for baseball went to Seiko High School or Naruto Tech.

"You should try to make it more fun," Christine said. "It's a game. I've seen those baseball players at the high school where I teach running around with tires hitched to their shoulders. They look like prisoners in a gulag."

"You don't understand," he'd told her. He remembered how he'd hated dragging those tires around himself, and yet what remained most vivid in his memory was a sense of brotherhood, of accomplishment.

On that morning, he had pulled his uniform out of his duffel bag. He'd been doing his own laundry, ever since his wife had gone into the hospital due to premature labor. He'd been washing her clothes, too: her underwear and pajamas; she didn't like wearing the hospital garb. As he turned on the washing machine, he remembered how his mother used to bend over the sink in the evenings, rubbing hard at the dirt smudging the knees of his uniform. She never complained, even though the bleach made her skin flaky and dry.

He stripped off his sweatshirt and changed into his uniform.

Outside, the rented bus rumbled into the parking lot. He went out to meet the driver. Miki, his assistant coach, was just getting out of his car.

"How's your wife?" he asked.

"She says bed rest is boring, but she's doing okay," Hideki replied. "And yours?"

Miki grimaced. He was leaving his harried wife home with three little kids, including a baby. Since he was his own boss at his trucking company, he made his own hours, but he didn't devote a lot of time to his young family. According to Miki, his wife was always ranting.

"You'll see." Miki chucked his shoulder.

Hideki allowed himself a momentary vision of Christine with their son and the new baby. He pictured them a little older: a little girl, demure in a pinafore, and a boy the spitting image of himself at four or five; a boy in a baseball cap bouncing with energy.

"I guess it's time to round up the guys," Miki said.

Hideki nodded. The phone in his pocket began to ring. He pulled it out and flipped it open. It was from the hospital, probably his wife.

"*Hai*?"

But it wasn't Christine. A nurse was on the line.

"Your wife is about to go into surgery for an emergency C-section," she said. "You'd better come quick."

A C-section? He stood there holding the phone, uncomprehending. It was way too early, only 26 weeks into the pregnancy. He watched, unable to move, as his players filed out of the clubhouse and onto the bus.

He thought about calling his mother and asking her to go to the hospital in his place. Men of his father's generation didn't take off from work for the births of their children. Women had their babies with their mothers urging them on. But what about Koji? Anyhow, Christine would never forgive him if he didn't show up.

"I'm on my way."

"What is it?" Miki asked, glancing at the phone in his hand.

"She's having the baby now. I gotta go. Do you mind?"

Miki nudged him toward his car. "Of course not. I'll handle it."

Hideki grabbed his clothes, figuring he'd change at the hospital, then got into his car and peeled out of the parking lot. He raced all the way to the hospital, his heart hammering.

She was lying on a gurney when he arrived in the ward. The obstetrician, called in on a Saturday, greeted him in a pink polo shirt.

"She's gone into premature labor," he said in a matter-of-fact tone. "At twenty-six weeks, it'll be a challenge, but we'll do what we can to save the baby."

So blithe, Hideki thought. *As if it were just a job.* For a split second, he wanted to punch the doctor, to make him feel the same kind of ache that was spreading in his chest.

The nurse handed him a plastic bag containing Christine's wedding ring.

"No jewelry allowed in surgery," she said.

Hideki shoved it into his pants pocket and went over to his wife.

"I'm sorry," she said. "I tried ...."

He shook his head, trying to smile.

"Don't worry. Everything will be all right."

And then they were rushing down the hall and around the corner to the operating room.

"You can't go in," the nurse told him. "There's a waiting room over there."

He saw the fear in Christine's eyes, saw her biting her lower lip so as not to cry. "I'll see you later," he said. Then he waved—a small, futile gesture—and sat down to wait.

He tried not to think about the scalpel slitting his wife open, the blood, the tiny body being extracted and lifted into the light. Instead, he held an image of her face in his mind, her face on the morning she'd come to him after taking the home pregnancy test.

"It's blue! It's blue!"

He'd hugged her and swung her around the room until he realized that maybe he should be a little gentler, considering her condition.

Her morning sickness had been especially bad this time. He had listened to her retch for weeks afterward, had watched her face go gaunt and elegant. They'd go out for spaghetti at La Pomodoro, or burgers at McDonald's: Christine, Hideki, and little Koji; then she'd come home and rush to the toilet.

Hideki had gone to the corner convenience store in the middle of the night to buy fruit-flavored milk, pork-filled buns, bananas, whatever she thought she might be able to keep down. On every errand he'd been filled with affection: for his wife, for his two children.

Now he reached into his pocket, fingers grazing the muted cell phone, and grabbed Christine's wedding ring. He rolled it around in his hand, remembering the day when she'd told him that she was pregnant with a boy. He'd missed out on the ultrasound that day because of baseball practice. After hearing the news, Hideki had allowed himself to imagine playing catch in the backyard with his son. He'd even gone out and bought a child-sized mitt.

He'd actually managed to make it to the appointment where

they'd found out they'd be having a daughter.

"A boy and a girl," Christine had said.

"We hit the jackpot!" Hideki chimed in.

He put the ring back into his pocket and propped his elbows on his knees. He really wanted a cigarette. He'd promised Christine that he'd quit for the sake of the children, but ....

Not too long ago he'd seen a documentary about preemies on TV, so he knew that at twenty-six weeks, his daughter's lungs and hearts hadn't fully developed. She wouldn't have any body fat at this stage. At twenty-six weeks, she'd be in all kinds of danger.

He glanced at the operating room door. There was no sign of movement. He thought briefly of going into the stairwell to call Miki and find out how the game was going, then decided against it. Miki would want to know what was happening at the hospital. Then he thought of all the other people he would have to call when this was over with: his mother, his sister, his closest friends. He'd call Shimizu first. He'd be sympathetic, at least; his wife had miscarried twice before finally delivering a healthy baby girl. He sighed, hoisted himself up and went to buy a pack of Marlboros.

Hideki was outside on a bench, lighting up his second cigarette when the call came from the NICU.

"Your baby is stabilized," a nurse told him. "You can come and see her now."

He took a drag, then put out the cigarette with the heel of his shoe and went up to the fourth floor. A nurse with bobbed hair and glasses—Nurse Matsumoto, according to her name tag—came out to guide him through the rituals of hand-washing and disinfecting. She opened a locker to reveal sterile gauze robes and slippers, and handed him a mask and a cap.

The NICU was all bright light and beeping monitors. A nurse, visibly pregnant under her pink smock, paced with a baby that was hooked up to an IV pole.

Nurse Matsumoto led Hideki to the back of the unit.

"Here she is," she said, gesturing to the incubator in the corner.

Hideki looked up at the nurse. She was smiling, as if there was something to be happy about.

"Yamada Baby" was taped to the incubator.

His heart sunk. Let her die, he thought as he peered into the Plexiglas isolette, saw all of those wires and tubes threading into her scrawny raw body. Her eyes were fused shut. Her tiny head was oddly shaped: narrow, not round. Her froggy limbs were covered with black hair. She didn't even look human. *Let her die.* She was too small; it was way too early for this. The doctor had filled him in on everything that might go wrong: bleeding in the brain, hole in the heart, blindness, mental retardation. That is, if she made it through the night. Let her die. They'd try again. There was no reason that they couldn't succeed again. They were both healthy, more or less, only in their thirties. They had money in the bank. And if it didn't work out, well, they already had a son. And if they decided that they really wanted to have another child, he might even consider adopting. It wouldn't be the same as having another child of his own flesh and blood, and he could just imagine how his mother would feel about it, but he would do it if it would make Christine happy, if it would make up for all of this. Hadn't she tried to talk him into adopting before?

"It's the ethical thing to do," she'd said, citing Third World poverty. She started a clip file: articles about infanticide and baby hatches in Eastern Europe for abandoned Romany infants. He'd come across her, late at night, surfing international adoption sites on the internet.

"Sarita," she'd read aloud to him. "'She has a sunny disposition and is very clever.' We could raise an Indian girl, couldn't we? Even if she has a club foot?"

He'd shrugged, at a loss about what to do to get her mind off the foreign babies. What could she be thinking, wanting to raise a child that didn't look even remotely Japanese?

But then she'd gotten pregnant. Twice.

One of the babies' monitors started to beep. Hideki started at the sound, but Nurse Matsumoto opened the door to the isolette, calmly jiggled a wire, and stepped back.

"Have you decided on a name yet?" she asked.

"Uh, no. Not yet."

They'd talked about names of course, he and Christine. It'd been almost a game. They'd come up with new names every week. Christine had lobbied for Amelia or Annetta, her great-grandmothers' names for the girl, but Hideki wanted to name her after a flower. Yuri, for lily. Or Sumire (violet).

His mother had advised them to go to a fortune teller. If they chose the wrong kanji, the effect could be disastrous, she'd said. She also told them that they'd be in trouble for hanging their laundry facing north, the land of the dead. She hadn't gone to a fortune teller. Hideki's grandfather had chosen his and his sister's names. That's the way it was done. But his father was dead, and his mother would never presume to take on the duties of the patriarch. Hideki was the head of the family now, the one she deferred to. The fortune teller was just a suggestion. He'd never bring it up to Christine, though. Just the thought of her sputtering in indignation about his mother's presumption, her superstitious mind, kept him from mentioning it. He remembered how incensed she'd been about the five-month belly banding cere-mony his mother had proposed.

"It sounds like Chinese foot-binding," she'd wailed. "How barbaric!"

Now, in the NICU, he ran his fingers over the label on his daughter's incubator and lightly rapped his knuckles on the hard plastic.

Nurse Matsumoto suddenly appeared with a Polaroid cam-era.

"How about a photo? For your wife?"

He shook his head, and put a hand up as if to cover the lens.

"No!" Then he reeled away and moved to the door.

The nurses exchanged glances. *This one wasn't taking it too well.*

"*Shikata ga nai*," the doctor had said. "These things happen."

Sometimes babies were born too early. Sometimes they didn't make it past the first few hours.

Christine was wan and pale against the pillows. She tried to work up a smile.

"How is she? The nurses won't let me go see her till I can walk on my own."

Hideki detected a touch of relief in her tone. Maybe she didn't really want to see the baby. Maybe she was as scared as he was.

"She's fighting," he said, thinking of those tiny hands grasping at air. "She's ... cute."

"Really?"

"Yeah. I mean, she doesn't look like those babies." He gestured to the stack of child-rearing books at her bedside, the plump infants on the covers.

She nodded.

"So what do you think about Emma?"

"Emma?"

"As a name for our daughter. After Queen Emma of Hawaii."

They'd visited the queen's summer palace on their honeymoon, and Christine, he remembered, had been captivated by her biography. She was both Anglo and Hawaiian: a multicultural woman who did good deeds.

"Sure." Hideki shrugged. What did it matter anymore? She would probably be dead by morning.

He went closer to the bed, thinking to embrace her, to comfort her, and she scrunched up her nose.

"You've been smoking," she said. "You promised."

He sighed.

"I'm sorry. It's been quite a day."

He stayed with her for a few hours, till feeling started to return to her legs, till she urged him toward the door.

"Go get something to eat. You must be starving."

Gratefully, he made his exit. He went across the street to a little curry shop favored by interns and nurses.

After he'd placed his order, he drew out his cell phone and checked his messages. Miki had called three times. He dialed.

"How's your wife?"

"She's doing okay," Hideki replied. "The baby is in the NICU. I'll tell you about it later. How'd the game go?"

Something rustled on the other end of the line. Papers. Game stats, maybe.

"We won."

"What?"

"Yeah, it was sweet. Ten to zero. You know how Abe's slider is always a little screwy? Well, today he nailed it. Seven strike outs."

As Miki went through the game play by play, telling of Inoue's stolen base in the second inning, Tanaka's double with a runner on third, and the home run that had sent the whole team swarming in joyful disbelief, Hideki felt something swoop and soar inside of him. He choked back his emotions.

"That's great. Thank you for being there."

"No problem, man. Glad I could help."

When the food arrived, he ate quickly even though the spices singed his tongue. He had to get back over there, to the hospital. He wanted to tell Christine that something good had happened that day.

His small, weak team had won. It was only a practice game; it wouldn't enter the official record books, but they had earned their first victory. Suddenly he was ashamed for having doubted them, for having written off the game before they even got on the bus. There were some things that you couldn't predict.

He pushed his plate back, paid the bill, and shoved out into the night air. The sky was full of stars.

He stepped into the elevator. His fingers hovered over the buttons. Christine was on the third floor. She wouldn't care about the game right now, not really. She would want to know how the baby was. He pushed "four."

When he arrived at the NICU, he went through the first set of doors and carefully disinfected his hands just as the nurses had instructed earlier. He yanked a blue gown out of the locker and pulled it on over his clothes. Then the paper hat, then the mask.

Different nurses were on shift now. They hadn't seen him falter, and it felt as if he was being given a second chance. One pink-capped woman nodded to him as he made his way to his daughter.

His baby girl, barely more than a pound, wriggled in her glass case. He reached inside to stroke her foot. She startled, and he quickly drew his hand away. Her heart beat steady and strong.

He touched the label on the incubator.

"Excuse me, nurse?"

The young woman tending the baby next to his looked up. "Yes?"

"Can I borrow a pen?" He took a deep breath. "I'm ready to give her a name."

The first win that counted had come the following March in the spring tournament, just before the start of the new academic year. They'd been pitted against a school whose team had once won first place at Koshien and had been living on borrowed glory ever since. Those national champions were grandfathers by now, but people still remembered the name, still associated it with baseball and the ephemeral beauty of youth. This year, however, the team was nothing to write home about. They'd been involved in some sort of scandal: a brawl that made it into the newspapers, and they had had to sit out the autumn tournament. Their team had been demoralized, and it showed in every missed fly, every grounder bumbled at first. But while they were not exactly the most worthy of opponents, a win was a win.

Hideki had held his breath when the last batter went up to

the box. The score was 3-2, in Kita High's favor. Ikeda had runners on first and third. If number thirty-two sent the ball over the fence, they'd lose once again. Even a base hit could change their luck. Anything could happen. *C'mon, Junpei.* Hideki had stared at the kid on the mound. He was clearly tired. His throws had been going a bit wild the last couple of innings, but Hideki hadn't dared put anyone else in. The first toss was a little high. Ball one. The batter took a swipe at the second, barely nicking the ball. Strike one. And then the third, a little low, but the batter swooped at it anyway. The ball popped up just over Junpei's head, like a day moon, and then fell with a resounding smack into his open glove.

A siren blared, signaling the end of the game. The outfielders immediately began dashing toward the mound, the basemen, too, and then Hideki was among them, hugging, pounding their backs, being lifted onto their strong, young shoulders, and heaved toward the dugout. Their faces were streaked with dirt and sweat and tears. A large knot clogged Hideki's throat. *My boys,* he thought. *My boys.* He couldn't imagine ever feeling that happy again.

Back at the dugout, they set him down and they all gathered in a huddle. Hideki dragged the back of his hand over his eyes, dabbed at his nose, and said, "I'm proud of you. All of you."

Then they rushed into formation, a straight line on the field. Ikeda's players lined up across from them, their heads all drooping toward the earth. Hideki could see that most of them were crying. The teams doffed their caps and bowed to each other, and then Kita High's players remained on the field as the school song, hastily composed by the principal a few weeks before, blasted from the PA system. None of the players sang along. This was the first time they'd even heard the tune.

At last, they lined up again before the scattered fans in the bleachers and bowed. *"Arigato gozaimashita!"*

The spectators cheered and waved their makeshift pom-poms.

Hideki looked up into the stands and saw Christine. She'd left the kids with his mother. She was wearing a floppy straw hat and sunglasses, the only woman without a parasol and elbow-length gloves. She was also the only woman in a bright red dress. After a certain age, Japanese women went for dark, somber colors, but her closet was a rainbow. He knew that dress. He'd rubbed the soft cotton between his fingers. He'd undone the buttons that ran down the front of it. He wished she were closer so that he could swing her up in the air. Instead, when she seemed to be looking his way, he waved to her.

She brought her fingers to her mouth and blew him a kiss.

A few sportswriters and a reporter from a local TV station were waiting to talk to him. He could already envision the headline: "Fledgling team wins first tournament victory." He would have to tell Christine to turn on the six o'clock news. He imagined her at home with their children, watching him on television.

When he looked back up into the stands, she was gone.

DAISUKE

That evening, when Daisuke went to his sister's room to borrow her textbooks, she wasn't reading about physics or doing extra credit homework. He found her punching out a text message on her cell phone. In other words, she was behaving like a normal thirteen-year-old girl. It occurred to him that she may be able to offer some insight on the opposite sex after all.

"So, Peaches," he said, using her Atlanta nickname.

"It's Momoe to you." She didn't look up from her keypad.

"Okay. Momoe," he tried again. "What would you do if you liked some boy?"

Surprisingly, this interested her. She put her phone down and cocked her head at him. "I don't know. I guess I'd give him chocolate on Valentine's Day."

"Valentine's Day is a long time from now," he said. He couldn't wait until February to find out if Nana liked him. A lot could happen between now and then.

Momoe shrugged. "What difference does it make? There's no one interesting in my class."

"Well, what if there was?"

She picked up her cell phone again, turned it over in her hand. "I don't know. I guess I'd write my e-mail address on a piece of paper and leave it on his desk."

He tried to picture Nana leaving a note on his desk, but nothing came into focus. Somehow, he didn't think that was going to happen. He'd have to make the first move. Trying to get advice from Momoe was obviously a waste of time. He gathered up the textbooks. "Okay, thanks."

But she wasn't finished. Her eyes started to go all far away, as

SUZANNE KAMATA

if she was getting swept up in a fantasy. "Maybe after I wrote down my email address, I'd fold the paper into a crane or a flower," she said. "Or a rocket. Depending on what kind of guy he was."

"That is so lame."

"You're such a dumb jock. No wonder that girl Angela wouldn't give you the time of day last year."

"What do you know, Geek Girl?" he said huffing out of the room. Ten seconds later, he was back. "Do you have any origami paper?"

He wrote his name and email address, the one that went to his cell phone, on a piece of red origami paper. Then he sat at his desk and stared at it for a while. What kind of shape would impress a girl?

He should have been studying, but he went downstairs to the room where the bookshelves were and dug up an origami how-to book. He looked through its pages for something sort of complicated that Nana might like. A grasshopper? Probably not. A rhinoceros? Something ugly and horned? Uh, no. Plus, it looked too difficult. A gazelle? Graceful and gentle and a little exotic? Maybe. He decided to give it a try, but it turned out looking like a beetle. He finally decided on a rabbit. He used the paper with his name and email address. It turned out okay. He tucked it into his school bag for tomorrow.

The next morning, he left the house a little early and got to home room before anyone else. He stood the rabbit on Nana's desk, then went back out into the hallway until at least half the class, including Nana, had taken their seats. When he entered the room again, he saw her playing with the paper rabbit, making it hop across her desk. She seemed to be deep in thought, didn't even look up when he brushed past her desk. Maybe she was trying to figure out who'd left it there. Good. But then it occurred to him that she maybe she wouldn't unfold the paper. *Crap.* He watched as she put the origami animal in her skirt pocket and he slumped back in his chair.

Much later, at almost midnight, he was sitting at his desk working on his math homework when his cell phone chimed. Someone had sent him a message. His body felt like a pile of rags, and he could hardly keep his eyes open, although Okaasan had brought up a cup of milky coffee a while ago. He took a sip, then reached for the phone. Nana had sent a message: "Let's skip school tomorrow. Meet me at the shrine gate."

His stomach fluttered. He'd never skipped school before in his life. But maybe it was time. He needed a break from Mr. Tanaka and the stress of trying to readjust to all the rules of Japan. It'd be nice not to have to wear a tie for once. Plus, he wanted to get to know Nana. He wanted to find out what she was like when they weren't at school. He knew the shrine she was referring to, the one on the way to school, among fat, old trees with branches that scratched at the sky. He'd meet her there, and then deal with the consequences later.

With his thumb, he punched a reply to Nana. "Okay. See you."

Sending it off gave him an adrenaline rush. Suddenly he had enough energy to finish his homework.

The next morning, Daisuke dressed for school as usual. It was too hot for the jacket, but they didn't officially switch over to the summer uniform (short sleeves, no jacket) until June first. As he pedaled toward the shrine, he wondered if Nana had bothered to dress for school. Maybe they'd just miss a couple of classes and show up late. He'd brought along his books, just in case. And his baseball gear. He wasn't going to miss practice. Coach would be dividing them into three groups later this week, in time for the game on Saturday. His goal was to get on the A Team, the most elite, the ones who would play in the tournament. The others were more like farm teams. At any rate, this wasn't the time to skip baseball practice.

When he got to the big orange *torii* gate, he could see Nana sitting on the stone steps leading up to the shrine. He stopped and just watched her for a moment. Her face was tilted to the sun, and her hair shimmered. She was wearing jeans, a frilly sort of blouse, and large hoop earrings.

She jumped up when she saw him and grabbed the long rope that hung down in front of the shrine. She pulled, and the gong of the shrine bell echoed through the neighborhood.

"Hey," Daisuke said softly, half-expecting a crowd to gather. "Don't do that!"

"Why not?" she asked, skipping down the steps to where he was standing. "You don't want me calling up spirits?"

"Maybe we shouldn't draw attention to ourselves."

She snorted. "You think people don't notice us? You, the boy from overseas? Me, the girl from a bad neighborhood?"

He had no idea where she lived. "No, I meant that we don't need for everyone to know that we're skipping."

She stared at him for a long moment. "So, do you want to see it?"

"What?"

"The bad neighborhood."

He shrugged, pretending that he didn't care. She was starting to make him nervous. Also, he wanted to get off the streets, far away from anyone who might recognize him by his school uniform and almost bald head. Even a bad neighborhood would be better than standing out there in the open.

"We can hang out at my house," she said. "There's nobody there. My mom's off with her boyfriend."

"Your parents are divorced?" He tried to keep his voice casual, tried not to show his surprise.

"Yeah," she said. "My dad left when I was about three. We weren't the right kind of people for him, if you know what I mean."

He didn't know, but he wasn't going to ask her to explain. He just nodded and waited for her to get on her bicycle, then followed her along back roads, past bright pink azaleas.

They rode by walled compounds where gardeners clipped trees and the gravel was perfectly raked, then smaller houses with dirt lots. After that, the houses became rickety and worn, small one-story shacks with a rusty tricycle here and there. Nana pulled up in front of one of the shacks.

"This is it," she said with a shrug. She stared at Daisuke, maybe watching to see if he'd recoil.

He parked his bicycle alongside hers and waited while she fished her key out of her pocket and opened the door.

It was cool inside, and dark. He caught a whiff of moldering *tatami* and cigarette smoke. Every surface seemed to be covered with cups, papers, and knickknacks. He couldn't help but picture his own mother in this place. She'd be wearing an apron and waving a can of air freshener around.

Nana stepped out of her shoes and up onto the floor. She set out a pair of slippers for him. "Come in."

He took off his tie, dumped his backpack and gym bag in the corner of the entryway, and followed her into the room. She motioned him toward the cushions around a low wooden table. He sat down cross-legged. She went to the refrigerator and poured barley tea into two glasses.

As far as he could tell, there were three rooms in the little house: the living/dining area where they were now, and two bedrooms hidden behind sliding paper doors. In the corner of the room, there was a compact stereo and a row of CDs. He crawled over and took a look at some of the titles. She had music by Princess Princess and Seagulls Screaming Kiss Her Kiss Her: noisy girl bands. Apparently, she wasn't a big fan of ballads. But wait. There were several soundtracks from musicals: *The Rose of Versailles, The Pirates of Penzance, Gone with the Wind.* Her mother's music?

Daisuke heard the tinkle of ice cubes as she came to the table. He went back to his cushion and she set down a coaster in front of him, then the glass. She'd brought out a bowl of chips, too. "Go ahead."

He felt shy all of a sudden. Not knowing what else to do, he put his hands together. "*Itadakimasu.*" He picked up one chip and put it in his mouth. The crunching seemed deafening.

Nana tilted her own glass so that the ice cubes rattled against it. She sighed. "I can't wait to get out of here."

Daisuke wasn't sure if she meant this house or this town or something else. Maybe she was planning on going abroad. He remembered how in the convenience store she'd asked him about America.

And then, as if she'd been reading his mind, she said, "I hate the way everybody's connected here, the way everybody knows everyone else's business. It's such a small town and no one ever leaves. Except you, of course."

Coming from anyone else, that might have sounded like a dig. But Nana managed to make being an outsider seem like something positive. Maybe he was better off not knowing what was going on around there.

"Where do you want to go?" he asked. "After we graduate?"

"I'm going to Hyogo," she said. She looked at him for a moment, as if she was trying to decide whether or not she could trust him, then grabbed a thick scrapbook from the shelf next to the stereo. She opened it and pushed it in front of him.

There were magazine pictures of women in different costumes pasted on each page. Some of them had short hair and wore men's clothes. In one picture, a woman dressed as a man, in a tuxedo and top hat, was dancing with a woman in a green ballgown. She wore a blonde wig of fat curls. Another was dressed as a pirate. A moustache had been painted on her upper lip.

"I'm going to be an actress," Nana said. "I'm going to take the exam for the Takarazuka Music School."

Daisuke couldn't help but feel impressed. He wondered if she would play the male or female parts. Probably male. He couldn't imagine her begging for help or wringing her hands. The male characters were always more popular anyway.

"So, Rhett or Scarlett?" he asked.

Before they'd moved to Atlanta, Okaasan had made Daisuke and his sister watch *Gone with the Wind*. He guessed she thought she was preparing them for life in the American South, but real life, twenty-first century Georgia was nothing like slave times. The streets were full of African-Americans, but they were in suits, clutching briefcases and cell phones. Instead of mansions with big white columns out front, the city was all skyscrapers and Starbucks. So no, the movie didn't help with understanding American middle school, but maybe it would help him understand Nana.

He didn't have to explain his question. He could tell that she knew exactly what he was asking: Given the choice, which role would she play?

"Scarlett," she said.

"Really?"

"Well, yeah. Rhett was always trying to get Scarlett to fall in love with him, but she was so strong."

"Wasn't she always thinking about that other guy?"

"Ashley? Yeah, I guess. But when the enemy soldiers came, she held them off. And she got to wear beautiful dresses."

He tried to picture her in one of those gowns with the big skirts, maybe twirling a frilly parasol. She'd look pretty, no matter what.

"I'll have a stage name, and no one will know my real identity," she said. "Do you know about the violet code?"

He shrugged. "What's that?"

"Takarazuka members aren't allowed to talk about their boyfriends or tell anyone their ages. We have to be pure, righteous, and beautiful."

She was talking like she'd already made it into the troupe, but even he knew that it was very competitive. But her dream wasn't any wilder than his.

"I'm going to be a professional baseball player." He said it in a joking voice, as if he didn't really believe that he'd be able to make it to the pros. After all, every other kid in Japan dreamed of playing in the J-League or the majors. Obviously not all of them were going to make it. But secretly, that was his plan. There was that player from Tokushima Commercial High School who was recruited by the Atlanta Braves; he was the first local player ever to go to America to play ball. It didn't seem like such a crazy dream. Besides, he'd heard a rumor that a Dodgers scout was going to be coming around to check out Kikawa's pitching. Daisuke was going to make sure he was batting well on that day.

"Tigers or Giants?" Nana asked.

He smiled. "Are we talking about Japanese baseball, or the Major League?"

She shrugged. "Either one."

Nine of out ten Japanese baseball fans followed the Yomiuri Giants. They were on TV the most. They had the most money, and many of the best players, sort of like the New York Yankees.

"The Tigers," he shot back. "In both countries. I like the underdogs. And besides, if I played for the Hanshin Tigers, I'd get to spend a lot of time at Koshien." That was their home stadium. They had to clear out and go on the road during the high school baseball tournament, but they spent a lot of time there.

"If you play for the Tigers, you'll be right down the road from me." Nana leaned across the table. "Will you come and see me onstage?"

"Yeah," he told her. "Every chance I get."

At lunchtime, Nana made rice omelets. They ate while watching a movie—vintage Godzilla—and then, almost as if she were trying to think of another reason for him to stay, she said, "Do you want to see my room?"

"Uh, okay." Daisuke glanced toward the door, wondering what would happen if her mother suddenly showed up and found them alone, together. And then there was the fact that he'd never been in a girl's bedroom before. Well, except for Momoe's, and she was his sister. Remembering the rumors, he half expected Nana to turn into a black widow spider and devour him, but he figured it was safe to take a peek. Then he would have to get out of there. He couldn't be late for baseball practice.

Nana slid open one of the paper doors and waved him into her bedroom. It was cramped compared to his, but it was ten times neater. There were no clothes on the floor or draped over a chair, and no empty plastic soda bottles or candy bar wrappers cluttering her desk. A narrow bed piled with stuffed rabbits was against one wall. Against the other wall was a desk and a chest of drawers, on top of which were more rabbits, made of glass, ceramic, and papier-mâché. He was pleased to see that his origami rabbit was tucked among them.

"You like rabbits, huh?"

Nana grimaced. "I did."

"Overkill?"

Her face twisted up. "Ugh. Don't say that word."

Daisuke waited for an explanation.

She sighed. "When I was little, all I wanted was a pet rabbit. I begged my mother, but she said that it was hard enough for us to take care of ourselves, let alone an animal."

She picked up one of the ceramic bunnies from her chest of drawers and tossed it from palm to palm.

"And then?" he prompted.

"Then, when I was in second grade, our class had a pet rabbit. His name was Snow. Just before summer vacation, our teacher asked for volunteers to take the class pets home for the summer. There was also a fish and a stag beetle. A whole bunch of us wanted to take Snow, so the teacher said we could take turns over the summer. We did rock paper scissors to see who'd take him home first, and I won.

"We kept him in the house with us and let him hop around. He nibbled pieces of carrots out of my hand. I took really good care of him, but it was hot. So hot. My mother forgot to pay the electric bill, or maybe she just didn't have enough money. Anyway, our power was cut off for a couple of days so we couldn't use the air conditioner. My mother filled up the bathtub with cold water so we could take a dip whenever we needed to, but the heat was too much for Snow. He didn't make it."

She set the ceramic rabbit back in its place and sank onto the edge of her bed, as if all of those memories were weighing her down. "I wasn't too popular at school after that," she said. "Not that I had tons of friends before. And my mom felt bad, so ever since then, she's been giving me rabbits as gifts. On my birthday, Christmas, Children's Day, you name it. It's her way of apologizing, I guess."

"That must have sucked," Daisuke said. Maybe folding an origami rabbit was a bad idea after all. Maybe he should have tried harder for a gazelle.

She tossed her head, as if she were shaking herself free of the past. "Sorry. I didn't mean to be such a downer. I really do like rabbits."

"You don't have to apologize," he told her. "And I know this is bad timing, but I really have to go to baseball practice."

She shrugged. "I have to go to work."

Technically, it was against the rules for students at Tokushima Kita High School to have part-time jobs. They were supposed to be concentrating on their studies. But maybe Nana had gotten special permission to work since her parents were divorced.

Daisuke got to the clubhouse at the same time as Junji.

"Where were you today?" he asked.

"I, uh, didn't feel well," Daisuke said. He felt bad about lying to him, but he got the idea that Junji wouldn't approve of him skipping school to be with Nana. Part of Daisuke wanted to tell him that he was wrong about her, that all of those rumors about her dating older men were untrue. But another part of him knew that it wouldn't be so easy to change his friend's mind about her. Junji had never been out of the country. He'd hardly been off the island of Shikoku.

Junji looked him up and down. He was still wearing his jacket. "You didn't come to school, but you stayed in your uniform all day?"

He decided it was best not to answer. The more lies he told, the more likely he would slip up.

"Did anything exciting happen in class?" he asked.

"No, not really. You didn't miss a thing."

Junji turned away, and Daisuke felt himself blending in with the team. No one else was likely to ask him about his absence. Or so he thought.

"Uchida! Come over here," Coach called out.

Daisuke jogged over to where he was standing.

"*Hai?*"

"Your home room teacher told me you were absent today." He pressed his lips together, waiting for Daisuke to explain.

It figured that Mr. Tanaka would be the one to rat on him.

"If you start playing hooky, I'm not going to be able to put you in any games," Coach said.

"I'm sorry, sir. Something came up with my ... grandmother."

He put his hand on Daisuke's shoulder. "Well, next time have one of your parents call or something."

"Yes, sir." He looked up into his coach's eyes. He was almost smiling now.

"Okay. Go on." He nudged Daisuke toward the field.

His heart was thumping, and he wasn't sure if it was because of guilt or shame or the fear of getting caught. Maybe a little bit of each. He silently vowed that he wouldn't miss another class. He wouldn't skip school ever again to be with a girl. Nana should understand. She had her violet code, after all.

The next day, after lunch, in Morality Class, Ms. Sano, a thirty-something teacher in a pale orange suit, came into the classroom and wrote some kanji on the board.

"Today," she said, "we will talk about the Dowa Problem."

The girls in the back began to whisper. When Daisuke glanced at them, he saw that they were focused on Nana, who was starting to wilt. She didn't look at Daisuke or anyone else. She stared at her desk.

Ms. Sano wrote a list of ancient occupations on the board,

starting with shogun. In the middle are samurai, merchants, and farmers. Down at the bottom she wrote, "tanner, butcher, executioner, grave digger."

"We Japanese are all of the same blood," Ms. Sano went on, "but people in the Edo Era wanted to have a hierarchy. This was the caste system that existed until the end of the feudal age. It's illegal now to discriminate based on caste, but there are still people who hire detectives to research their children's prospective brides and grooms. There are still secret lists circulating among companies."

And probably secret lists going around among teachers and students, he thought. Or at least people talked. Suddenly he felt sick to his stomach. He understood why his classmates were so cold to Nana. He'd finally figured out what she was trying to tell him at the shrine the day before. Nana was part of the "Dowa Problem." Her ancestors were at the bottom of the social ladder and some people thought that she and her mother were still there.

He wanted to stand up and shout that none of this mattered. He wanted to tell everyone that Nana was his friend, to show his solidarity. But of course, he didn't. He remained silent, glued to his chair. He didn't even look at her, not wanting her to feel embarrassed, or think that he was giving her away. And besides, he was just getting to know her.

NAHOKO

Jun called that evening.

"I think our daughter has fallen in with a bad crowd." Nahoko twisted the hem of her nightgown in her fist as she spoke, feeling ashamed because she couldn't keep the kids in control, the household in order.

Her husband merely grunted on the other end.

"Did you hear me?" She felt a flash of irritation. "Her homeroom teacher called me this morning. She said that Momoe has been missing classes. Sometimes she doesn't show up at all." She wasn't even going to mention the phone call she'd gotten about Daisuke skipping school.

"What do you want me to do?" She could hear him sigh over the wires. "Should I come home? Do you want me to talk to her?"

Yes, she wanted to say. But she could read the sarcasm in his tone. He was preparing for a business trip to China to launch a new product, and he couldn't possibly return to Tokushima that weekend or the next. And, quite frankly, he didn't know how to talk to teenagers. These were rhetorical questions. It was her job to manage the home front, while he made the money that supported their comfortable lifestyle.

"How's Daisuke?" he asked. "How's the baseball?"

Typical. Change the subject. And yet, he had a right to ask about his son, and she was grateful for his interest.

"He's fine. You should see him. He oils his baseball glove every night before he goes to sleep, just like Ichiro. He's really good, you know. There's a tournament coming up in July. If you could come down for even one game, he'd be so happy." She was babbling, trying to fit as many words in as possible before he lost interest.

"I'll think about it. Is he studying?"

"Yes," she assured him. "He's getting great marks in English and his math is improving." Why did she have to work so hard to sell these children to their father? Why couldn't he just ask them himself?

"And your mother?"

Nahoko paused for a few beats. She knew that Jun wasn't overly fond of her mother. He thought she was silly and hysterical. His own mother was an ice queen.

"One of her neighbors called me," she said slowly. "She's been digging holes in her yard and burying things. She thinks someone has been stealing her dishes."

From Tokyo, only silence.

"I've been thinking she should move in with us for a while. She needs company. Her doctor says that she's losing her grip on reality."

He knew about responsibility. He could hardly deny her this, and yet, even as she waited for his consent, she knew she was giving him yet another excuse to stay away.

He sighed again. "As you wish."

While they'd been living in Atlanta, Nahoko had worried about her children's education. Sure, their English improved; after three years abroad, they spoke better than she did; she couldn't understand them when they were talking to their American friends, but their Japanese skills had deteriorated. She'd sent them to Japanese school on Saturdays at first, but Daisuke had wanted to play baseball, and Momoe pleaded that she wanted to go to so-and-so's pool party, or to the mall with somebody else, and finally she'd given up. When in Rome ... Her husband had insisted that they keep up with their kanji. Nahoko had sent to Japan for workbooks and CD-ROMs, and every now and then she'd asked if they'd done their homework, but she hadn't pressured them too much. Like her kids, she'd been seduced by the relaxed, anything-goes atmosphere, the freedom of America. She'd let them eat cornflakes for breakfast and sandwiches for lunch.

But now, she understood that she had been wrong. If Daisuke and Momoe were going to succeed in their native country, they needed discipline. They needed a thousand kanji to read the newspaper. They needed to blend in with their peers. And she needed to be a better mother. And daughter.

In spite of her resolve, she missed the following Monday's visit. Two weeks later, she got a phone call from one of her mother's neighbors.

"I think you'd better check in with your mother," the woman said. "She's had her locks changed two days in a row. She seems confused."

"Busybody!" Nahoko muttered to herself after hanging up the phone. And yet, she felt guilty. For the past three years, she'd been relieved to be on the other side of the globe from her mother, too far away to be at her beck and call. Her sister had been in Japan, in Tokyo, but at least she was in the same time zone. Their mother could call her and rant about the neighbors without worrying about NTT long-distance fees. Now that Nahoko was back in the same prefecture, just twenty minutes away by car, her mother had started calling daily, on the slightest pretext. For the most part, she tried to pre-empt these calls, phoning her as soon as the kids had gotten off to school. But sometimes her mother forgot that they had spoken and called a few hours later, wondering why she hadn't heard from her younger daughter.

Nahoko took her time getting ready. She put on make-up—it was rude not to—and cut some daffodils from the little garden she'd started at the side of the house. She wrapped them in a cone of newspaper and set out for her mother's house.

When she got there, she found that the door was locked. She rang the bell. As she waited, she gazed around the yard, noting the weeds that had grown up on the pebble path leading to the door. Her mother had always been so meticulous, weeding and sweeping the concrete driveway almost daily. From inside, she heard the sound of footsteps. The door opened just a crack.

"Who is it?"

"Okaasan, it's me. Nahoko."

The door opened wider.

Nahoko breathed in sharply. Her mother's hair was all snarly as if it hadn't been combed all week. The air, when she stepped inside the dimmed room, was stale, slightly putrid. Obviously, the windows hadn't been opened in days.

"Mother, are you okay? Have you been sick?"

"I'm fine," she said. She grabbed Nahoko's sleeve and dragged her toward the kitchen. "I have to show you something." She opened the refrigerator. The shelves were laden with small, unwrapped dishes of moldy leftovers. Bowls of rice covered in bluish fuzz. Egg salad that had turned green. "Look here. Someone has been putting rotten food inside."

It was still morning, but Nahoko felt a wave of fatigue coming on. "Mother, I think you must have put this stuff in here and forgotten about it."

"I would never do such a thing," the older woman said. And then she looked at her daughter and gave a little cry. "You did it, didn't you? It was you!"

With a sinking heart, Nahoko realized that nothing she said at that moment would make any difference.

Later, at home, she realized she would have to call Mariko. Just the thought of her sister filled Nahoko with exasperation, and maybe a little envy. In Tokyo, she was oblivious to their mother's decline. She had no idea that her mother's refrigerator was filled with rotting food, that she'd padlocked all her cupboards shut and lost most of the keys, that she was convinced someone, a prowler, was creeping into her room every night and touching her feet. But Mariko needed to know these things. Nahoko sighed deeply and picked up the phone.

Since it was a weekday afternoon, she knew that Mariko would be at work, awake and sober. Sometimes when she called her sister on her cell phone, she could hear music in the background, or trains, or voices. It was hard to talk if she knew that Mariko was at a party or using public transportation. But if she was at her desk, at least she would be still.

The phone rang once, twice, and then, "Sis! What's happening?"

"Mariko, it's about Okaasan. She's not doing so well. I think she has Alzheimer's or something."

"I just talked to her yesterday," Mariko said. "She sounded fine to me. We got into this long conversation about that white dress that Marilyn Monroe wore while standing over the grating. Do you remember? That famous photo of Marilyn trying to hide her underwear?"

"I'm serious, Mariko. Last week when I went to visit her at three o'clock in the afternoon she was still wearing her nightclothes." She'd seemed disoriented. When Nahoko had pointed to the clock, she'd cried out in surprise. In Nahoko's childhood, their mother had gotten up before anyone else in the household, and she'd always been dressed when the girls stumbled into the kitchen for breakfast.

"Ha! Pajamas at three o'clock. That sounds like me!" Her hand went over the receiver for a moment, and Nahoko could hear her speaking to someone else, a co-worker perhaps.

When she came back on, Nahoko said, "Yeah, well, Okaasan isn't out in Roppongi until the wee hours of the morning. She goes to bed at about eight, in case you forgot."

Mariko sighed into the phone. "Listen, sis. Work is busy right now. We're heavily into the fall collection and I can't get away. I'll send her a robot."

"A robot? What are you talking about?"

The line went dead. Nahoko threw her cell phone across the room. It cracked and yet minutes later, it began to ring.

A package was delivered a week later. As soon as it arrived, her mother called, wanting help.

"I can't get this box opened," she fussed. "I think it must be locked."

Nahoko sighed. She was in the middle of making pickles. She couldn't just up and leave. "What box, Okaasan?"

"From your sister Mariko," she said. "A present from Tokyo." Her voice was filled with impatience, like a kid held back from the booty on Christmas morning. "When can you get here?" she whined.

If Nahoko waited until the next morning, her mother would probably call several more times that day. She'd forget that she'd already made the request. Or maybe she just did it to spite her daughter. "Give me an hour," she said, surrendering another afternoon to her mother's "emergency."

When she arrived, she found that her mother had managed to peel off the brown wrapping paper to reveal a large box. There was a picture of a fluffy white stuffed seal—no, a robot—on the side of the box. So this is what Mariko had been talking about: the latest rage, therapeutic robotic animals meant to comfort the sick and elderly.

Nahoko wondered if it would work, if it would keep her mother company, and distract her enough so that she would stop calling ten times a day. She went into the kitchen and got a knife and then she opened up the box. She showed her mother how to charge the robot, using an adapter that went into the seal's mouth like a pacifier.

"So soft," her mother said, stroking the fur. And then she made cooing sounds, the same sounds that she used to make with the little Pomeranian they'd once had.

Nahoko sighed. At best, it would buy her some time. Clearly, a robot seal was a stop-gap measure, something that *might* slow down her mother's dementia, if they were lucky. But Nahoko suspected it was too late.

"Do you want to give it a name?" Nahoko asked.

Her mother clasped her hands together, suddenly girlish. "I think I'll call her Mon-chan," she said. "After Marilyn Monroe."

When it was finally all juiced up, the baby seal began to move her head. She let out a small yelp, as if she were seeking her mother. Her flippers flapped like wings.

"Here I am, my darling Mon-chan," the elderly woman said. "I'm right here."

It's just a stupid toy! Nahoko thought. Filled with a sudden, aimless fury, she scooped the seal robot into her arms and held it, away from her mother's grasping hands. The thing kept moving, as if trying to squirm out of her grip, but she held on tightly, burying her face in its fur.

CHRISTINE

The American Wives' Club meeting was on a Saturday. They'd decided to gather at the McDonald's on Highway 17 because it was the only contained place where the moms could sit and drink coffee while the kids ran amuck. All the kids except, Emma, of course. While Trina counseled Sophia on the best places to buy organic food, Christine honed in on Emma, who was halfway through the plastic tunnel leading to the slide.

"Oh, just let them play," Elizabeth had said, when Christine made a motion to join the kids in the climbing structure. "The bigger kids will help Emma."

She knew that Trina and Elizabeth saw her as overprotective. Scraped knees and bumped elbows were part of childhood, they thought. And Emma—look at her! She was vigorous and determined! The other kids crawled over her, eager to move along, but she was undaunted!

Christine could see Koji, nudging her up toward the slide, and then the two of them came down together, Koji sitting behind, his arms wrapped around his sister's waist. They were both laughing, both wild-haired and bright.

She tore her eyes away and bit into her cheeseburger.

"I have something to tell you," Elizabeth said then.

"What?" Christine and Trina asked at once.

"We're being relocated. To Maryland."

Elizabeth's husband worked for a pharmaceutical company with branches around the world. She'd been pushing him for a transfer for a couple of years now. He finally had enough seniority for a plum assignment abroad. Plus, he spoke English, and his employers were no doubt sympathetic to the needs of his wife.

Trina held up her hand for a high five. "That's great! Congratulations!"

Christine wasn't in the mood to be happy for her. "What about your research?" she asked stupidly. "About foreigners in Tokushima?"

Elizabeth laughed. "Well, maybe I'll just turn it all over to you!"

When Christine had first arrived in Japan, she'd had a different set of friends: young, globe-trotting English teachers. They were all gone now, even the diehard Japanophiles, off to careers in foreign service, international law, and corporate event planning. For most of them, Japan had been a brief interlude. Only she had fallen in love and stayed behind.

In the intervening years, she'd met other foreigners, who had also returned to their home countries or moved on to the next adventure, and she'd even had a couple of Japanese friends, one of whom who'd eventually moved to Tokyo, another to San Francisco. And now her mom friends were leaving. Trina had a house in Oregon and an unfaithful husband. No doubt she'd be next, and then Christine would have to make friends all over again.

"When are you leaving?" she asked.

"June."

"We'll have to have a party," Trina said.

She was overly cheerful. Christine wondered if she was having an affair, too. Then, remembering all of her love for Elizabeth, all of her gratitude to her for helping get Koji into the private school where he was surrounded with English every day, she rallied: "We can have the party at our house. It would be my honor to host this one."

On the way home, they stopped at the video rental store. A drop of rain splattered on the windshield just as Christine pulled into the parking lot. Shit! Wheelchair in the rain. In spite of the sky full of clouds, she hadn't packed any rain gear or umbrellas.

There was no awning between the car and the shop. She'd have to work fast to unload and unfold the wheelchair, haul Emma out of the car, and get them all inside. If Emma's hearing aid got wet, it might be ruined. And the last thing they needed was a wet wheelchair.

Christine considered abandoning the mission and going back home. They'd play board games and dress up Barbies, which was more wholesome than watching animation anyway. She looked into the back seat where Emma and Koji were itching to get out of the car.

"Hey guys, it's raining ...."

Koji frowned. "Mom, you promised."

Emma would throw a fit. Videos were her big escape. She needed a relief from stress once in a while, a world of image, where nothing was demanded from her.

"Okay, but let's be quick. I don't want to get stuck in a downpour." She parked and opened the door. *Choose quickly,* she signed to Emma. *It's raining.* Once inside, she let them wander by themselves down the aisles. She could always feel the clerks' disapproval when she let Emma go off by herself, but the kid needed to feel independent. She could wheel herself. She could choose a video by herself. The store wasn't all that big, anyhow. She kept track of her kids, made sure nobody bothered them.

She drifted over to the new release shelf and sighed. She needed a little escapism herself. A little romantic comedy, an adventure in the jungle. Or maybe something old. Vintage Hitchcock. She moved to the next aisle, where a Japanese woman was perusing the Marilyn Monroe shelf.

The woman read the back of a video case, then put it down: "Some Like it Hot." Then she glanced at Christine, did a double take. "Excuse me, aren't you Mrs. Yamada?"

Christine startled at the mention of her name in English. "Uh, yes." The woman looked vaguely familiar, but she couldn't remember where they'd met. Was she a previous student? The mother of one of the kids she'd taught? Someone from the PTA?

"I'm Nahoko. My son is on your husband's baseball team."

"Oh!"

"*Itsumo o-sewa ni natte imasu.*"

Christine bowed in response to the standard greeting, just as Emma approached in her wheelchair.

"This is my daughter," she said. She wondered if the mothers of Hideki's players knew that Coach Yamada had a disabled child. If not, they'd probably know by tomorrow. Word traveled fast. He'd be annoyed, probably. He always said that he wanted to keep his personal life private, but she wondered sometimes if he was ashamed of Emma's imperfections. At any rate, his personal life, foreign wife, crippled child, was too sensational to keep secret for long.

"Are you a Marilyn fan?" Christine asked, hoping to deflect attention from Emma.

"Oh, not really. My mother is. She's ... visiting."

Christine nodded. Nahoko's English was quite good. Was she the mother of the boy who had lived in Atlanta? The one Hideki had mentioned? Maybe they could have coffee together, or lunch.

"My mother saw Marilyn Monroe when she was young," Nahoko continued. "She has a photo of Marilyn and Joe at the airport in Tokyo."

"Really?" Christine remembered reading somewhere that the actress had come to Japan on her honeymoon. She'd always thought that Marilyn was too full-blown, too sexy, for the Japanese. It was odd to imagine a little old lady as a fan. She was about to ask more, to ask for Nahoko's phone number, but Koji came tearing around the corner, clutching at his crotch. "Toilet!" he said.

Christine raised her eyebrows to Nahoko and shrugged. "Sorry. I've got to deal with this. It was nice meeting you!"

She looked toward the front window. By now, the rain was falling in sheets. The entrance to the toilet was on the side of the building, outdoors.

DAISUKE

That night, he got a text message from Nana: "Wanna hang out Saturday afternoon?"

Saturday afternoon. Hmm. They had a practice game in the morning, which meant he'd be finished with baseball by lunchtime, but Okaasan wanted him to spend time with his grandmother. It was important for her to be with people, his mother said. It helped to keep her from drifting off, or wandering away. His mother had even made out a chart. Daisuke's name was in the Saturday afternoon slot.

But he didn't want Nana to think he was avoiding her because of the caste thing.

"Do you want to come over to my house?" he texted back.

Within seconds she replied. "Sure."

The next morning at school Nana didn't look at him when he walked past her desk. She probably wanted to keep the fact that they knew each other a secret. To tell the truth, he was a little relieved. He'd rather not have the whole school know that they were friends, or whatever. He'd rather not have to explain to Junji or his other teammates when he was just figuring things out himself. It wasn't like America where girls and guys hung out together. Here, everybody was segregated. That's just the way it was.

On Friday, when he left for school, the sky was overcast. Rain started falling at the start of first period and didn't let up all day. Instead of practice on the field, Coach told them to stay inside and lift weights.

The weather cleared by morning, so their game with the Tokushima Hawks was on, as planned, but they had to gather at six a.m. to prepare the ground.

"Grab some buckets and rags," Kikawa said. "We need to sop up those puddles."

Daisuke picked up an aluminum pail and an old towel and found himself a puddle. He crouched down and dipped the towel into the muddy water, then wrung it out over the pail. He couldn't imagine Coach Harris ever making the Bobcats do such a thing. He would have wanted them to save their energy for the game. At his school in Atlanta, there was someone else who watered the grass and smoothed the dirt. Someone who got paid for doing it.

He soaked up some more water with the towel, wrung it out again. It was tedious, and probably meaningless, but it didn't require any thinking. He let his mind fill up with pictures of Nana: her eyes, her shiny hair, her smile. When he thought about seeing her later, his heart beat a little faster. He hoped that Obaachan wouldn't go all freaky on him while Nana was there. And he hoped that Nana didn't start dancing on the table or something. There's no telling what she would do.

Actually, Daisuke thought he should probably worry more about himself. He hoped *he'd* know how to behave. What if he blurted out something stupid? Or what if he did something that she really hated? It's not like he'd ever had a girlfriend before, or even gone on a date. Maybe he should send an email message to Rico and ask him what to say. Then again, Japanese girls were different from Americans. He was on his own.

The game time had been delayed for a couple of hours to give them a chance to make the diamond presentable. After the team had been crouching long enough to cramp their legs, and their buckets were full, the first years were sent to fill a wheelbarrow with fresh dirt and fill in the holes. After that, the raking.

Today Daisuke wasn't even on the roster. He and the rest of the first years would just be watching. The upperclassmen were the only ones who would get to play.

When the Hawks' bus finally pulled up, his teammates seemed to shrink a little. He suddenly felt smaller, too. Their guys swaggered, while Daisuke and his teammates were scuttling around like beetles. Speaking of which, he'd heard about their four a.m. practice sessions and their special rites of passage. Rumor had it that the upperclassmen made incoming first year players eat a live cicada before they could play on the team. Although Daisuke would have hated to have to put a bug in his mouth, he couldn't help thinking that the Hawks were the tougher team. And besides, they might have brains, but his school's baseball team had never beaten the other guys in a tournament.

Daisuke sat down in a folding chair on the sidelines with the rest of his first-year teammates. Spectators usually didn't show up for practice games in Japan, but some parents came to watch and help out. His mom sometimes did, but today she was busy taking care of his grandmother. He looked around and saw some mothers in folding chairs, and a big, hulking guy behind home base. With his fingers hooked through the chain link fence, he looked like a tiger trying to get out of his cage. Daisuke realized that it was Shintaro's dad.

Shintaro, two seats down from him, didn't look happy. He was frowning and his shoulders were stiff. Daisuke watched for a while to see if he'd acknowledge his father. Shintaro's eyes darted to the side from time to time, as if checking to see if his dad was still there, but he never turned his head.

Before the start of the game, both teams rushed out to the center of the field, lined up, and bowed to each other. Daisuke noticed that the Hawks' bows were short and shallow. Apparently, their coach wasn't big on humility. But as the game got underway, it became clear that they had no reason to be so cocky.

The two teams were pretty evenly matched. Not a lot happened in the first several innings, which made the game kind of boring. The folding chair seemed to get harder and harder under Daisuke's butt. Next to him, Junji's knee jittered up and down.

Yuji, the first-year catcher, seemed lost in some daydream. By the seventh inning, there were still no runs. If only someone would get on base!

And then Shima, their number four batter, got a nice line drive into right field. The ball nearly grazed the foul line, but it was in play. As the outfielders scrambled after it, Shima rounded first base and went on to second. He was cutting it close.

"Slide!" the third base coach called out.

The rest of the team jumped up to cheer him on.

"Go, Shima!" Daisuke shouted, his feet pounding the ground as if he were running with him.

Shima went into a skid, but somehow, he got tangled up with the second baseman. Limbs were going every which way. A cloud of dust bloomed. Shima went down in a heap, with his leg at a weird angle. Daisuke heard a crack. Shima started to howl.

A time-out was called, and the coaches and managers rushed onto the field with a first aid kit. From the sidelines, Daisuke couldn't really see what was going on. All he could hear was Shima roaring like a lion, and then Coach saying the words "ambulance" and "don't move him."

A few minutes later, Kikawa ran over to tell them that the game was over. Final score 0 – 0. It was only a practice game, anyhow. It didn't really matter if they finished the game or not. It wouldn't go down in the record books. Still, Daisuke noticed that Shintaro's dad shook his head in disgust and slunk away. As soon as he was gone, Shintaro loosened up.

"We could totally beat them," Shintaro said in a loud voice.

It was true. They hadn't lost. Those guys were legendary, but they couldn't even score. That meant that they had the chance to win in the summer tournament. Daisuke thought that he should feel happy that his team hadn't been bitterly defeated, that their guys had held their own, but all he could think about was the commotion on the field.

They sat there waiting until the ambulance came.

HIDEKI

The game was going well. It was just a practice game, a little over a month before the start of the summer tournament, but every win helped to build morale. Hideki allowed his mind to ease off a bit. He vaguely remembered that he had something to do afterward, that evening. He'd made some promise to Christine. The score was still 0-0. His guy Shima was flying toward second base. He tried to go into a slide, but somehow twisted his leg.

Hideki heard a crack, though maybe he just imagined it, like he imagined the pain after seeing Shima's facial contortions. The kid let out a roar just as the second-baseman tagged him. Clearly, the out didn't matter to him. In that moment, Hideki suspected, the kid couldn't have cared less about the game.

The umpire called a time-out. Hideki ran onto the field, the manager right behind him with a first aid kit. Shima probably needed more than spray, though. He was breathing heavily, trying not to cry.

"Can you move your leg?" Hideki asked, bending down next to him. A sudden breeze sent clay particles swirling around them. He blinked the dirt out of his eyes and laid a hand on the kid's shoulder. "Do you think you can limp off the field?"

Shima made an effort to move, then roared again. "I don't think so, Coach. I think my leg is broken."

"Call an ambulance," Hideki said over his shoulder.

The manager nodded and dashed toward the dugout.

"Hold tight. We'll get you to the hospital and have a doctor look at it."

They'd have to call his parents, too, and the principal.

The rest of the players remained frozen in play, waiting

for the obstruction to clear.

Hideki stayed on the field until a siren sounded in the distance, then became louder and louder, and then finally died down. The medics, spiffy in their white uniforms, hustled a gurney over to second base and eased the kid onto a trauma board. They got him into the back of the ambulance in about five minutes flat, and then they were out of there in a cloud of dust.

Hideki made a few phone calls, then headed over to the hospital himself.

Shima's mother bowed to him as he walked in the door. She was wearing an apron.

"How is he? Anything broken?"

"They're taking x-rays now," she said.

He went over to the vending machine in the corner to get her a cup of coffee. She accepted it with two hands. They chatted until the doctor called Shima's mother in for a consultation.

While he sat there alone, his mind drifted back in time. He remembered glancing toward the dugout, hoping for a sign. But no one was warming up on the sidelines, and Coach sat grim-faced in the shadows, his arms folded across his chest.

Hideki's arm screamed with pain. He bit his lip. Just one and a half more innings and he would have served his penance.

The catcher flashed him the sign for an inside strike.

He lifted his knee, going into the wind-up. As he brought his arm back, the pain almost dizzying, he focused on that sweet spot on the corner of the plate and let it fly.

The batter hopped back. An exaggerated reaction, Hideki thought, but the umpire called it a "ball."

And then the count was full with bases loaded and one out. No relief pitcher in the wings, only him and his aching arm.

He whispered the lotus sutra under his breath and thought of his teammates arrayed in the field, straining forward on the bench, counting on him for a scrapbook memory. He thought of his parents and his girlfriend in the stands, the newspaper reporters who swarmed around the winning pitcher after every game. And then he threw.

The next pitch made it over the plate, a little low, but the batter swung and managed to connect. The ball bounced into the short stop's mitt. He tagged second, tossed to first, and the inning was over.

Hideki heaved a sigh. He just wanted to curl up on the dirt and go to sleep. A couple of guys patted him on the back as they made their way back to the bench. He summoned his last bit of strength and shuffled off the field as well.

The manager handed him a cup of water which he downed in one gulp. Out of the corner of his eye he saw Coach, his arms still folded. Not a word to him. Not even a grunt.

Somehow, they had made it through the last inning without incident, winning the game and advancing to the quarter-finals. Hideki would be named to the Japan Collegiate All-Star team, but his arm would never be the same after that day. With every throw of his over-exercised arm, he'd torn his tendon a little bit more, cracked the bones just a little bit more. He would go through two or three rounds of surgery, the first a botch job, and then he would spend six months on the disabled list, a bench warmer.

Professional clubs snapped up his teammates in the draft the following winter, but no one had wanted him. His options were to go it alone, try to get a position on a company team, attend try-outs, maybe have a little more surgery, or go home, like a good *chonan*. He'd take the teacher's exam and coach high school baseball. Get a wife, have kids. Take care of his parents in their old age. That had been the plan.

It was ten o'clock by the time he got on the road toward home. He hadn't eaten, but all he wanted to do was grab a beer and throw down in front of the TV: sweet oblivion. But there was that feeling in his gut, a queasiness that churned with the hunger, and when he turned the corner just before the house, he remembered why. Another car was pulling out of the driveway, and as he waited for it to ease onto the road, he remembered. Company. They were having guests for dinner: The American Wives' Club and their families. He was supposed to sit around and talk with the Japanese husbands of the American women. About baseball or Tokushima trivia, or foreign wives.

Christine would be pissed. He could imagine the groove between her eyebrows, the tightness of her mouth as she put his clean plate and glass back in the cupboard. Or maybe she'd saved some dinner for him, under plastic wrap, that she would shove into the microwave as soon as he walked in the door.

He had let her down, once again. He should have called. He knew that. But he hadn't, and now a wave of exhaustion passed over him, dragging him under. He thought about taking off, going to some bar and drinking until he passed out, sleeping in his car. But that would just make it worse. The lights of the last of the guests' cars disappeared around the corner. Hideki sighed and maneuvered his minivan into the carport. He glanced toward the house, saw the twitch of the curtains. What he really wanted to do was smoke a cigarette and listen to the radio, decompress a bit before going in. But already she was turning off the porch light, a clear sign of her displeasure.

He lumbered up to the door. At least she hadn't locked it. "I'm home!" he yelled out.

Silence.

"I'm sorry!"

He slipped off his shoes and went to the bathroom, washed all those hospital germs off his hands. A splash of cold water on his face brought him back to life.

She was there in the kitchen, loading the dishwasher. A couple of empty wine bottles stood on the table alongside a bakery cake box. The scent of curry hung in the room. She'd made honey mustard chicken, his favorite.

"I'm sorry," he said again, when she didn't look up. "One of my players was injured and I had to take him to the hospital."

"You could have called," she muttered. She rubbed her wrist over her eyes. And now he saw that she was crying.

"I know. I'm sorry. I had to switch off my phone."

"What if one of us was injured? What if we needed you?"

He sighed. Had she forgotten about all the nights he'd spent at his father's bedside as he lay dying? Or the nights he'd spent on the floor of her hospital room when she was pregnant and bedridden? And what about the midnight visits to the NICU? How could she possibly imply that he didn't take care of his family?

"I hate it when you're like this," he said. "You know I'd be there."

She was silent for a moment. She grabbed the detergent without looking at him, sprinkled some into the dishwasher, then mumbled, "I'm sorry."

He looked back at the door, yearning, but forced himself to stay there, rooted, bathed in her disappointment.

"So how was dinner?"

"Awkward," she said. Then, "Fine."

"Well, maybe you could invite them again sometime," he said, though he hoped that she didn't.

"It was a farewell party for Elizabeth Tanigawa and her husband," she reminded him. "They're moving to the States, so I won't be inviting them again. Obviously."

With his buddies, guys he'd known since high school, or even elementary school, he was at ease. He didn't have to chat, if he didn't want to. With new people, or people he didn't know that well, like Christine's friends and their husbands, he couldn't shake off his public persona. All day long, he had to deal with parents and coaches and colleagues, had to follow certain codes of behavior according to age and rank and gender. Being on guard all the time made him tired. Christine didn't seem to understand. She didn't pay attention to the codes. As a foreigner, she could get away with it, but for him, it was ingrained. And yet, he understood that she was lonely, and that it was stressful to try to follow Japanese customs and conversations. She needed to be with other expats from time to time. He just didn't want to be involved.

Upstairs, the kids were sleeping. He crept into their room and stood at the threshold for a moment, listening to them breathe. As usual, Koji had kicked his blankets off. Hideki tucked him back in, and then smoothed his hair against his scalp. Emma was tunneled under her comforter. He peeled it back, baring her head, and kissed her soft cheek. When she was at rest, sitting on the sofa leafing through a picture book, or asleep in her bed like this, he could sometimes imagine her as a normal child. At those times, she was pure beauty: cinnamon curled, fair skinned, her mouth a perfect bud. He fantasized about the words that she would say, the churning of her legs as she ran through the park. He pictured her in a pink tulle skirt, dancing on a stage.

Christine refused to listen. Her fantasies were different. "Well, look. She likes to draw. Maybe she could be a comic book artist. Or a paralympic champion. Her arms are so strong."

She liked to fly down slopes in her wheelchair. She could go faster than any of them.

But he hated the chair.

He'd seen that doctor on TV, the one who performed near miracles. He knew how to cut tendons, at just the right age, so that kids like Emma could learn to walk. At first, it would hurt a lot. She would need extensive therapy. They would have to travel to Tokyo or Kyushu, maybe live there for a while. But if it would get Emma onto two feet, it would be worth it. Once the summer tournament was over, he'd work on Christine, get her to agree to a consultation. For now, he stood there in the dark listening to his children breathe. If only he could have gotten home in time for their mad welcome, their small bodies leaping at him, their arms around his neck. Tomorrow he would be early. Tomorrow he would prove his love.

DAISUKE

Okaasan was at her French cooking class. She'd started that as a way to make new friends. And his sister? He didn't know what she was doing. She was probably up in her room making a board game out of the periodic table or plotting her escape to Cape Canaveral. Daisuke was sitting at the kitchen table with Obaachan with a pack of cards and a bowl of rice crackers, waiting for Nana to arrive. He figured when she got there they could play a nice game of Concentration or Old Maid, something to keep his grandmother's mind from turning into total mush.

"My friend is coming," he told her, straightening up a pile of mail. Earlier he'd vacuumed and lined up the guest slippers at the door.

Obaachan got up and went over by the sink. She started washing up some cups. He'd already told her two or three times about their visitor, but she tended to forget.

"*Hai, hai,*" she said, a little impatiently. "Your friend Nana is coming. So tell me, Daisuke, where did you meet this girl?"

"I met her in homeroom. We go to the same school."

"She must be pretty smart then," she said.

"She is." He thought about all the test scores he'd read over her shoulder. She'd never gotten anything below an 80. "And she smells really good, too," he couldn't help but add.

From outside he heard the squeak of bicycle brakes and then, a few seconds later, the doorbell rang. A flash of panic went through him. Sweat broke out in his arm pits and at the small of his back. For a second, he considered hiding in the closet or faking a sudden fever.

Obaachan made a move toward the entryway.

"I'll get it," he said, jumping up. He took a deep breath, slid open the door, and there she was, standing in the dusk. She was wearing a white skirt and a pale blue T-shirt with a white lacey jacket thing over it. Wisps of hair floated around her face. She looked beautiful. His hands went all clammy.

"For you," she said, handing over a cardboard box from a nearby cake shop.

"Come in," he said.

When she stepped out of her ballet-type shoes, he saw that her toenails had been painted a sparkly blue. And then she slid her feet into the vinyl slippers that he'd set out for her.

He kept staring at her feet. He heard barking behind him. Mon-chan flopped into view, with Obaachan following.

"How cute!" Nana said. Her face lit up like a candle. She bent down and gathered the baby seal in her arms. "What a fuzzy wuzzy thing you are!"

Maybe she thought the robo-seal was weird, but she didn't let on. She was a great actress. He felt a whoosh of relief.

Obaachan was beaming and he could tell that she liked her.

"What's its name?" Nana asked.

"Mon-chan."

Daisuke knew that at some point, his grandmother would tell her the story about Marilyn Monroe. He'd heard it a million times himself. For now, they went into the tatami room where there was a low table surrounded by cushions. Nana settled across from Obaachan. While the two of them were getting to know each other, Daisuke threw some tea leaves into a pot and poured hot water over them. He got out some plates, the gilt-edged Wedgewood ones that his mother rarely used, and three tiny "princess" forks. There were six pieces of cake in the box: enough for each person in his family, plus a slice for Nana. Each wedge of fluffy white cake was decorated with a strawberry, a bite of kiwi, a few blueberries, and a sprig of parsley. He eased a piece of cake onto each plate, wiped up a bit of stray whipped cream with his finger and licked it when no one was looking, then put the plates on a tray along with the forks, a pot of tea, tea cups, and coasters. He brought it all over to the table where Obaachan and Nana were now bent over a photo album.

"How cute!" Nana said again.

Daisuke leaned in to see what she was looking at. It was a photo of him as a baby, strapped to his grandmother's back. Even though it was just a baby picture, he felt oddly flattered that she found him cute. He could feel his face turning red.

Nana turned to the next cellophane-covered page. There was a photo of him, at about three years. In this one, he was wearing a Yomiuri Giants baseball cap, and holding a plastic bat. Ojiichan, his grandfather, crouched next to him.

"My mom and dad were both working," he said. "My grandparents took care of me all day. They pretty much raised me."

Nana nodded, but she didn't say anything. Daisuke wondered what her childhood had been like. Did she spend a lot of time with her grandparents?

On the next page, there was a picture of him in a *hakama*, traditional Japanese dress for boys, taken at the shrine for Shichi-Go-San. That was when families took seven-, five-, and three-year-olds to pray for their good health. In this photo, he was with his whole family, his grandparents, Momoe, Okaasan and Otosan.

"Is that your dad?" she asked.

He was just a normal-looking guy with black-framed glasses. "Uh, yeah."

"Must be nice," she said.

He remembered that her parents were divorced.

"Do you ever see your dad?" he asked her.

"No." She sighed. "He has a new family now."

There was this kid on his team in Atlanta whose parents were divorced. He spent every other weekend with a different parent. He had his own room at each house. Every game, he had two sets of parents cheering in the stands. But in Japan, the laws were different. Kids usually lived with one parent all the time. There was no such thing as "shared custody."

Nana stared at the photo a little while longer.

"Someday I'd like to have my picture taken in a kimono," she said quietly. "Maybe when I'm twenty. For the Coming of Age ceremony."

Daisuke wanted to tell her that she'd look beautiful in a kimono, or that she looked beautiful now, in Western clothes, but he couldn't say anything like that in front of Obaachan.

Nana flipped through his elementary school years, more pictures of him with bats and gloves, and then she got to the photos sent back to Obaachan from Atlanta: all of them standing in front of Martin Luther King's birthplace, the Coca Cola Museum, the Braves' stadium. There were also some pictures of his friends from school. She stared at one of him with his baseball team for a long time.

"Were you the only Japanese kid?" she asked.

"On my team? Yeah. But there were all kinds of kids. There was one kid who'd been adopted from Russia. Nobody cared that I was Japanese. The only thing that mattered to them was whether or not I could play baseball." For a second, he felt a flash of homesickness, or whatever it is when you feel a longing for a place that you've left behind. For a second, he wanted to be with Rico and the guys in Atlanta just as much as he wanted to be here with Nana.

She nodded slowly, then looked up from the album. Her eyes were sad as if looking at the album had brought up bad memories for her. It was time to forget about the past and change the subject. Daisuke searched his mind frantically for a new topic, and then he remembered the cake.

"Maybe we should eat," he said.

"Let's!" Nana put her hands together, once again, all perky and cheerful. "*Itadakimasu!*"

Obaachan nodded, then they all picked up their forks and dug in.

After cake, they played cards. Nana won at Concentration,

Old Maid, and Uno. Whenever she won and a gleeful beam came across her face, Daisuke felt like throwing confetti in the air. He could sense that Obaachan wasn't trying too hard. Maybe they'd worn her out.

At nine o'clock, Nana looked at her watch. "I'd better get going."

"Already?" His stomach dropped. Had she been bored? Disappointed? To tell the truth, this wasn't supposed to be their big date. He'd been thinking they'd go someplace together after his mother came back. He was about to say as much when she smiled and tilted her head.

"I've got the wake-up shift tomorrow," she said. "Gotta be behind the counter at six."

"Oh, okay." Daisuke had baseball practice at seven, but he would have stayed up all night with her, if he could have. He tried to think of a way to keep her from leaving, but she was like sand falling through his fingers. *Do something*, he told himself. His brain wasn't working right. His mouth stayed shut.

She stood up and carried her empty plate to the sink. "Bye. Thanks for having me over." She waved at his grandmother, who was still seated at the table.

"*Mata kite, ne!*" she said. *Please come again.* "And thank you for the cake!"

Daisuke followed her to the entryway, mute and stupid.

"I hope it wasn't too boring," he finally said in a low voice.

She shook her head. "It was fun. Your grandmother's really sweet."

"Uh, thanks, I guess." She must have noticed how flaky Obaachan could be. She'd called him by his father's name at least twice.

"You're lucky, you know," Nana said, "to have your grandma around."

Lucky wasn't quite the word he would have used. "What about you? Do yours live far away?"

She stepped out of the slippers, into her shoes and moved

toward the door. At first, he thought she wasn't going to answer, but just before she shoved off into the night, she turned back and said, "My mom's parents are dead. My dad's parents live near here, but they don't want anything to do with me. They hate my mom."

"Oh." Daisuke felt like he was supposed to be doing something here, but he wasn't sure what. And he didn't know what to say about her family. He realized that Obaachan's little quirks, her robot pet and memory lapses, were nothing to complain about, not compared to Nana's grandparents.

She opened the door. He stuffed his own feet into a pair of loafers and followed her outside. Should he offer to ride his bike to her house with her, to make sure she got back okay? But then what would his mother say if she found Obaachan home alone, or worse, what if she wandered away?

"So I guess I'll see you on Monday," Nana said. She pushed back the kickstand on her bicycle with her foot and climbed onto the seat.

"Yeah. Or maybe I'll stop by the store tomorrow on my way to baseball."

She studied him for a moment. "Okay, then. See you tomorrow." And then she was off, her white skirt almost glowing in the dark.

Daisuke felt like he was losing something. He ran out into the street and watched until she was out of sight.

CHRISTINE

Christine poured herself a cup of coffee and picked up the newspaper. The headline jumped out at her: VIOLENT TEEN HAD MASS MURDER IN MIND. In Osaka, a seventeen-year-old had attacked a four-year-old boy in a park, hitting his head with a hammer. A shudder rippled through her body. She glanced over at Emma and Koji, who were just dipping spoons into their bowls of cornflakes and slammed the paper face down on the table.

"What's wrong, Mommy?" Koji asked.

"Nothing, sweetheart. Just some bad news. In a place far away."

Hideki, who was engrossed in his Japanese-language newspaper, grunted. She knew he thought Christine was overprotective. He didn't like the way she switched off the news as soon as something disturbing flashed on screen: tanks in the desert, the detritus after a tsunami, a house on fire. He didn't understand how sensitive Koji was, how he'd fret all day, tears pooling in his eyes. The nightmares. He was afraid to go down the hallway to the bathroom by himself. Whenever Christine took her little boy's hand and walked him to the toilet, her husband shook his head.

Now, she was tempted to ask him to tilt the paper away from their son, even though he wasn't looking at the photo of the police at the scene of the crime. He couldn't read the characters for "kill" or "hammer." Neither could Emma, who was less fearful, anyway. Christine wondered if her deafness shielded her somehow. Or maybe the cerebral palsy ... maybe the part of her brain that registered fear had been damaged at birth.

She nibbled on a piece of toast and tried to think of other

things. Emma's presentation, for example. She had to go up in front of all the other deaf school kindergarteners and talk, well, *sign*, about her spring vacation. Christine had blown up digital photos of Emma sitting in Grandpa's boat with a fishing pole. There was another photo of her in a wagon being pulled by Koji in her parents' big backyard. In Japan, that much land would hold an entire neighborhood. She couldn't help thinking that the other mothers would be impressed.

After breakfast, she quickly filled the dishwasher and rounded up the children's bags and thermoses. Hideki carried Emma to the car and buckled her into her car seat. And then they were off.

The presentations were scheduled for the morning. The kids went straight to the Playroom and lined up their little chairs in rows. The first kid up was Naoki. He folded a beetle out of black origami paper, narrating all the while, then showed photos of a real stag beetle, clinging to a tree. He drew a net out of a paper bag and demonstrated how he'd caught the beetle. Lastly, he pulled a small terrarium out of the bag, and showed his classmates his new pet.

Everyone clapped. The other women leaned in toward Naoki's mother and congratulated her. "What a good job!" "He did it all by himself!" "His speech is so clear and easy to understand!"

Now it was Emma's turn. Naka-sensei scooched Emma, chair and all, to the front of the classroom. Christine knelt beside her, handing up the props and photos, one by one.

Emma pointed to a picture of an airplane. "Uh..uh..uuuuh." She signed "airplane" and "Grandpa and Grandma" and "America."

Then the next picture, the boat. Here, Emma tugged on the orange life jacket they'd bought at K-Mart. Christine handed her a fishing pole they'd made together out of a chopstick and a piece of string with a magnet tied to the end. She tossed some paper fish affixed with paper clips onto the floor and Emma "caught" them.

Finally, Emma tacked the blown-up backyard photo to the white board.

"*Amerika hiroi na!*" Naoki blurted out. America is wide! He waved his hand like an American flag, the sign for the country. Then he pointed his index finger and said, "Pow! Pow!"

Christine sighed. Everyone here thought of America as the land of guns. How was it that a four-year-old deaf Japanese kid had developed such an idea anyhow? Did his parents let him watch the news? Did his mother tell him that in America everyone packed heat? She glared at Naoki's mother, who wasn't even paying attention. She was whispering behind her hand to the mother sitting next to her. She wanted to tell Naoki's mother that every time a toy gun found its way into her house, she threw it immediately into the trash. She was trying to teach Emma and Koji about peace and love.

Back when she'd been teaching English in the local adult education program, she'd invariably had at last one student, smugly confident about his or her language ability, who'd gone on about how fat foreigners were, and how the United States was such a violent country. Christine had always snapped that her family was on the thin side, and that she'd never laid eyes on a handgun and there hadn't been any pistols in her house.

The truth was she'd grown up in a family of deer hunters. Every November they'd convened—cousins, uncles, and aunts— and gone out into the woods behind her grandmother's house. During the summer, Christine had loved to wander through those trees. She'd carved her initials, and those of whichever boy she liked at the time, into half a dozen trees with the Swiss Army knife that she still carried in her purse. She'd once come across a beaver building a dam in the pond out there. Another time, she'd stumbled upon a doe and her fawn. She'd looked straight into their big, brown eyes. During deer season, she avoided the woods. The men and boys, and sometimes her aunts, went out to their blinds where they'd wait until they were ready to shoot. Christine had never joined them. She and her mother had stayed in the house reading novels and playing Scrabble. But sometimes she'd venture out to the barn and stare at the carcasses hanging from the beams. The blood made her stomach turn.

When hunting season was over, her father and brother stored their rifles in the back of the coat closet. Although she didn't like the killing, knowing those guns were there, and that her dad could shoot a six-point buck at 100 yards made her feel safe. She slept soundly, guarded.

She remembered waking one night to footsteps thudding on the lawn. The motion-sensitive light at the edge of the driveway had flashed on, and then a sliver of light seeped under her door. She'd stumbled into the hallway, blinking against the glare, to find her dad reaching into the back of the coat closet.

"Go back to bed, Chrissie," he'd whispered.

She'd slipped back into her room and parted the curtains. She could see someone in dark clothes crouched by the bushes, and then, at the window, the silhouette of her dad's rifle. The prowler suddenly bolted off toward the road, and then there was the sound of an engine revving, fading, the closet door shutting, her father padding back to bed.

Later, Nishioka-sensei, the head teacher at the deaf school kindergarten, announced that in response to the Osaka incident involving the boy with the hammer, there would be a new drill. In addition to periodic earthquake and fire drills, from now on the children would practice evading *fushinsha*: suspicious strangers. Although the mothers wouldn't be taking part in the drill, which would be held for the first time after lunch, they were invited to watch from a second-story window.

The children were playing outside during their afternoon recess, digging in the sand, soaring on swings, scrambling over the jungle gym. Christine could see Emma down below filling a plastic bucket with a small shovel. Everything was peaceful until a teacher disguised in a trench coat, stocking cap, and sunglasses lunged into the play area. She reached into a pocket and pulled out a knife. No one noticed at first, then Naoki shrieked and pointed and another kid started to cry. They all ran to the teachers; all except for Emma, who couldn't run, couldn't even walk. If this were real, she would be the first victim. But Emma didn't look all that alarmed, at least not at first. Christine saw that she was curious. She watched the weirdly dressed teacher until her own teacher, Naka-sensei, swooped down and picked her up and carried her to the verandah where the others were huddled in fear.

Christine shook her head. They'd done nothing but scare the children. She remembered what her Sunday school teacher had said long ago about the devil: He wouldn't be some ugly red ogre with horns; he'd be handsome and friendly and he'd come bearing candy.

Christine envied the other mothers at Koji's school who could drop their kids off and then go on to yoga classes or aromatherapy or jobs in climate-controlled offices; such activities were not an option when she took Emma to school. Christine thought the rule requiring mothers to hang out at school was meant to throw them together and force them to bond. Left to their own devices, they might fall into depression over their disabled children. They might be too ashamed to talk about their problems. They might try to hide their deaf kids and develop ulcers from accumulated stress.

So the mothers were stuck at school, and the teachers thought up little tasks to keep them busy. They had to clean the toilets on the second floor, pull weeds from the playground, sift pebbles from the soil before rice planting. It was like work, Christine thought, one of those menial minimum wage jobs she'd had in high school or college, yet she didn't get paid and she wasn't bonding.

The next big project would be designing and sewing costumes for the annual Culture Festival. Nishioka-sensei called a meeting to discuss the event. The mothers knelt at a low table, with

Nishioka-sensei at the head. Various photocopies were distributed: schedules, memos, diagrams.

"This year's theme is ninjas," Nishioka-sensei announced. "The children love ninjas."

The other mothers nodded, but Christine squirmed. Ninjas went around hurling death stars. They carried knives. They killed people in the dark of night. How could they even think of putting these children onstage as killers when there were all these stabbings in the news? She'd read that in the United States, after Columbine, a child had been sent home from school for picking up a chicken drumstick and saying "bang bang."

Nishioka-sensei paused. "Yamada-san, is there something you want to say?"

Here was her chance. She had to speak out. She remembered how, a couple of years before, she'd convinced a teacher that the children shouldn't feed rice to the pigeons in the park. The grains, she'd explained, would absorb moisture in the birds' stomachs, swelling and killing them. That's why no one tossed rice at weddings in the States anymore. The teacher had been moved and they'd wound up feeding the pigeons bread crumbs instead.

"Well," she began, trying to arrange her thoughts in Japanese, "ninjas killed people, right? And there was that guy in Osaka ...."

Nishioka-sensei stared, uncomprehending.

"It just seems that with these problems of violence, maybe something more ... *peaceful* would be better."

Nishioka-sensei nodded. "I see. Well, that's one opinion."

Obviously, no one else felt the same. Down the table, someone snickered.

When the meeting was over, the other mothers began discussing costumes. Naoki's mother went off to the library to look for illustrations of ninja attire. Christine remained in place, her face red, her legs cramped, her lips pressed together. Why didn't they get it? How could they not care?

She was still irritated two hours later when she pulled into the parking lot of Koji's school. He came running out of the gate as soon as he saw her, and she felt her spirits lift. So much energy! He handed his backpack over to her, hugged her legs, and then went spinning off to join his friends.

As she waited at the edge of the school lawn, she looked into his backpack and found a sheaf of memos, making her worry about the depleting rainforests in Indonesia, and what was this? A tightly rolled newspaper insert, looped and taped at the end into a handle. Another saber, she thought with a sigh. Every morning when she brought Koji to school, she saw the boys parrying like musketeers with their homemade swords. Once a kid had even pretended to slash her thigh. Koji'd told her before that his teacher helped make them.

That evening, after the children were in bed, she brought up the matter of the ninjas with Hideki.

He sighed. "Ninjas weren't evil. They were just trying to protect their masters."

"But the weapons ...."

He shook his head. "You think too much, Christine."

The next week, she brought her sewing machine to the deaf school. Up in the mother's room, she ran the yellow fabric under the needle. Real ninjas wore black, but the mothers had decided that more vivid colors would be better onstage.

At home, Emma folded death stars out of origami, something she had learned at school. She slid them between her palms, making them fly across the room.

The morning of the event, she staked out folding chairs for herself and Koji in front of the stage. She'd brought along a camera and a video recorder. Hideki was off coaching baseball; he would watch later.

She sat through the sixth graders' taiko drum performance, the high school girls' fashion show, and then the first little ninjas came onstage, flinging death stars into the audience, little cardboard daggers tucked into their sashes.

Christine readied her video camera. Emma came out in her wheelchair. She twirled a long pink ribbon in spirals, her face alight with joy. She looked so fierce and confident up there in her ninja costume in front of all those people. Watching her daughter through the viewfinder, Christine felt a surge of love and pride. Emma looked almost like she could take care of herself. Almost, but not quite.

When Emma had left the stage, she lowered the camera and began to clap. She thought of all the things she would do to protect her children.

DAISUKE

"So who was that girl?" Okaasan asked as she set a bowl of miso soup in front of Daisuke on a Saturday morning in June.

"What girl?" He dribbled a little soy sauce onto his fried egg.

"Obaasan told me that you've been having visits. From a girl in your class?"

"Oh. Yeah." Why had he thought that she wouldn't tell? He should have sworn her to secrecy. Then again, he had nothing to hide. She was just a friend. They played cards and ate cake. Totally tame stuff.

"Her name's Nana," he said. "Nana Takai."

"Hmm. I wonder if she's any relation to the Takai lady in my French cooking class. She said that she has a granddaughter about your age. I think she even said that you're both at the same school."

Well, that was interesting. Maybe Nana's grandmother wasn't as oblivious to her as she thought. If this woman was her grandmother, that is. After all, Takai was a pretty common name.

"Could be," he said. "Is she nice?"

His mother looked at him oddly. "What kind of a question is that?"

Uh, oh. Maybe he'd said too much. "Never mind." He filled his mouth with rice before he had a chance to say anything else stupid.

He stopped at Lawson's on the way to practice. Even though he'd just had breakfast, he was hungry again. But more than that, he wanted to tell Nana what he'd heard about the lady in his mother's cooking class. When he pushed through the door, he saw that she was busy with a customer, so he hung out in the candy aisle until she was free. He walked up and laid a Ghana bar on the counter. She smiled at him, but the manager was standing right next to her, listening in. It didn't look like the time to chat.

"Thank you. Will that be all for today, sir?" she said with a smirk.

"Yeah, that's it." He was about to say something about her maybe grandmother when he heard his name.

He turned to see Junji waiting in line behind him, a couple of rice balls and a carton of juice in the bowl of his hands.

"Hey, did you hear about Shima?" he said.

"No, what happened?" The last they'd seen of him he was being loaded into an ambulance.

"He broke his leg," Junji said. Then he smiled.

"That'll be a hundred and ten yen," Nana broke in.

Daisuke fumbled with his change, his thoughts suddenly caught up in Shima and his broken bone. If he was out, that meant there was an opening on the team. Coach would have to find someone to replace him. Judging by the smile on his face, Junji was thinking exactly the same thing.

Daisuke handed over the money. "See you later, Nana."

"Bye, Daisuke." She started ringing up Junji's breakfast.

Daisuke waited for him by the door and they walked out together.

"You know her?" Junji asked, once they were outside, out of earshot.

"Sure," he shrugged. "She's in our homeroom."

"Yeah, but ...."

He wasn't ready to tell Junji that he was hanging out with Nana. Junji was his buddy and all, but he had a big mouth. He'd told Daisuke everything that was going on with everybody else. Who was to say he wasn't telling them everything he knew about Daisuke?

"I sit behind her, you know," he said. "She dropped her pencil once and I picked it up."

"Oh, okay." This seemed to satisfy him. At any rate, Junji didn't say any more about Nana. He tore off the plastic wrapping from one of the rice balls and stuffed it into his mouth.

They rode the rest of the way to school together. Thinking about Nana made Daisuke's stomach go all woozy. Why didn't he admit that she was his friend? What did it matter if people knew? When they'd parked their bikes, he tossed the chocolate bar into Junji's basket. He'd lost his appetite. He didn't want it anymore.

CHRISTINE

The next big event at the School for the Deaf was the annual sleepover, held in June.

"Why does our daughter have to take a bath with her teacher?" Christine asked Hideki during dinner a few nights before. "As a Japanese teacher, please explain it to me."

On their last family vacation, months before, they had spent a weekend at a spa. They had indulged in a "family bath," a private hot tub under the stars. Bathing as a family seemed intimate and appropriate. After all this time in Japan, she'd lost much of her American prurience. She no longer thought it was perverse for fathers to bathe with their young daughters as per Japanese custom. But Emma taking a bath with her teacher and unrelated kindergartner boys?

"Do you know Dewey?" Hideki asked. He stared ahead, his profile still almost as sharp as it had been at twenty-four, when she'd met him.

"As in John, the philosopher? Yes." Christine had once been a teacher, too. She'd probably studied the same pedagogical theories that he had, but learned to apply them in different ways.

"Dewey said that education should occur in all areas of life."

"Hmm. So you're saying it's an American idea."

She tried to wrap her mind around this, while thinking that the following weekend's school sleepover was a quintessentially Japanese activity. No one in her native country would think it necessary for a four-year-old to bond with her classmates, at least not to the degree that was intended. Emma would be cooking, eating, sleeping, bathing, and doing just about everything else with her group, the Stag Beetles.

The weekend was intended to be a family event, but Christine was supposed to stay out of the way. She and her son would be eating at another table, sleeping in another room, bathing at another time. It seemed odd and unnatural to Christine to let the teacher help Emma brush her teeth and shampoo her hair instead of having her mother do it.

When she'd first told Hideki about the sleepover, he'd said, "You should cancel." He wouldn't be going himself because he had a game. He had no time for deaf school events or concerts and festivals at their son's school. But it quickly became clear that everything at Emma's school was now geared toward the sleepover. Three weeks before, the first orientation meeting had been held. The three-, four- and five-year-olds in the school's kindergarten, were divided into groups the children named themselves: the Ghosts, the Melons, the Stag Beetles. From that moment, they ate lunch in their groups every day. Almost every school activity—making curry and rice, preparing skits, planting flowers—was conducted as a group.

The mothers were suddenly spending all day together, too. The next day, after spending half an hour wandering among the blooming roses in a corner of the park, Christine opened the door of the Mother's Room to find all the other women cutting out colorful, felt shapes and threading needles. She nodded a greeting and made an effort to wedge herself into the circle. They were making name tags for the sleepover. Somehow she had missed the memo.

"What should I do?" Christine asked, trying to appear eager. If she were Japanese, she would know. She would just plunge in.

Akaishi-san, mother of Maya, a girl in Emma's class, handed her a few scraps of felt. "Stitch these brown pieces onto the yellow one."

Christine craned her neck to see what the others were doing. One had almost finished sewing a brown felt stag beetle onto a small square of yellow.

"Oh, this stitch is too big," she said. She began to tear it out.

Christine wanted to roll her eyes. Who cared if one teeny tiny stitch was not exactly the same as the others? Wouldn't this time be better spent studying sign language or lobbying for an elevator? (There were several students, including Emma, who couldn't walk, but the three-story school didn't have any ramps or elevators.) She could already tell that this was going to be a week-long project. They would spend more time making the name tags than the children would wearing them. But that was the wrong attitude. She should admire them for their attention to detail, for their insistence on perfection. They were doing this for their beloved children, after all. Sewing was a way to demonstrate their affection. Isn't that what the head teacher had preached at the beginning of the school year when she'd ordered the mothers to make the required tote bags and aprons for their children by hand?

"What's the stitch?" Christine asked.

"Chain."

How did that one go? Back in the day, when she'd been a Girl Scout, she must have learned all those stitches: the slip stitch, the satin stitch, the chain stitch. But her hobbies ran more to reading and traveling and studying foreign languages than embroidery. Now, she was stumped.

"Does everyone here know how to do the chain stitch?" Christine asked.

The women looked at her: six pairs of dark eyes filled with scorn (or so she imagined). She could almost see the speech bubbles over their heads: "A woman who doesn't know how to sew. Hmmph. Well, what do you expect? She's American."

"We learned it at school," Maya's mother finally said.

"Oh, really?" Did the boys learn it too? she wondered. Probably not. Christine had to have someone teach her. She tried, she really did, but her stitches weren't even. Everyone would know which one she'd made.

Later in the day, after they'd all had lunch followed by green tea, Nishioka-sensei appeared with a stack of print-outs about the sleepover. As usual, she handed out copies to everyone, then proceeded to read every single word aloud, something that never ceased to annoy Christine. With the exception of herself, they were all literate, and responsible enough to read the pages on their own.

One of the sheets featured a chart showing the names of the participants and every father's estimated time of arrival. Some would be dropping by after work, others were coming after the bonfire on the beach, in time for a parent and teacher drinking party. Next to Hideki's name (actually, "Emma's Father"; they only existed in relation to their children, apparently), there was an X.

Another paper listed participants' duties. Every task had been designated, down to who would put the smallest children's hearing aids in airtight cases at bedtime and who would wield the hair dryer after the bath. Christine had volunteered to spread a blue plastic sheet on the ground before dinner, thinking it was something she wouldn't mess up. How hard could it be? They were all going to eat outside, under the tall pines in front of the Youth Hostel, within earshot of the whispering sea.

The next page was of the bath schedule. Emma, Christine noted, would be going in just after dinner. Everyone was allowed twenty minutes in the bath, from start to finish. There was a photo-copied image of the bath as well: a large room with a tiled floor and a tub the size of a small pool. They would sit on small wooden stools to wash with soap outside the tub, then rinse and soak in the nearly scalding water.

A final sheet listed exactly what items the children should bring and exactly how they should be packed; each outfit in a separate see-through plastic bag, each bag labeled: pajamas, change of clothes, after the bath. They were to bring a small pack of tissues, a handkerchief, a plastic bag for the shells and stones that they would collect at the beach on the last day. The plastic bag was supposed to go in a pants pocket.

On the one hand, Christine was impressed by this attention to detail. On the other, she hated it. Living in Japan brought out her inner adolescent. She often felt that the teachers were trying to control her daughter's entire life—and hers—and she wanted to rebel.

Even before Emma was born, she'd had a pretty good idea of how involved teachers were in their students' business. After all, she'd taught English as an extracurricular subject in public schools and she knew about the yearly visits teachers made to students' homes (and just how nervous this made the mothers, who spent days cleaning and fussing over what sort of snacks to serve). Plus, her husband was a teacher. More than once he'd been called away near midnight to deal with a student caught drinking in a karaoke box or shoplifting at a Lawson's convenience store. If one of his forty home room students was in the hospital, he was obliged to visit.

She'd thought the teachers' involvement excessive and ridiculous then, but now that she was on the other end of it, she found it unbearably intrusive. The deaf school produced reams of memos telling parents what time to put their children to bed, what they should eat and drink, what kinds of books they should read, on and on, as if the parents themselves had no common sense. Meanwhile, among themselves, the mothers were hypercritical of everything the teachers did: This one only used finger spelling as opposed to proper sign language. That one had no idea of how to discipline unruly four-year-old deaf boys.

When Christine brought Emma to the school for early intervention, back when she was three, she packed a lunch; sometimes it was sandwiches on whole wheat bread with a side of potato chips, which she quickly learned were beyond the pale. *Snack food.*

"What does she drink with her lunch?" the teacher asked one day, eyeing Emma's imported Bob the Builder thermos.

The teachers ate in their own room. Christine, Emma, Maya,

and Maya's mother, ate in the classroom together.

"Water," Christine answered, pouring out a cup.

"Mineral water?"

"No, just tap water."

The teacher frowned. "You really shouldn't give her tap water. She could get food poisoning."

Was this woman for real? Christine glanced at Maya's mother, expecting a look of mutual disbelief but Akaishi-san quickly looked away. What was the big deal? She knew that the local water was potable; she'd been drinking it for ten years. It's not like the Ganges was gushing through their pipes. She was too taken aback to argue, though, so she said nothing. Red-faced, she listened as the teacher complimented Akaishi-san for giving her daughter cold barley tea: "I hear it's really healthy."

After the teacher had gone off to her own lunch, Maya's mother leaned forward and said, "You don't give her carbonated drinks, do you?"

Remembering all this made Christine want to rant about the caffeine in the tea the older kids were given at lunch. Instead, she sipped her own green tea till she felt calm again.

They finished making the name tags with a few days to spare, but then the mothers had to rehearse a dance. On the evening of the sleepover, everyone would perform by the light of the bonfire. The children were practicing skits. The mothers, it had been decided, would sing and sign a Hawaiian song. The mother of Rai, a five-year-old boy who'd recently gotten a cochlear implant, was choreographing the whole thing. Maya's mother had designed costumes: hula skirts with strips of colored plastic hanging from the waistband.

Although it was only June, it was hot as dragon's breath, and humid, too. The deaf school, like every other school in Tokushima, had no air-conditioning. In the Mothers' Room there was an oscillating fan, but it gave only the suggestion of relief. It was in this room, in this heat, that they pulled the plastic skirts over their clothes and practiced moving in unison, hips swaying as their fingers formed words.

Christine could feel rivers of sweat soaking her T-shirt. After they'd run through the song a couple of times, there was a discussion about the final moves. Should they drop to their knees and throw their hands in the air: "Ta da"? Twirl? Bow? None of this mattered to Christine. All she wanted to do was throw herself into the cool pond across from the rose garden.

That Saturday, Christine packed the car with bags, thermoses, and kids. Then, with gritted teeth, she set out for the sleepover. Although she jammed a reggae tape into the cassette deck, the only song in her head all the way there was "Kamehameha," the one that she'd heard over and over in the Mothers' Room for the past few days.

The Tokushima International Youth Hostel was at Omiko Beach, a popular spot for barbecues and ocean swimming. "Don't think hotel," the head teacher had warned. Christine told her son it would be like camping. When she entered the building and made her way up the dark stairs, she had a flashback to all the twenty-five-dollar-a-night European hostels she'd slept in on her junior year abroad. The stained pillows and futons made her cringe now. These days she was more of a Nikko Hotel kind of person.

Christine and Koji found that they'd be sharing a room with Maya's mother, her five-year-old sister and baby brother. The room was empty except for a small coin-operated television on a table. The bedding was stashed in the closet. It smelled vaguely of mold and cigarettes.

Emma, of course, would be sleeping down the hall on futons with the other Stag Beetles, and her teacher. For a moment, Christine imagined teacher and children curled up together like kittens and felt a stab of jealousy. She'd never spent a night so far apart from her daughter.

After stashing their bags and thermoses, they returned

downstairs for a meeting. Emma was already with her group. Christine tried to catch her eye, but her teacher seemed to be blocking her from sight on purpose. Well, she was supposed to be paying attention. This was an extension of school, after all. Christine sat down at the back and pulled Koji onto her lap.

Next, everyone moved to the picnic area to begin preparing curry for supper. There was an open pavilion under the pines with grills and workspace. Emma's job was to peel the onions. Christine could see her sitting in her purple wheelchair, pulling the papery skin away. She was intent on her task, oblivious to her mother's watchful eyes.

Now that dinner was underway, it was time for Christine to spread the blue plastic sheet on the ground. She found it in the meeting room and, after clearing away a few sticks and rocks, laid it out on the pine-needled ground. Here and there were little hills of plastic, and Christine stamped around in her stocking feet, tamping them down. It was a small job, but she couldn't help feeling that she had done something wrong. The Japanese mothers would lay it out perfectly and they would know if she had not. Finally, she shook her head in disgust. She was becoming paranoid. The blue plastic sheet really did not matter so much. She looked up, then, for her son. He was nowhere in sight.

Maybe he'd wandered down to the beach, she thought. Christine strolled through the pines, calling out his name. She scanned the groups making curry—the Melons, the Ghosts, the Stag Beetles—looking for Koji's chestnut head. Then she looked again toward the water and her heart began to bang.

"Koji? Where are you?"

"I think I saw him go into the hostel," Rai's mother called out.

Christine ran toward the building. She found him alone in their room, drinking from his thermos in the fading light of late afternoon, and nearly fainted with relief.

"What's wrong, sweetie? What are you doing in here?"

He dropped his head to his chest. "I feel shy," he said.

He doesn't feel like he fits in, Christine thought. *Like me.* She ruffled his hair and pulled him close. "We'll just sit here for a little while," she said.

Later, as they sat on the blue plastic sheet with their bowls of curry, Christine looked across at her daughter, eating with her teacher. She was smiling, shoveling in the food like it was the best thing she'd ever tasted. The other Stag Beetles signed something to her that Christine didn't understand, and Emma nodded and signed back. She's having a great time, Christine thought. She wondered if her daughter understood that she would be reunited with her family when the weekend was over.

Christine watched as Emma, assisted by her teacher, washed her bowl and spoon. Then the teacher pushed Emma in her wheelchair to the hostel for a bath. Christine imagined the teacher's fingers tangling in her daughter's long hair, squeezing out the shampoo suds. She had a vision of the teacher's hands sliding over Emma's soft skin, into her crevices and hollows, the tender way she might blot the girl's back with a towel. She remembered how, just after Emma's premature birth, she had stood by as the nurse swabbed her body clean in the incubator. She hadn't been allowed to hold Emma without permission. It had taken such a long time to feel like her mother.

After dinner, when they were all once again assembled in the meeting room, Nishioka-sensei announced the beginning of the *Obake Taikai.*

Koji looked up at Christine with alarm. "Ghosts?"

"Just people dressed up as ghosts, sweetie. The mommies and daddies will be wearing costumes. They'll be giving out presents."

Koji shook his head vigorously, tears already pooling in his enormous brown eyes. "I don't like ghosts!"

"Okay, we won't join in." Christine's heart sank. She at least wanted to see Emma's thrilled expression. Her daughter was the brave one, her son the hyper-imaginative cautious child.

Sometimes, like when Hideki dangled Emma upside-down over a pond, she wondered again if those shrieks of delight weren't abnormal. Maybe her lack of fear was another manifestation of brain injury. Being afraid of the ghosts in the woods at dusk (or talk of earthquakes, or being swung by the ankles) seemed normal for a kid of that age.

They watched the other kids and mothers and teachers embark on the ghost hunt, and then Koji turned to go back to their room. Christine sighed, wishing she'd brought a picture book or pack of cards to amuse him with.

The final event of the evening, before the children were sent to bed, was the bonfire on the beach. If this were America, Christine thought, they'd sit in a circle around a teepee of kindling, prepared for marshmallow roasting and singing. But this was Japan, and the campfire was referred to in the printed schedule as a "firestorm." She anticipated something grand and theatrical. Koji was biting his fingernails.

Plastic sheets were laid over the sand. They would sit there, away from the fire, and watch. When everyone had gathered, Rai, master of ceremonies, stood up at the front of the group and announced the start of the fire ceremony.

Some fathers laid fat logs in a square.

"Look!" One of the teachers directed everyone's attention further up the beach. "The goddess of fire is coming."

Nishioka-sensei, wearing a mask and headdress, was advancing with a torch and two attendants, also in costume. It reminded Christine of the Olympic ceremony, or some ancient Mayan rite. The teacher was well disguised and she wondered if the children actually believed that she was a deity.

The "fire goddess" lit the logs, slipped away into the night, and the main attraction began. Each group—Ghost, Melon, Stag Beetle—had prepared a skit. Christine knew that the kids had spent weeks practicing, just as the mothers had. The air was filled with nervous tension.

Emma and her group took their places on the sand. They were wearing costumes made of strips of plastic. Emma held a tube of tightly rolled paper that was probably meant to be a wand or a sword. Other than that, Christine had no idea what was going on. In the dark, with the chirr of crickets and cicadas filling the night, it was difficult to make out the children's imperfect pronunciation and to follow their sloppy signs. But no matter. Emma was smiling, pleased as ever, to be onstage and the center of attention.

For the finale, Christine and the other mothers shimmied into their hula skirts and lined up in front of the fire. With the Hawaiian music blasting from a cassette player, they swished and swayed together under the sequinned sky. It was fun, after all; Christine found that she couldn't stop smiling.

She'd meant to join the other parents for drinks in the meeting room after she got Koji to sleep, but she'd nodded off herself. When she did wake, in the early hours of morning, he was hogging her pillow and crowding her off the futon. For such a fearful boy, he slept in an attitude of absolute trust: arms flung open, belly exposed.

On the other side of her, Maya's baby brother had rolled off his own mother's futon and nestled against her back. Christine carefully nudged the children, clearing some space for herself, and tried to go back to sleep.

In the morning, Christine and Koji dressed and packed up their belongings then headed downstairs for breakfast. Emma was already in the dining room with her teacher, spooning up scrambled eggs. Christine noted, somewhat ruefully, that her daughter's pigtails were tighter and neater than usual, her part perfectly straight. She herself felt rumpled after a night spent fending off thrashing toddlers. Koji was sleepy and sullen.

After breakfast, the plan was to go down by the water and explore. Nishioka-sensei had scissored her fingers in the sign for crab and shown the kids pictures of water insects they might come across. There might be shells, too, she said, and interesting rocks.

They all set out in a loose column along a well-trodden path. But instead of continuing to follow the path, which was bordered by railing, Nishioka-sensei veered off through the underbrush, down a steep slope to jagged rocks below. There were no steps, but a few fathers were positioned to give a hand to anyone who might need help getting down.

Christine was surprised to see that Emma, who could not walk, who would never be able to make it safely down such a treacherous incline by herself, was already on the rocks, grabbing at frogs and beetles. She realized that the treads on her sneakers were worn flat and that she would probably slip. Koji, at her side, had grown stiff with fright.

"We'll just stay up at the top of the hill and watch," she murmured. "Unless you want one of these nice daddies to help us get down there."

He shook his head, already working his way back to the official trail.

Before she went after him, she took another look at her daughter: happy, curious, poking between the rocks, leaning down for a closer look at a bug. She watched as her little girl caught a crab with her small fingers and held it up to the sun.

DAISUKE

On Saturday afternoon after Daisuke had finished practice, show-ered and changed, and after Nana has finished her shift at Lawson's, they meet up at the karaoke center. The guy in the booth handed them a plastic card with a room number on it.

"If you want to order food, just push the intercom button," he said.

Nana took the lead. Apparently, she'd been here before. Daisuke followed her down the hallway, his eyes on her swishing skirt. He could smell her hair.

"Here we are," she said. She opened the door to the little chamber and flopped down on the maroon crushed velvet sofa. There was a table stacked with songbooks in front of the sofa, a couple of mikes, a karaoke machine and a TV screen. Up in the corner, he noticed a security camera.

Nana opened the songbook, and Daisuke grabbed the menu.

"I'm starving," he said. "How about you?"

"I could eat some yakitori."

He ordered the grilled chicken on skewers, rice balls filled with sour plums, a plate of French fries, and Lemon Squash for both of them.

"I want to hear you sing in English," Nana said. "How about the Beatles? Do you know any Beatles songs?"

He shook his head. He wasn't a singer. To tell the truth, he wasn't crazy about karaoke, and no, he didn't know any Beatles songs. Back in Atlanta, his teammates had introduced him to rap and hip hop. They sometimes listened to Eminem. But he knew there weren't any Eminem or Tupac tunes on this karaoke machine.

"How about the Carpenters?" Nana pointed out a couple of song titles in English. "Please, Mr. Postman" and "On Top of the World."

"My mom likes the Carpenters," Daisuke said. "She used to sing those songs around the house."

"Okay. I'm entering this into the machine."

The music started up, along with some cheesy video featuring a Japanese woman in a bikini walking along a beach. Nana handed him a microphone.

He tried to sing along, but his voice was flat and off-key. Finally, he shrugged and launched into a rap version.

Nana burst into laughter.

"I'd rather hear you sing," he said, handing the mike over, even though the song hadn't finished.

She rose, diva-like, and, without looking at the words streaming across the monitor, belted out the rest of the song. Her voice was rich and pure, sliding easily between octaves, steady on the high notes. And her face, while she was singing, seemed lit up somehow. Daisuke felt the hairs at the back of his head stand up. If he'd had any doubts about her ability before, they were all gone. Nana was the real deal. She was a true contender.

When she reached the last note, he started clapping and whistling.

She did a little curtsy.

To Daisuke's relief, she didn't try to make him sing again.

"Any requests?" she asked.

"How about 'Can You Keep a Secret?'" It was a song originally sung by Hikaru Utada, who had been born in New York City. She lived in Tokyo now, and she was hugely famous.

Nana nodded. Piece of cake. She cued up the music and stepped in front of the monitor, swaying to the intro music. For the next hour or so, Nana put on a performance, becoming more and more uninhibited as the night wore on. Daisuke sat there chowing down on grilled chicken and French fries, thinking that she was as good as any singer he'd ever seen on TV. As good as Hikaru Utada, even.

When her voice started to go hoarse, they settled up their bill and rode their bikes to a game center. They played a couple of games of air hockey, Dance Dance Revolution, and pinball. He managed to win a Hello Kitty doll for her in the UFO catcher game.

It was after dark by the time he took her home. The porch light was on, and he could make out the blue glow of a television inside. When they pulled up in front of her house, he saw a figure at the window. Her mother, he guessed.

Nana dismounted her bike and parked it at the side of the house. "Well, see you later," she said, hugging the Hello Kitty doll. "I had a good time."

"Me, too." He shifted from foot to foot.

She approached him, the doll still in her arms.

Did she expect him to kiss her? He wanted to, but ... he caught the faint, dizzying scent of girl sweat and shampoo. He leaned a little closer. Then the front door burst open, and she backed away.

"Nana, 'zat you?" a voice slurred.

"*Hai!*" She didn't introduce him to her mother. Instead, she put a finger to her lips and gestured that he should go. He waited in the shadows until she had disappeared into the house, locking the door behind her. The porch light went dark, and he got back on his bike and rode home.

CHRISTINE

Less than a week after the sleepover, the mothers at the School for the Deaf had a new craft project. This time, the eleven mothers and one grandmother, proxy for a mother who had refused to give up her job as an elementary school teacher, gathered to make cards. The cards were to be presented to student teachers from a nearby college on the last day of their practicum to show the mothers' appreciation.

Christine knelt at the low table, trying to ignore the cramps in her legs. The tabletop was a flurry of colored tissue paper, sheets of origami, glue, and glitter. Across from her, Rai's mother was folding an impossibly complicated panda, while to her left, Maya's mother was carefully lettering a greeting. They worked in reach of cups of instant coffee and bowls of rice crackers, chatting and writing and folding.

Christine was silent. She listened, a fly on the wall, as one mother talked about sex, how she was never in the mood but her husband was always nudging her, and then she'd give in just to get some sleep. It was the kind of thing women might talk about among close friends, Christine thought, but here? At school? With Kaori-chan's grandmother listening in? Not to mention the foreigner. But then maybe she didn't count. They probably thought that she didn't understand what they were saying.

She didn't really want to talk about her sex life, or lack thereof. Hideki was usually exhausted. He often fell asleep in an easy chair, with the TV on, and a beer can clenched in his hand, pages with baseball stats strewn across his lap. The few times per week that he made it up to bed, he often flinched when she touched him. "How about tonight?" she'd say, sliding her hand down the front of his boxers. "Christine," he'd say in an irritated voice, grabbing her wrist and flinging her hand aside.

But maybe she should try harder to get along with these women. She should make an effort for Emma's sake, so that she would be able to negotiate playdates with their daughters or ask them for advice when buying a new hearing aid for Emma. Maybe if she shared something personal, they would stop thinking of her as an outsider. They would trust her. When there was a lull in the conversation, she forged ahead, in a shaky voice.

"Something strange happened last night," she said.

The mothers looked at her, curious, waiting for her to go on.

So she told the story, as best as she could, starting with finding Hideki asleep on the floor, his head lolling on the hard wood. The TV was on low. Christine tucked a pillow under his head, turned off the TV, and went to bed herself. She tended to be an insomniac, so she didn't really understand how he could fall asleep anywhere. She'd seen him nod off while sitting on a bench at an art gallery, and he'd even fallen asleep at a restaurant while they'd been waiting for their food. On that occasion, he'd blamed jet lag—they were on a ski trip to Vancouver—but even if she'd gone twenty-four hours without sleep, Christine didn't think she'd be able to fall asleep while sitting in a public place. She couldn't even sleep on airplanes.

Anyway, last night, she'd dozed for a while, then awoke to some commotion in the next room. She groped beside her: nothing; Hideki still hadn't come to bed. Then she heard a sound like water pouring. Was it raining? Was there a leak in the roof? Better go check. She dragged herself out of bed and pushed the door open to find Hideki urinating on Emma's Licca dollhouse. Licca was a well-known Japanese doll, as famous as Barbie. Her backstory was that her father was Japanese, and her mother European, which made the family bicultural, just like theirs.

"What are you doing?" Christine flicked the light on.

"Huh?" He woke then, as surprised as she was.

"Look at what you did!" she said. "You peed all over Emma's dollhouse!"

He blinked at the sudden brightness. "I'm sorry. I didn't know what I was doing."

"Were you drinking?" she asked.

"No, nothing."

She went to get some old towels to sop up the mess. Meanwhile, Hideki carried the dollhouse out onto the balcony, careful not to spill, and dumped the liquid out onto the ground below.

Christine wasn't sure what kind of reaction she'd expected from the mothers. Laughter, maybe? But when she finished her story, there was an awkward silence, as if they were embarrassed for her. Maybe they hadn't even understood, what with her accent and inevitable grammatical mistakes in Japanese. Finally, one of the mothers smiled kindly at Christine and said, "Your husband is under a lot of stress."

They uttered a few words of sympathy, and then turned to Aoyama-san, who was the mother of Sayuri, a blind-deaf girl.

"I've been checking my husband's cell phone messages," she said. "He's been getting love letters from some woman." This was obviously worse than too much marital sex or peeing on a dollhouse.

When Christine had gotten married, some of her woman students had thrown her a bridal shower because they knew it was an American custom. As part of the fun, they'd taken turns asking her questions. What was her "signature dish?" How many kids did she want to have? What would she do if her husband was unfaithful? Her honey mustard chicken was pretty good, she'd replied, and she wanted to have two kids; a boy and a girl would be ideal. And if her husband ever had an affair, she would file for divorce. (In fact, she had told Hideki just this: "If you ever hit me or cheat on me, I'll leave you.")

The women had been shocked. After all, men played around, and if it was just recreation, not real love, then what was the big deal? A mistress would never have the same status as a wife. Christine had wondered if their husbands had cheated, if it was true, as she'd read, that Japanese wives tucked condoms into their husbands' suitcases when they went on business trips to Thailand.

Now, she wondered what kind of advice the other mothers would dish out. She wanted to express her own outrage on Aoyama-san's behalf. What kind of a man could justify fooling around when his wife devoted virtually every minute of every day to her multiply disabled daughter's development?

Actually, it turned out to be more than a brief fling. Aoyama-san broke down and confessed that her husband hadn't been home (the home that he and his family shared with his parents) for days. She was getting a lawyer. She wanted out.

"Good for you," Christine muttered under her breath.

"I'm worried that he might want to keep our oldest son," Aoyama-san said.

Another mother pushed a box of tissues toward her. "Well, his mistress won't want Sayuri," she said.

The other mothers nodded knowingly. Christine wondered if they saw this as a consolation or a booby prize. In Japan, it seemed unlikely that she would be able to remarry. She now had serious baggage.

What would you do if your husband cheated on you? Christine thought back to her student's question. She imagined Hideki with one of the baseball mothers, or with some snack hostess, while she was trying to coax Emma through physical therapy or drilling her in sign language. *I'd go after him with a butcher knife. I'd hack off his balls and leave him for dead.*

When it was time to pick up Koji, Christine followed a gleaming black BMW into the school parking lot and pulled in beside a sparkling white Mercedes Benz. She wished she'd gone to the car wash to get rid of the pollen dusting her little Nissan hatchback. Hopefully, none of the smartly dressed, perfectly made-up mothers would peek into her car's interior where balled-up fast food wrappers littered the floor. She really shouldn't let her kids eat in the car.

It was almost time for the kids to come streaming out the door. She considered leaving Emma in the car while she ran up to get Koji, then decided against it. It was hot, for one thing, and Emma was unpredictable. Although she kept the child lock on the rear door, Emma had been known to crawl into the front seat and open the driver's side door. At the very least, she'd start messing with all the levers and dials. With a sigh, she got out of the car and heaved the wheelchair out of the back, unfolded it, and hefted Emma into the seat.

Emma started wheeling away before Christine had a chance to lock the car. What the hell. She left it unlocked and dashed after her daughter. A couple more cars were turning into the parking lot. Emma was oblivious to danger, intent on movement. She didn't know she was supposed to look out for traffic. Emma grabbed the wheels in protest when Christine took control.

"Please," she said under her breath. "Cooperate with me just this once."

A large part of her admired Emma for her strength and determination, but on days like this, when she was hot and tired and still unsettled by the discussion in the Mother's Room, she wanted maybe a hint of compliance.

They made it across the road, and Emma's attention turned to the high school baseball players out on the diamond. It had rained the day before, and many of them were out there with buckets and rags, mopping up puddles. They doffed their caps and bowed when Christine walked by.

Emma pointed and signed. "Papa."

"That's right," Christine said. "Your dad is Mr. Baseball. Twenty-four seven. Baseball, baseball, baseball."

Up ahead, Christine could see the older elementary school boys trickling out of the classrooms in their white shirts and neckties. The students wore white T-shirts emblazoned with the school symbol and navy shorts all day, but they were required to wear their formal uniforms going to and from school, even if they were just riding in their parents' cars. The boys dressed in gray shorts, while the girls wore gray skirts and blouses with Peter Pan collars. At least they didn't have to wear the jackets anymore, now that it was almost summer.

Emma rolled ahead just as Koji came out the door. A few girls flew out after him, then stopped in their tracks when they saw Emma in her wheelchair. "What's wrong with her?" one girl asked. "Can't she walk?"

The girls started closing in on Emma. One of them had picked up a stick. They were looking at Emma, jeering at her orange leg braces, as if she were a bug on the sidewalk. The little girl with a stick stepped up to Emma.

"No!" Christine shouted, rushing forward. "Get away from her!"

The three girls tittered, then skipped away. Emma, who couldn't hear the taunts in their voices, waved to them. She'd thought they were being friendly, Christine realized with a sinking heart.

Koji appeared then and patted Emma on the head. "Are you okay?" he asked her. Then he took charge of the wheelchair and began pushing it toward the parking lot. "Come on, Mom. Let's go."

A week later, Hideki took Koji to the bath while Christine cleaned up in the kitchen. She waited until he called on the bath's built-in intercom before bringing Emma to him to be bathed. As she pulled Emma's shirt off, she could hear Hideki's voice, gruff and angry, beyond the shower door.

"*Dare?*" he demanded. "Who?"

"I forgot," Koji whimpered.

"Who did this to you? Tell me!"

Christine quickly tugged off the rest of Emma's clothes, then pushed open the door to the bath. She caught a glimpse of Koji's bare back and gasped.

Five red gashes ran down his back. As if he had been clawed. As if someone with long fingernails had raked his tender flesh.

Christine suddenly felt sick to her stomach. "Oh, honey. What happened?"

Her mind scurried back to pick-up time when he'd clambered into the car, a little quieter than usual. Why hadn't she noticed that something was wrong? And why hadn't he told her?

She'd insisted on sending him to this expensive private school thinking he'd be safe from bullies. With his foreign mom and the sister in the wheelchair, he was so different from most other kids. At a public school, he had an been an obvious target. But at this small private school with just over twenty kids in a class, she'd figured the teachers were keeping an eye on things.

"I'll deal with it," Hideki said, dismissing her.

She nodded and closed the door. *I'm negligent,* she thought, suddenly sick to her stomach. *How could I not have noticed?*

On the other side of the door, Koji remained stubbornly silent.

Christine remembered a conversation she'd once had with one of her students. The woman's son had been singled out by a bully, but she hadn't reported the kid to the teachers or called his parents. "If I say something, the boy will become angry at my son for tattling and the violence will escalate."

Of course, this was possible. In a classroom of thirty-five kids, it was hard for a teacher, especially a rookie, only a year out of college, to keep track of what was going on. So much of the bullying was under the radar: a deliberately kicked shin during a game of soccer, a shove into the recessed toilets, a hat or bag swiped on the way home from school. Plus, reports of bullying were bad PR. Most schools preferred to ignore and deny abuse among children.

Now, Christine could hear Hideki advising Koji to be strong, to fight back. Her small, sweet son. Tears came into her eyes.

Later, after the kids were in bed, Hideki came to her, his face still clouded, and said, "He said it was Masaki."

Christine's heart sank. "Masaki?" She'd thought they were friends. She remembered how, on Parents' Day, Masaki had followed Koji around, trying to engage him. Koji had firmly disregarded him.

"That was so rude," she'd scolded afterward. "He just wants to be your friend."

Koji hadn't offered any explanation. He'd scowled at her, and she'd felt disappointed at being mother to such an unfriendly little boy.

Now she realized that she'd entirely misread the situation. Masaki had probably been picking on Koji even then. No wonder he hadn't bothered to talk to her.

"That's it," she whispered to herself. "We're getting out of here."

When she told Hideki that she wanted to take Koji and Emma to the States for a few months, he was surprisingly agreeable. Well, it'd be easier for him. He could concentrate on getting his team in shape for the summer tournament.

"What about school?" he asked.

"Koji's only in first grade. He won't miss that much." Neither one said anything about the school fees that his mother was paying. She would deal with her mother-in-law's displeasure. She would find a way to pay her back. Meanwhile, she promised Hideki she'd find a tutor, some Japanese exchange student or an expat housewife, to speak to their children in Japanese and teach them kanji. And she'd drill them in addition and subtraction. She'd find a therapist for Emma, too. It would only be for a little while.

Hideki drove them to the airport, dropping them off at the curb. Koji cried for a few minutes about leaving him.

"Pretty soon you'll be able to play with Max," Christine said, hoping to distract him. Max was her brother's son. He was a year older than Koji and they'd gotten along well on previous visits. "Can you help me with the suitcase? Or maybe push Emma's chair?"

They checked in, ate an expensive lunch at one of the airport restaurants, and perused the goods in the duty-free shops. Finally, they made it to the gate and waited to board. Koji sat on the edge of his chair, swung his legs back and forth, then sprang up and dashed off to the window. He pressed his nose against the glass, watching the baggage carts ferrying luggage to the plane. Christine said nothing to reel him back. He needed to unloose some of that boundless energy before the twelve-hour plane ride ahead.

Emma let up the brakes on her wheelchair and went after him. When another child, a girl with a Totoro backpack, got in her way, Emma tapped her on the shoulder and motioned for her to move. The girl stared at Emma, sitting there in her purple wheelchair with hearing aids nestled in her ears. Her mouth fell open, and her hands started fumbling as she reached for her mother. Emma forged on ahead.

Christine could sense the other passengers' concern: a little crippled girl in a wheelchair, all by herself—where were her parents? Who was taking care of her? But she remained steadfast and leafed through her magazine. Emma was fine.

Mixed in with the Japanese families going on vacation were a dozen or so young American men with crewcuts. She heard one of them mention Okinawa with a Southern drawl. These guys were probably on furlough, on their way to see friends and family in the States. And then she heard "Baghdad" and she wasn't so sure. She took a long look at the young man sprawled in the seat across from hers. Earbuds from his iPod blocked out the noise of shrieking children and the chatter of passengers. His foot tapped to some secret melody. His eyes were closed. She studied him, trying to memorize his features: crooked nose, a scar just over his eyebrow, his jug ears. She wondered about his mother. Was she sick with worry? Was she beaming with pride? How could she let her son join the army during wartime?

Her gaze skittered to Koji, still at the window. She had an urge to grab him and hold him against her heart. At least she would never have to worry about her daughter being shipped off to do battle. At least not that kind of battle, but she might need others to protect her. No matter how independent she was now or turned out to be, she would never be what others thought of as perfect. Christine had always identified as a pacifist, a would-be conscientious objector, but now, remembering what had happened to people like Emma during World War II, she understood the importance of armies. There had to be young men like that guy in the departure lounge to save them from Nazi "euthanasia" programs and other such evils. She shuddered imagining.

"Emma!" she called out. "Koji! Come back over here!"

PART TWO

HIDEKI

Now that Christine and the kids were gone, he could concentrate on his job, on coaching his baseball team and getting them to the final game of the summer tournament, and then to Koshien. He knew that it was possible.

The day after Hideki's team had lost to Seiko in the spring tournament, a huge photo of his boys, their heads drooping, had appeared on the sports page of the local newspaper. Their shame and humiliation had been on display for all to see. He'd felt even worse when, the next afternoon during practice, he got a call on the school office phone.

"I saw that game yesterday," a man's voice growled. Then the line went dead.

Hideki had held the phone for a moment, listening to the buzz of the dial tone. What the hell? Was that supposed to be some kind of threat? Was he going to find his tires slashed? His windows broken? Sports made people crazy. He thought of that Colombian soccer player who'd been assassinated by a fellow countryman for an own goal during a World Cup match. Why couldn't these baseball dads get a life?

Now, here he was at the end of a practice session, on the verge of the summer tournament. The boys were streaked with sweat, their uniforms smudged with red clay. The sun was edging toward the horizon. When the last of the batting cages had been stowed away, and the boys had taken off on their bicycles, his assistant Miki ran a handkerchief over his forehead and turned to Hideki. "Hey, Coach. Wanna go have a beer somewhere? Grab some dinner?'

Hideki shrugged. "Sure. Why not?" There was no one waiting

for him at home anyway.

They made their way to an izakaya a few meters from the school. The owner called out his greetings from the kitchen when they walked in. The air was heavy with grease and cigarette smoke. They kicked off their shoes, crawled up onto the tatami, and settled at a low corner table. At the center of the table there were a few plastic flowers stuck into a vase, next to the soy sauce dispenser.

"Two drafts," Miki barked as soon as the server appeared.

"Tempura ramen," Hideki added, glancing at the hand-scrawled menu posted on the wall. "And some fried chicken."

They chatted a bit about practice: so and so's batting was looking better, wasn't it? And so and so's ankle seemed to be healing nicely after a sprain. When Miki's face was as red as a pickled plum from the beer, he lit a cigarette and said, "You've done a good job with these kids, but I think you're a little soft."

Hideki didn't say anything. He knew that he'd done an amazing job. These kids were on track for college, not baseball, and yet he'd managed to turn them into contenders. He didn't hold practice at five a.m. like the coach of Naruto Tech, or deprive them of water during training sessions like his own high school coach had done, in the misguided belief that it would make them tougher. He didn't hit them, and he wasn't about to go retro and become some sort of drill sergeant. As Christine always reminded him, baseball was a game, and he wanted them to enjoy it.

"You want to go to Koshien, right?" Miki went on. He caught the server's eye and beckoned for another large mug of beer. "You want one?"

Hideki shook his head. He'd had enough. "Of course, I want to go to Koshien," he said. "Doesn't everyone?"

"I can get you there. If you make me head coach, I can get these boys to Koshien."

Hideki didn't reply at first. He waited until the server had set the foaming mug in front of Miki, until Miki had taken a big gulp, and then belched. They both knew that Miki had been the one to oversee his team's first victory, on that day when he'd been called to the hospital for his daughter's birth. That first win had always hovered between them, like a ghost, but neither had ever mentioned it.

Finally, Hideki laughed and shook his head. What an arrogant bastard. Sure, he'd gone to Koshien when he had been a high school ball player, and Hideki had not. Miki probably had his little sack of dirt sitting on the family altar. And sure, he'd coached his son's Pee Wee league team to a championship, but he had to admit that there was something dirty about Miki. His love of baseball was impure. He wanted power and glory.

"Look, I'll take your ideas into consideration," Hideki said, knowing that he wouldn't, "but this team is my responsibility. Coaching isn't just about winning. It's also about building character." Granted, there had been some bumps in the character-building department. Just the week before, one of his players had been picked up for shoplifting. And another kid, his second string first baseman, had stayed out all night with his girlfriend the week before, prompting frantic calls from the kid's parents. But still, Miki was a truck driver, not a teacher. He didn't understand the job.

Miki snorted. "You want to win, and you know it." He ground his cigarette out in the ashtray more forcefully than necessary. "But you, my friend, are never going to make it to the national tournament."

There was still beer in Miki's mug, but Hideki grabbed the check from the table and eased toward the edge of the tatami. "I'll see you tomorrow," he said. "Thanks for your help today."

When he got home to the too dark, too quiet house he had another drink at the kitchen table. He thought about calling Christine, but it was still pretty early in the morning in South Carolina. He sat there alone trying to chase Miki's words, that tinge of contempt, from his mind. Miki was right: he wanted to win and go to Koshien. But what would he have to sacrifice to get there?

CHRISTINE

"It'll be expensive if you don't have insurance," the woman said on the phone.

"Money is no object," Christine replied. That wasn't entirely true, but if these people could help Emma learn to stand or even walk, she'd be willing to sign over all of her earthly goods.

There was a pause on the other end of the line, then the woman came back on, slightly hesitant, and said, "I can schedule your daughter for Friday morning at ten."

"Perfect." She wondered if they'd accept credit cards.

Well, if it was really so expensive, she could get some sort of job. They'd be here for a few months. It might be worth her while. She could do some freelance writing. Maybe write some travel articles for the local newspaper. And, of course, she had experience teaching English to non-native speakers. She could tutor Mexican kids at the area schools. The area was suddenly swarming with immigrants from south of the border. Christine wasn't sure if they were legal or not, but judging by the Spanish she saw everywhere, at least some of them needed help with English. Or maybe she could teach the Somali Bantus. She'd read in the newspaper that a number of area churches were sponsoring refugees from Somalia. She could help.

They'd been back in South Carolina for almost a month now. When she'd first called her parents and asked about a prolonged stay, they'd been welcoming, if a bit guarded.

"Is everything all right with you and Hideki?" her mother had asked.

"Yeah, sure, Mom." Christine knew that her parents didn't approve of Hideki's long hours. They were quietly puzzled by

Hideki's absence when Christine brought the kids over. "Doesn't he get vacation time?" they asked. "Why don't you move over here? He can coach Little League, and still have time for his family." Once, when Christine had been describing her husband's heavy workload, her mother had said, "Are you sure he's not having an affair?"

At any rate, they were sympathetic to Christine's heavy burden, more than happy to put up their beleaguered daughter and her two nearly fatherless children; at least, in the beginning. There had been a flurry of outings—Riverbanks Zoo, the children's museum, a trip to a swamp where an alligator had been sighted— but now the honeymoon period was over. Her father was starting to grumble about the Lego blocks always underfoot, and the seemingly constant blare of the Cartoon Network. And her mother was itching to get back to her ladies' lunches, her church circle and Bible study groups, her book club meetings. It was time for Christine and the kids to stop being guests and develop some sort of routine.

After she'd scheduled a therapy appointment for Emma, she called Hideki.

"How long are you planning on staying there, Christine?"

"Just a few months. We'll be home by New Year's."

"And what about school?"

"They can go to school here. It'll be a great experience for them."

"And what about me?"

"You can always take a week or two off and come over here."

"You know I can't do that in the middle of the school year."

She did know that. In Japan, there was no such thing as a substitute teacher. If Hideki took time off, his classes would become the responsibility of the other teachers in his department. She remembered how Hideki had complained about a younger colleague's honeymoon. While the guy had been off snorkeling in the Maldives, Hideki's workload had been even more punishing than usual.

"You could come here for the winter holiday," Christine said, more gently. And then maybe we could stay longer, she thought. We could finish out the school year.

He sighed loudly. "You know I can't. I have responsibilities."

Christine sighed. He'd probably already settled into a bachelor lifestyle: boxed meals from Hotto Motto, socks on the floor, online mah johng at midnight. He could stay at baseball practice for as long as he liked, and she would never call him on his cell phone, asking him to pick up a carton of milk on the way home.

As soon as they reached the door to the therapy room, Emma went into rebel mode. She grabbed the rims of her wheelchair, effectively putting on brakes. Her wails echoed down the corridor.

"Iyaaaah!"

"Emma! Shh!" Christine put a finger to her lips. As if that ever did any good.

The door opened.

"Emma!" Janet, the physical therapist who'd worked with her the week before, stepped into the hallway. "I thought I heard someone out here calling my name."

Her hair was in cornrows today. Emma caught sight of the multicolored beads at the tip of each braid and shut up. "Pretty," she signed, and pointed. She motioned for Janet to move in closer so that she could get a better look.

"We've got a girly girl here, haven't we?" Janet grinned. She held still while Emma fingered the beads, cooing.

"Why don't you wait out here today, Mom," Janet said. "Sometimes it works better when the parents aren't around."

Christine nodded, relieved. She knew that Emma always looked to her for rescue when the stretches hurt, and she was sure that Emma behaved better when she wasn't standing there, watching.

Janet grabbed the wheelchair handle and started to push. "Bye-bye."

"Do your best," Christine signed. "Ice cream after!"

She waited till the door had swooshed shut behind them before taking a seat on the bench in the lobby. Assorted magazines were strewn on the low table: dog-eared copies of *Exceptional Parent, Ability Magazine,* an old issue of *People.* She grabbed a couple magazines and settled in to read.

A man on crutches swung into the room. The first thing Christine noticed about him was his pant leg, folded and pinned just below his left knee. She looked away quickly, then glanced back, watching as he reached into his pocket, inserted a coin into the vending machine, and bent down to grab a can of Coke. His sun-bleached hair was short, above his ears, and when he'd leaned forward, a pair of dogtags had tapped gently against the machine. There was something familiar about his profile.

"Andrew?" She said it softly in case she was wrong.

He looked up. "Christine?"

"Yeah." She felt oddly guilty that she hadn't informed him of her impending visit. Then again, their online flirtation was just that. She hadn't ever meant to carry it over into real life. She had deliberately not told him that she would be spending time in South Carolina.

"Wow, what a surprise! What are you doing here?"

"Emma's here for therapy," she said, gesturing to the door, ignoring the bigger question. "And you?"

"I have rehab at the V.A. hospital," he said, raking his fingers through his hair. "But I come here sometimes to cheer on the kids."

He settled on the bench beside her close enough that she could feel the heat of his body. Maybe she should have walked away.

HIDEKI

"I put Emma on a horse today. You should have seen her. She looked so happy!"

He closed his eyes for a moment. He could see Emma with her wide-gapped grin (she'd lost her front baby teeth in a tumble down the stairs), arms flung out, astride a slick, black beast. She was totally lacking in fear, unlike Koji, who'd probably whimper and cling to the reins. A wave of tenderness washed over him, and he had to swallow a lump in his throat.

"Can you put them on the phone?"

"Yeah, in a minute. I wanted to tell you that I've signed Emma up for hippotherapy."

"Hippo-what?"

"Horse therapy. I think it'll be great for her. It'll help with her balance and give her confidence and—"

"Okay. Sounds good." She was always glomming on to new therapies and treatments: yoga, Botox injections, most of which were unavailable in Tokushima. So far, therapy hadn't done Emma a lot of good. She was still crawling around, still dependent on Christine for a trip to the bathroom. He wondered if it was a good time to bring up the orthopedic surgeon in Fukuoka again.

"Here's Koji."

Hideki heard a rustle and clatter, as if the phone was being dropped, and then a blast of heavy breathing. "Hey, there. What have you been doing?"

"Ummm, I played T-ball."

"T-ball? Was it fun?"

"Yeah. I'm going to play on a team while we're here."

"Well, it's not real baseball, you know."

"Oh. Guess what? We saw an alligator."

"An alligator?"

"Yeah, we went to the swamp with Grandpa."

"Were you scared?"

"Umm, a little. It swam away. Do you want to talk to Mommy again?"

"No," he said. But Koji had already handed the phone back to Christine.

After he'd hung up, he cracked open a beer and boiled water for instant ramen. Christine had frozen individual helpings of stew and pot pie for him. "Don't eat those convenience store *bentos* the whole time I'm gone," she'd said. "They're full of MSG." He knew the food she'd prepared would still be in the freezer, covered with ice crystals, when she got back.

He'd just started hacking at a head of cabbage when the doorbell rang. Probably another delivery guy, he thought, wiping his hands on his shirt. This was the season for *O-chugen*. He'd already gotten three cases of beer and a package of steaks from parents of boys on his team: offerings of gratitude.

He flicked on the porch light and slid open the door. It wasn't a delivery guy. Daisuke's mother was standing there, a gray skirt swirling around her ankles, her lips freshly colored.

"*Konbanwa*," she said, with a trembling smile. "Since your wife is away, I thought you might like some home-cooked food." She held up a platter wrapped in an indigo-dyed cloth.

He could smell fried food. His mouth watered.

"It's tempura," she said. "I'm sure it's not as good as your wife makes, but ...."

For a moment, his hands hovered in mid-air. He remembered that her husband was in Tokyo and that she often wore skirts at baseball games. She had nice legs.

"Thank you," he said, taking the plate with both hands. "It smells wonderful."

Christine never prepared tempura. "Think about your arteries," she would say.

Daisuke's mother bowed then. "Please give my regards to your wife," she said. "*Ja, ne.*"

"Uh, good-bye. See you next weekend." He knew she'd be there, serving cold tea and juice during the practice game with Tokushima Tech.

She backed out into the evening and slid the door shut.

Hideki waited in the entryway until he heard her car engine sputter and start. When he got back to the kitchen, the pot of water was boiling furiously.

He wolfed down his dinner, piled the dishes into the sink, and grabbed another beer. Then he went upstairs and booted up the computer. Miki had told him about a baseball chat room. Players from different high school teams in Tokushima were posting, often under fake names.

"What do they write about?" Hideki had asked.

Miki had shrugged. "Gripes. Gossip. This coach is too strict. That manager has big breasts. This player might be gay."

It didn't sound like the chatter had a lot to do with baseball, but Hideki was alone, bored, and maybe just a little curious. He pulled a piece of paper out of his pocket and studied the URL Miki had scribbled there. He keyed it in.

There was an active thread about Tokushima Kita.

ninja 457: I'm third year junior high school, second base. I want 2 go 2 Koshien. What school is best?

iluvtigers324: Tokusho has number one ace pitcher this year.

ninja457: How about Tokushima Kita?

batboy16: Forget it. They always choke under pressure.

iluvtigers324: Yeah, 2 x in semifinals. They have a complex. Can't compete.

ninja457: What about the coach?

koko997: Kind of a tyrant. Plus, he takes a lot of time off for "family matters." His head's not in the game.

Hideki pounded his fist on the desk. Who the hell was writing this trash? He'd taken maybe three days off in as many years. He hardly spent any time with his family. *Miki.* He swigged his beer, trying to wash away his unease. Maybe Miki was logging in as a player and planting rumors. Maybe he was still ticked off about not being made head coach. If Miki knew about these messages, he'd have to know that Hideki wouldn't be happy about them. So why would he want to make him feel bad? Maybe he was trying to sabotage Hideki. All right. So be it. He wasn't going to trust the guy anymore. He'd pay attention, and if Miki gave him the slightest cause, he'd boot him out.

Hideki drained the rest of the beer, then clicked on to hotasianbabes.com.

He got a phone call a few days later from an old friend. They'd taught at the same school back when Hideki was a weightlifting coach. Now Asama-sensei was teaching at Joto, in the city, the high school next to the School for the Deaf. It had been rebuilt just before the economic bubble burst. Instead of the typical white ferro-concrete featureless block of years past, the school was actually beautiful. The outer walls were a terra cotta suggestive of Mediterranean villas. And what's more, the parents had pitched in for air conditioning, making it one of the most comfortable postings in the school district.

"What's up?" Hideki asked.

"That guy Miki is your assistant coach, right?"

Hideki felt a sinking in his stomach. "Uh, yeah. So?"

"I just wondered what he's been doing, hanging around here. You haven't sent him to spy on us, have you?"

"I don't know anything about it," Hideki said.

"Hmm. He seems to be vying for an assistant coaching position over here."

"Well, you can have him."

That treacherous bastard. And, of course, he had to pull this right before the start of the summer tournament.

"Is there something we should know about?"

"We've had our differences. But he's not going to be working with me anymore."

"Okay. Just checking."

As soon as the line disconnected, he dialed Miki.

He picked up on the first ring. "Yeah?"

"Don't ever come around here again," Hideki said. "We're through."

At practice, he told the players that Miki would no longer be helping out. He saw a couple exchange glances, but they were stoic for the most part. They were curious, no doubt, but he wasn't about to explain.

He put the team captain in charge of batting practice, then went into his office to decompress. The fathers would be willing to assist until he found a replacement. He'd make sure that they whooped Joto the next time they met on the field.

As he sat at his desk, filling his lungs with air, he realized that under his fury was relief. He'd had enough of Miki's second-guessing and the subtle cuts he made in the players' presence. They'd gone to the same college and played on the same team, but Hideki understood that they had never been friends. Not truly.

CHRISTINE

Christine woke to the ringing of the phone. She grappled for the alarm clock: six a.m. A few seconds later, knuckles rapped on the door.

"Telephone," her mother said. "Someone speaking Japanese."

Hideki, Christine thought. But no. He would have spoken in English, would have identified himself. She heaved herself out of bed and took it in the kitchen.

"Christine! I haven't heard from you in ages," her mother-in-law shrilled. She sounded like she was hopped up on green tea. Christine gripped the receiver tightly. "Okaasan. How are you?"

She tried to remember if she'd left this number with Hideki's mother, and for the briefest moment, she admired the woman for her pluck in dialing overseas, in risking English conversation with foreigners in order to speak with the mother of her grandchildren.

"Well, my blood pressure is a bit high. The doctor says I need to avoid stress, and to try not to worry too much, but other than that, I'm doing as well as my old bones will allow. And you? Didn't Emma have a little cough when you set out?"

"We're fine." Christine tested the phone cord, but it was too short. She wouldn't be able to get the coffee started.

"That's such a relief," her mother-in-law trilled. "And have you spoken to Hideki? Is everything all right between you two?"

Christine gritted her teeth. "Everything is just fine, Okaasan." What if she'd said otherwise? What kind of advice would a Japanese mother-in-law deliver to a foreign wife?

"Well, I thought you should know that my son's been having a visitor."

"Oh?" Christine thought about putting the receiver down and letting the woman gab to air while she filled the coffeemaker. "A visitor, you say?"

"Some woman dropped by a couple of evenings ago. An attractive, slender woman. I think she was a couple years younger than you."

"And how would you know this?"

"Oh, I have my sources."

Nothing like nosy neighbors, Christine thought with a sigh. "It was probably the woman who collects for the newspaper," she said. "Or someone circulating a petition."

"Hmm. That may be true, but I believe she arrived with a bottle of wine. And I'm told that she stayed for quite a while."

Christine was already in a bad mood when Koji started going on about the corn. One of her parents' neighbors, an elderly woman with a face like that of those apple dolls Christine had made long ago when she was a Brownie in Michigan, had rolled into the driveway on a bicycle with a paper bag full of fresh-picked corn. Corn brought back more memories of Michigan, of sitting on the back porch with the bushel baskets before her, husking and de-tasselling with her mother, of suppers at the picnic table under a parasol on the patio, of sweet yellow kernels shiny with butter, studded with salt crystals, summer in her mouth.

Christine thanked the woman effusively, accepted the bounty, and brought the cobs into the house. She stood at the sink peeling back the green leaves, stripping the silky strands, while Koji and Emma played with blocks in the next room. He was talking to himself while he played, narrating in Japanese. Sometimes he played in English. It seemed to depend on the context: for instance, English when he was pretending to be Spiderman, Japanese, when he was imitating a samurai.

When she'd cleaned the corn, Christine gently tugged a cookbook off the shelf. It was tattered by now, the middle pages now loose sheaves; her mother had consulted it over and over, looking up recipes for meatloaf, macaroni and cheese, and chocolate cake, all the foods that Christine made in Japan in order to comfort herself when she felt homesick. Now, she flipped to vegetables, then to corn: Add one tablespoon sugar and one tablespoon lemon juice to each gallon of water. Heat to boiling; boil uncovered two minutes. Remove from heat; let stand ten minutes before serving.

She followed the instructions, and then she prepared a salad with cucumbers and tomatoes that another neighbor had brought over the day before, and pan-fried a piece of salmon. When supper was laid out, she called her parents, Koji, and Emma to the table.

Christine admired the colors: the yellow of the corn, the cucumbers with pine-green skin, the flash of red tomato. Her mouth watered.

"This looks delicious, honey," her mother concurred.

"Sure does," her father said.

Koji was already picking up his fork, but Christine shot him a look and he put it back down. They lowered their heads while Grandpa said a blessing.

"*Itadakimasu*," Koji said, pressing his palms together.

"Honey, we're in America," his grandma said. "You need to speak English."

Koji glowered at her.

"Mom, please."

Christine tried to put a cob of corn on Koji's plate, but he held out his hand as if he were stopping traffic. "I don't like corn."

"You should try it with butter and salt," she said. "It's really good."

It was then that he shook his head and said, "Japanese don't eat corn like that."

Christine sighed. The summer fifteen years ago when she'd first arrived in Japan as an assistant English teacher, she'd been instructed on many occasions about the peculiarities of the natives. Her boss, a middle-aged woman who'd just returned from a four-day trip to visit Beatrix Potter's birthplace, had laughed when Christine complained about the incessant shrill of cicadas.

"We Japanese find the sound beautiful," she said. "Japanese hear insect sounds in a different part of the brain than foreigners, you know." She'd wanted to challenge the woman. Which foreigners? Does that include the Chinese? Koreans? Japanese-Americans? But being new to the country, she'd kept her mouth shut and nodded politely as if in agreement. Another time, on the way to watch a *bunraku* puppet show, they'd passed a Western hamburger restaurant and the teacher had frowned saying, "We Japanese have shorter intestines than you foreigners. We can't digest meat as easily as you." It was as if she believed her countrymen were of another species entirely.

Christine had felt both annoyed and excluded whenever the teacher made this kind of pronouncement. Now, in her parents' dinette with her son, she said, a little bit more coldly than she intended, "Koji, there are many ways to eat corn." She picked up a cob and took a big bite.

She remembered what Koji had said in the car, on the way to Osaka to renew his American passport the previous fall.

Hideki had been driving. Christine had lain back against the headrest, looking out the window at the tiny islands scattered across the Inland Sea. She listened to father and son talk, glad to not be, for once, the center of Koji's attention.

"Which do you like best," Hideki asked. "Soccer or baseball?"

Christine smiled. She knew what their boy would reply. They both knew. He was, even at that age, a diplomat, and his dad was a baseball coach.

"Baseball!"

"Who do you like better? Mommy or Daddy?"

Koji giggled. "I like Mommy *and* Daddy."

"Are you American or Japanese?"

Koji paused for a moment, then said, "When I'm in Japan,

I'm Japanese. When I'm in America, I'm American."

Good enough, Christine thought. When he was twenty two, he would have to choose sides, unless the law changed. But for now, he was a dual citizen.

They were a bit confused by all the one-way streets in the city of Osaka, but they finally found the consulate, just down the road from a Portuguese restaurant. When they'd gone through the glass doors and up the elevator, Christine leaned down and whispered in Koji's ear, "You're in America now." The navy passport that arrived in the mail a week later was the same size and color as his Japanese passport. But this one listed his middle name (Benjamin, after his grandfather, Christine's dad) and gave him rights to a country that his father didn't have.

"Pretty soon you'll be able to play with your cousin Max," Christine said, hoping to distract him from the corn. They were going to drive upstate for a visit after lunch.

This visit started out well enough. Max was there to greet them, as soon as they walked in the door. "I'm going to be a rocket scientist or the president when I grow up," he said. "What about you, Koji?"

Anne, Max's mother, leaned in and said, "Excuse him. It's Career Week at school, and he's all fired up. By the way, I volunteered you to speak to Max's class about being a writer. The day after tomorrow. That's okay, isn't it?"

"Uh, yeah. I guess." Christine didn't really think that the kids would want to hear about the kind of writing she did: rewriting manuals for electronic goods in the middle of the night when her family was fast asleep. Once, long ago, she'd published a few poems in her college's literary journal and she'd even started a novel or two, but she could hardly call herself a writer. Then again, maybe she could just talk about Japan. Surely kids would be interested in hearing about life in a foreign country. She could talk about volcanoes and sumo wrestling and how the Japanese kids ate whale meat in their school lunches. They'd get a kick out of that.

Christine sat at the table with Emma, who was filling in outlines of unicorns in a coloring book. She watched her son through the window. He and his cousin were running around the expansive back yard, dodging between fat, towering pines, and rolling around on the plush grass. Oh, what Christine wouldn't give for a lawn like that.

At home in Japan, they had just enough room behind their house for a sandbox and a patch of grass. They had a skinny maple and a quince tree that bore heavy, hard yellow fruit Christine couldn't figure out how to eat.

That evening, Christine's brother Pete fired up the grill out on the big wooden deck overlooking the lawn. Christine remembered how their father had grilled steaks on the back patio every Sunday. How she had missed that smell. In Japan, they owned a small hibachi, but Hideki said that the smoke from a barbecue would disturb the neighbors, so they rarely used it. They only grilled at the beach, or at the riverside where dozens of other families did the same. Christine watched her brother tend the hot dogs until they were plump and oozing juice. She helped Koji fix a sandwich.

"Look at that," Pete said, as Koji bit into the bun. A bit of ketchup was smeared on his face. "He looks just like an American."

"He *is* an American," Christine said. "He has an American passport."

"Well, why don't you get that husband of yours to move over here? There's a Japanese auto plant in the next town over. He could get a job there easily."

Koji put down his hot dog then and scowled.

"He's a teacher and a baseball coach," Christine said. "And he loves what he does."

"He could teach, then. He could even coach Little League."

Christine sighed. He thought of Hideki, back in Japan, out on the field. While other coaches maintained poker faces, Hideki was known for being expressive. More than one sportswriter had mentioned tears in his eyes after an important victory. And she'd heard someone call in on a radio show to comment on Coach Yamada's obvious joy in the game. Christine had seen it, too, on TV when the games were broadcast on NHK or the public access channel, and around the house. After a tournament win, or a victory over a perennial favorite like Toku-sho or Seiko, his good humor would last for days, or at least until the next defeat. He'd be on his cell phone for hours, laughing and talking with friends from way back in junior high school, going over key moments: the home run at the bottom of the ninth, Inari's two stolen bases, the narrow escape in the fifth. He'd stop by Mister Donut and bring home treats for the kids. He'd be adventurous and generous with her in bed. Coaching high school baseball made him happy. So how could she ever ask him to quit?

Her family believed that anyone would be happy to live in the United States of America, land of plenty, land of opportunity. And it was true, she missed her home country and her family. But she wasn't sure that Hideki could ever be truly content outside of Japan. Sure, he loved the cheap golf, but here, he stumbled through conversations and didn't get jokes. He was more confident in his own country. And then, of course, there was the issue of his being an only son, and the question of health insurance.

Christine glanced over at Koji, who was still frowning at his plate. She gave him a small smile.

"Our home is in Japan," she said.

Koji picked up his hot dog and started eating again.

At Max's school, Anne, Christine, Emma, in her wheelchair, and Koji went into the office to get visitors' passes. Christine was pleased to see big, leafy plants and an aquarium full of fish. And the colors! The walls, the furniture, even the teachers' clothes were in shades of yellow, orange and red. Such a bright, cheerful place!

Anne led them down the corridor to Max's classroom where the eighteen kids sat at two long tables. Christine was pleased to see that they came in all shades. There were at least two children of African descent, another couple who appeared to be Mexican-American, and an Asian girl, maybe Vietnamese.

Mrs. Brown, the teacher, who had emigrated from Mexico herself, greeted them at the door. "Everyone, let's welcome today's special guests," she said. "Max's aunt and cousins have come all the way from Japan."

"They don't look Japanese," a blond boy said.

Mrs. Brown let the comment pass, but Christine felt Koji stiffen at her side.

The children gathered on a bright green carpet and Christine settled in a chair. She positioned Emma to her left. Koji knelt beside her. She'd brought along a map and a picture book about a Japanese boy. She held up the map and indicated a few key spots: Tokyo, Mt. Fuji, and Nagano, site of the winter Olympics. Then she had Emma point out the island where they lived. After she read the book, with Koji turning the pages, she asked the children if they had any questions. A few hands shot up.

"Did you write that book?" the Asian-American girl asked.

"No, I'm sorry. I didn't."

"Have you ever seen a volcano?" another kid asked.

"Yes, but not when it was erupting." She had seen Mt. Fuji from planes and distant hotel rooms.

"Do you have a robot?"

"Uh, no."

They seemed increasingly disappointed. Max, there in the back row, looked embarrassed. She felt like a failure.

Finally, Mrs. Brown stepped in. "Let's all give our special guests a big hand!"

Christine stood and bowed and they were escorted from the room.

Later that evening, Anne put a hand on Christine's arm and led her into the next room.

"Why don't you rest? I'll call you when dinner's ready."

Dozing on the sofa, she could hear bits of Max and Koji's

play. At first, they were pretending to be firemen, but then Max said, "Hey, I've got an idea. I'm George Washington and you're a British soldier."

"George Washington?" Koji asked.

"Don't you know? He was the first president."

Christine's stomach went a little queasy. Was he supposed to know about the Founding Fathers? The Revolutionary War? Had she known that in first grade? Then again, Max was fairly precocious. She knew that he was beyond picture books, and that he entertained himself by writing poems and stories on the computer.

Christine felt a twinge of jealousy. She'd done everything she could to interest Koji in learning to read English. She'd even set up a chart for him: a star for every ten minutes spent practicing writing the alphabet, a small toy for every ten stars, and an expensive computer toy—the one that his best friend had with the fighting beetles—if he mastered the stack of easy readers she'd bought for him. Bugs and violence: she was willing to stoop that low just to get him sparked. But it hadn't worked. He'd learned to read Japanese with almost no help at all, and now he sat in rooms with books by himself, sounding out the words with greater and greater proficiency.

She'd done her best to fill him in on American culture, though she had felt he was too young to learn about war. He sometimes asked her about photos on the front page of the newspaper, and she answered evasively. He was never allowed to watch television news. But now, she could hear the "bang bang bang" in the next room as "George" took out the soldier.

Christine was leafing through an American parenting magazine ("How to Fire Your Nanny," "Time Outs for New Moms") when Koji suddenly appeared, brow furrowed, chin against his chest. His lower lip jutted in a classic pout.

"What's wrong?" Christine put down the magazine, which didn't anyway tell her how to raise a bicultural child, or deal with bullies, or advocate for her disabled kid, and patted the cushion beside her.

Koji burrowed into her side. "I want to go home."

She sighed. Home was living so close to others that you could hear the phone ring three doors down. Home was having her mother-in-law telling her how to store her broom and chiding her about the dust on top of the television. Home was not understanding half the things that people said; it was doing everything wrong. Here, Koji was in a huge house full of playthings, with a yard big enough for a full-scale soccer game, a treehouse, cousins who understood his love for Scooby Doo and macaroni and cheese. Why wasn't he having fun? Sure, he missed his father, but it had to be more than that.

He plucked at the cushion for a moment then looked up at her. Tears pooled in his eyes. (His father's eyes, she had to admit.)

"Max said that there was a war between Japan and America."

"Yes, there was, but it was a long time ago. Japan and America are friends now. Daddy and Mommy got married, right?"

He sniffled and dragged a sleeve across his nose. "Max said that America won and Japan lost."

Oh. So that was it.

"Well, honey, I don't think anyone really wins a war."

She could have told him how Japan had been rebuilt, how it was now a prospering and peaceful country, but all that she could think about was his apparent rejection of his second country, her country. Even as he sat there snugly, warmly against her, his hand toying with hers, she felt disowned.

DAISUKE

Daisuke had heard a rumor that Coach's wife had gone back to America. She'd taken the kids with her, and as far as anyone knew, she wasn't coming back. It was no big surprise. Marriages between Japanese and foreigners didn't last long. He thought of Irabu, that guy who'd pitched three seasons for the Yankees. His father was American, but his parents had divorced when he was a little kid. He was *hafu*. Sportswriters insisted that that's why he was always so angry, because he was conflicted about his identity. It was hard to be *hafu*, in Japan. Hard to be a Korean, even if you were born in Japan; hard to be *burakumin*: the descendant of tanners or butchers; hard to be a second-generation Japanese. He saw a documentary on TV once about those Brazilians living in Hamamatsu. They were descended from Japanese who'd emigrated years ago, looking to make their fortune on the sugarcane plantations of South America. In recent years, many had been welcomed back to Japan because officials thought they'd fit in well, what with their pure blood and Japanese faces. The problem was, they were actually Brazilian. They couldn't write kanji or speak proper Japanese. They didn't sort their garbage correctly, and the neighbors complained that tin cans were mixed in with combustibles, and plastic bottles mixed with milk cartons, and they had to divide the trash all over again. They had barbecues, those Brazilians, that lasted all day long.

Daisuke worried that he had become too American to ever fit into Japan again. Coach had once said that he swung like an American: feet flat on the ground, bat cocked high. He wasn't sure if it was a good thing, or not. After all, Coach's wife was American, and a few weeks ago a scout from the Los Angeles

Dodgers had come by to take a look at their pitcher. His batting average was pretty good, so Coach didn't tell him to change his style or anything.

He wondered if Coach had a hard time fitting in. He wished he could sit down on the bench someday and just talk. Not just about baseball, but everything. The way he wanted to talk to his father.

When he first heard about Coach's wife, he'd imagined his own parents getting divorced, and his mother marrying the coach. It didn't seem so far-fetched. Whenever his mother spoke about Coach Yamada, there was a lilt in her voice. And he thought that his mother was still good-looking. She was slender, and she kept the gray out of her hair. There were hardly any wrinkles around her eyes. She was as pretty as Mrs. Yamada. And it didn't look like his father would be back anytime soon. Now that his grandmother was living with them, his father didn't come home at all.

CHRISTINE

The next time she saw Andrew, he was on two feet, gray sweat-pants covering his legs.

"Hey!" She said, before she could stop herself.

Andrew sat down next to her on the bench, where she waited for Emma.

"How's your daughter doing?"

Christine shrugged. "Still waiting for a miracle." Lately, Emma was in love with her wheelchair. Whenever she saw someone else rolling along on TV, or in print, or in the aisles of Walmart, she became excited. "Same!" she signed, bringing her thumb and pointer fingers together. Christine was dismayed by this sense of solidarity. Sure, wheelchairs were great, but if she didn't have any desire to walk, then she wouldn't even try.

"How are your kids doing?"

Andrew reached into his pocket. He opened his wallet to a photo of two tow-headed girls in the arms of a blonde with bee-stung lips.

"Your daughters are beautiful," Christine said. "So's your wife."

"Ex-wife."

"Oh. I'm sorry." She wondered if the leg had anything to do with it. "So. Any plans for the Fourth of July?"

"Actually, no. I figured I'd kick back with a beer and watch a ball game on TV."

"Do you want to barbecue with us?" She hadn't planned to say it, the words just flew out of her mouth. She could feel herself blushing.

He looked at her, a little suspiciously, and she realized that her invitation had sounded like charity to him. Maybe he could see that bleeding heart on her sleeve.

"I just meant, well, I'm not good with a grill, but barbecuing seems like such an American way to spend the holiday. I thought it might be good for my kids."

He didn't ask any questions. He didn't say anything at first, then finally, he nodded. "Okay. When and where?"

As it turned out, Andrew was a master at the grill. Christine stood by as he prepared the coals, watching him lift the burgers from the platter with a spatula.

Emma had gotten down from her wheelchair and was sketching in the dirt with a stick. Koji had a stick, too, but he was using his to whack a tree trunk. From time to time he paused to glare at Andrew, who was too busy monitoring the meat to notice.

He was wearing baggy shorts that fell over his knees. It was too hot for jeans.

Christine spread a checked tablecloth over the picnic table and set out ketchup and mustard and a bag of whole wheat buns. She inhaled the aroma of cooked beef mixed with lake water and pine. It was like old times, she thought. Like when she was a kid. Her dad had grilled burgers and hot dogs at the state park near Lake Michigan, or in the backyard.

When Koji saw the chips, he ran over to grab a handful.

"Sit down," Christine said. "It's time to eat."

He plopped in the seat next to her. She settled Emma next to Andrew's place. "Do you mind?" she asked him. "You might have to help her a little."

"No problem."

Koji kept his eyes on the table as Christine put together his sandwich. Across the table, Emma was swatting flies away from her chips. Andrew didn't seem to be paying much attention to either child. They ate in silence for a while. A motorboat buzzed along the shore. Christine fussed about Koji's posture, then reached across the table to cut Emma's burger into manageable pieces with a plastic knife. Koji gobbled up the chips on his plate before reaching for the bag. His hamburger sat untouched.

Christine took a big bite, and showed him her burger. "Mmm. This is perfect, Andrew. Look, Koji—no pink. It's just the way you like it."

Andrew grunted and forced a smile.

It must be hard for him, Christine thought. He's probably missing his own kids. Then, Emma tapped him on the shoulder and pointed to his artificial leg. "Why?" she signed. Screwing up her face and scrunching her fingers together, she asked, "Does it hurt?"

"What's she saying?" Andrew asked.

Christine shook her head at Emma and put a finger to her lips. Her mind raced, chasing after some conversational gambit that would distract the kids. She'd talk to them later about Andrew's prosthesis and what kind of questions were polite. But then Koji spoke up for the first time since the outing had begun: "She wants to know what happened to your leg."

Andrew nodded. His gaze strayed from the table, went out onto the lake where a family of ducks were settling on the water. He took a big bite out of his hamburger.

At first, Christine thought that he wasn't going to answer, but after a few more seconds he swallowed and turned to the little girl at his side. He brought his arms up together as if he were holding a rifle. And then he was up from the table, miming a slow, careful entry into danger, the rifle held in front of him. Emma and Koji watched wide-eyed as he froze. Suddenly his hands crashed together and flew apart. His body bolted backwards. He fell onto the ground, his mouth an "O" of surprise.

Christine hesitated. Should she help him get up? But before she could make a move, he was on his feet, brushing pine needles off the seat of his pants, and back at the table, taking another bite.

Emma started to giggle.

"It's not funny," Koji said with a glare.

Well, that was weird. Christine reached for the Tupperware container she'd brought along. She'd have a talk with the kids later. "Anyone want a chocolate chip cookie?"

DAISUKE

Today is the day, Daisuke thought as he pedaled to school, his mitt nestled in his bicycle basket. He had a temple charm tucked into his back pocket. This afternoon, Coach Yamada would announce the starting line-up for the summer high school tournament. All of their practice games since the beginning of school in April had been leading up to this moment. Had he managed to impress Coach with his speed ("cheetah boy," his mother called him)? Had he won a space on the roster? He'd memorized all the coach's complicated signs. He'd never messed up in reading a sign during a practice game. He'd even mastered the bunt.

Daisuke couldn't concentrate during English class. He didn't really need to bother. He could speak English better than anyone else, including the teacher, since he'd spent the previous three years in the United States.

Now, he looked over at Junji, whose fuzzy head was nested in his arms. He was gently snoring, but no one tried to wake him up. He'd noticed that the teachers were always easy on the ballplayers. They knew how hard the guys practiced, sometimes till nine at night. Coach Yamada had told them that starting two weeks before the tournament, they'd have morning practice, before classes, as well. They'd be expected out on the diamond by seven a.m. even on weekdays.

Junji would probably be on the team. He played third base, and he could whack the ball if he wanted to, if he was in the zone. His father helped out a lot at weekend practices. He sometimes invited Coach Yamada out for yakitori and beer after Saturday's practice sessions. "Butter up," was what the Americans said. Junji's dad "buttered up" the coach so that his son would get to play.

Kikawa, there at the back of the room, had been personally recruited by Coach Yamada. Three or four different coaches had gone out to the seaside junior high school where he was a student to see him pitch. Kikawa's parents had convinced him to go with Yamada. And now Coach Yamada was responsible for him, and Daisuke was sure he'd get to start. Another colloquialism leftover from America jumped into his head: Kikawa was Coach Yamada's "pet."

But Shima, who'd been the starting shortstop in the spring tournament, had broken his leg. He wouldn't be able to play. There was an opening.

Daisuke had been a walk-on. He didn't have anything going for himself, aside from his own ability. His dad was too busy with his work to ever help out. He'd never seen Daisuke play, not even in America. In fact, he'd been against Daisuke's joining the middle school baseball team in Georgia, where they lived. It would take time out of his studies, said his father.

Daisuke's dad hadn't played any sports himself. His mother had once dug an old photo album out of a drawer. She'd pointed out the photos of his dad as a kid, wearing glasses and prissy clothes. He wore bow ties. "Your father wasn't very athletic," his mother told him, trying to explain why he wouldn't play catch like the other fathers. "He had asthma when he was a child. He was sick a lot. He spent a lot of time reading."

Daisuke knew that his dad had graduated at the top of his class and gone on to study at the University of Michigan and then M.I.T. By bringing his son to America for three years, he'd been hoping to give him the language of science—English—not apple pie and baseball.

"But it's only for a few months," Daisuke had argued. In the States, baseball was a spring and summer sport. Even the star players gave it up in the crisp, cool days of fall. When the maples turned scarlet, they'd put on helmets and pass footballs. And after that, there was basketball. Daisuke promised that he'd buckle down in the autumn. He wouldn't play any other sports. He wouldn't join the newspaper club or learn to play any musical instruments. And he would keep his grades up; he'd make his father proud.

Only his mother had attended those games in America. He remembered her sitting alone in the bleachers, the only one in a skirt, too shy about her English to strike up a conversation with the other spectators. She'd been at every single home game, and when he came back from the away games, she asked him to describe everything he could recall. Did he hit the ball? Did it go far? Did his teammates call out his name?

When his dad was late coming home, they sometimes watched pro baseball together on TV. They kept an eye out for the Japanese players: Nomo, Ichiro, Matsui.

They sat silently at desks in their crisp white shirts and dark pants, like prisoners awaiting a sentence. Sure, some of them knew already that they'd be on the team, but a few spots were up for grabs. There'd be twenty boys in the dugout during the summer tournament, twenty boys swinging and throwing their hearts out under the merciless July sun. The rest would be stuck in the stands, with mothers, girlfriends, and maybe a few *senpai*, where they'd try to mash down disappointment and cheer into megaphones.

For the third-year students, this would be their last shot at Koshien, or the quarterfinals, or any other kind of tournament play. After this, after whatever happened during these sweat-drenched days, they'd be retiring their high school uniforms and opening the books. In the season to follow, the third-year students would be studying for college entrance exams or for the tests that guaranteed entry level positions in top companies or local government offices. From autumn on, it'd be bye-bye baseball.

Daisuke would be around for a couple more years. If he didn't make this summer's team, there was still next summer, and the one after that. But he knew he was good, and he knew he'd be disappointed if his number wasn't called. He wanted his dad to fly down for the tournament. If he was sitting in the bleachers, it'd be business as usual up in Tokyo. He wanted his dad to know that he was special. He could hit that ball over the fence, and run bases like Ichiro. If they made it all the way to Koshien, maybe then his father would finally respect him.

Coach Yamada stepped up to the front of the classroom. He was wearing a tie with a baseball motif and his cheeks were shaved smooth. There were bags under his eyes, though, and Daisuke wondered if he'd stayed up all night fretting over the twenty. Or maybe something had come up with his kids, or that foreign wife.

Coach never talked about his private life, but there were rumors going around: He and his American wife were on the verge of divorce. His son was getting pushed around at school. No wonder Coach spent so much time at the ball field.

Daisuke's home life wasn't all that much fun either. His mom was always arguing with his sister, or she was tired and snapped at them for no good reason. But when he was on the baseball diamond, his entire body was focused on that white ball with red stitches. He didn't think about anything else.

Coach cleared his throat. "Good afternoon."

They responded in chorus.

"As you know, the summer baseball tournament begins next week. You've all played your hearts out for this moment, and I've been moved by your efforts. If it were up to me, you'd all be in the dugout, taking your turns at bat. But you know the rules. Only twenty names are allowed on the roster." He paused and slowly surveyed the sun-bronzed faces. When his eyes met Daisuke's, he held his gaze steady. "But even if I don't call your name today, you should know that you are still a valuable member of this team. We need you to keep up the spirits of the players on the field. Your job is very important."

The managers brought in a stack of jerseys.

Coach rattled off a little more about team spirit and sacrifice and then he read the first name.

"*Hai!*" The third-year first baseman stood up, his back soldier-straight, walked to the front of the room, and bowed first to the rest of the team, then to Coach Yamada. He extended both hands and accepted the uniform as if it were a diploma or an award. He bowed again.

"I will fight hard for everyone!" His expression was stoic, blank, but Daisuke could imagine the wild joy leaping inside of him.

Pick me, he thought. *Pick me.*

He remembered the moment Coach Harris in Atlanta had read his name, and how he'd felt as if he could hurl a ball all the way to the moon. He hadn't thought he had a chance. After all, he was an outsider, a foreigner, some stranger from Japan. He wasn't a part of the system, hadn't grown up going to the same schools and playing on the same Little League teams as everyone else. But in America, none of that mattered.

A bunch of boys had shown up for the first practice sessions and Coach Harris had put them all through the paces. There were white kids and African-American kids and Asian-Americans and boys who spoke to each other in Spanish. Daisuke was inconspicuous among them, at least until he picked up a bat. When he blasted the ball, jaws dropped. *Wow!* They said. *This kid is magic.*

"Kikawa Ryohei," Coach called out.

Of course. They couldn't do anything without him.

"Okada Kenta."

And then, finally, "Uchida Daisuke."

"*Yes!*" He wanted to bump fists or slap hands with someone, but when he looked around, there was no joy. A few of the upper-classmen who didn't make the team were actually glaring at him. Junji was sitting there with his shoulders slumped, looking down. Shintaro's name wasn't called either. He was good enough to make the team, Daisuke knew, but he didn't seem to be angry at him for taking his place. Instead, he was looking out the window, biting his thumbnail. If anything, he looked worried. Daisuke wondered if his dad would cuss him out because he wasn't selected. Or worse.

The room was silent. He was suddenly embarrassed for having shouted. "*Sumimasen*," he mumbled. *I'm sorry.*

He stood and approached Coach Yamada, who handed him the uniform that he would wear for tournament play with a reverence usually reserved for folded national flags. Daisuke bowed to his coach and his teammates, being careful not to smile. "I will do my best to help this team get to the championship round," he said.

Coach explained that from now until the tournament, only the chosen players would be participating in practices. He had a list of tasks for everyone else, which he turned over to Kikawa, team captain.

"Okay, now, get out there on the field."

The ceremony was over. The guys shuffled out of the room. Daisuke expected Junji to congratulate him, or at least walk to the clubhouse with him, but he hung back with Shintaro. He didn't say a thing.

The big freeze continued throughout afternoon practice and on into the next day. At lunchtime, Junji pushed his desk next to Shintaro's. Daisuke moved his desk over by theirs, but they ignored him. Shintaro had a lacquer box stuffed with rice balls, fish, and boiled vegetables. He didn't offer anything to Junji, who was dining on a bag of rolls. He'd probably bought them at the convenience store on the way to school. Daisuke ate his *bento* without saying a word.

He looked across the room and saw Nana sitting by herself, as usual. In one hand, she was holding a book, in the other a pair of chopsticks, her black lacquered *bento* open before her. Although she was alone, she looked more aloof than lonely, but maybe it was just a front. He'd already discovered that Nana was good at acting. And maybe he'd been lying to himself about why he'd been keeping their friendship a secret. Maybe he *was* afraid of what others—Junji, for example—might think. Which was stupid. And Junji wasn't even talking to him anyway, so whatever.

Junji and the rest of his classmates obviously knew nothing about her. They didn't get that she was smart and serious. They should give her a chance. Who cared about her family's history, or the house she lived in?

Daisuke glanced over at Junji and Shintaro. They were laughing about something, and he wasn't in on the joke. Why were they being such jerks? Maybe they thought he was getting special treatment from the coach just because he'd been to America. Or maybe they thought his father had intervened and given Coach a "gift" or something. They didn't seem willing to concede that he'd earned his place on the bench, that he was better than them. Whatever. Daisuke was tired of downplaying his skills and trying to fit in.

Nana looked up from her book just then and their eyes meet. He saw a challenge in her eyes and sucked in a deep breath. Why not? Screw those guys.

He pulled his desk away from theirs and pushed it across the floor. Other students looked up at the screech of dragging furniture.

CHRISTINE

Andrew had his daughters the following weekend. He suggested that they all meet up at the zoo. Emma and Koji had been there only a couple of weeks before with Grandma and Grandpa, but Christine figured it would be good for them to spend time with other kids. Good for them to be with a man, too. Besides Grandpa, they didn't interact much with adult men even in Japan. Hideki was hardly ever home.

Andrew and the girls were waiting at the entrance when Christine and her children arrived. The younger girl stared at Emma's leg braces until her sister elbowed her.

"This is Brittany," Andrew said, placing a palm on the younger girl's head. "And that's Elena."

"Hi, girls. Meet Koji and Emma."

The kids eyed each other shyly. It would take them a while to warm up.

The adults paid the entrance fee and they all made their way into the park. African drumbeats blared from a loudspeaker, mingling with the chatter of birds and the conversation of monkeys.

Emma, always quick to suss out who was most sympathetic to her, caught up with Elena and made the sign for "peacock."

The older girl nodded, her blonde braids swaying.

Koji started signing animal names then, too, showing off for the girls. And then they were all using their hands, repeating the signs that Emma taught them and making up new ones.

"Looks like they've hit it off," Christine said. She and Andrew were lagging behind.

He nodded. "That's good."

They wandered through the animal exhibits, taking an especially long look at the gorillas, with their almost human gazes. When Emma's arms got tired, the other three kids took turns pushing her wheelchair.

At the entrance to the reptile house, Brittany balked. "I hate snakes," she said.

Christine glanced at Andrew. Did he know this about his daughter? Was that one of the things that he'd missed out on during his deployment? "Maybe we can just wait here," she said. "Is that okay with you, Andrew?"

"Sure." He held the door open and the other three went inside.

Christine and Brittany settled on a bench.

"Are you my dad's new girlfriend?" she asked.

"What? No! We went to the same school. We're old friends." And yet she felt that there was a spark between them.

It had been such a long time since she'd felt even remotely attractive. In Japan, she was a large, pasty-skinned foreigner, an asexual being. Although Hideki sometimes—rarely—grabbed for her in the early hours of the morning, his attentions of late always seemed born more of instinct than a specific desire for her.

Sure, she found Andrew attractive, but what she had relished most about their encounters was the feeling that she was understood. Like her, he had gone far away and come back, different.

"My mom has a new boyfriend," Brittany went on. "He's nice. He never yells. And he buys us paper dolls and stuff."

"Your dad is nice, too," Christine said. She wanted to stick up for him, this lonely, broken man. "And he really loves you. I can tell."

She thought about what might get back to Andrew's ex-wife. Maybe it'd be better if she didn't say too much. "Hey, why don't we go have a look at the elephants?" she said. "The others will catch up."

When they'd been reunited, they all fed the giraffes, then visited the barn with the farm animals.

"*Uma*," Emma said, pointing to the horse. It was one of the few words she could pronounce.

By the time they'd seen the last of the animals, the kids were hot and cranky. They broke for ice cream in the shade near the gift shop. Andrew sat next to Christine. He leaned close so that her hair was brushing his nose. "Dinner next week?"

She felt the hum of his voice all the way to her groin. "Yes," she whispered without looking at him.

DAISUKE

Nana didn't show up at school on Monday. Daisuke was thinking maybe she'd caught that bug that was going around. He texted: "Where are you?"

"Damage control," she replied.

Daisuke: "Huh?"

Nana: "Stuff with my mom. Don't ask ...."

Two weeks before the start of the summer tournament, they found out who they'd be up against. In game one, they'd be playing Ikeda, a school in the western part of Tokushima Prefecture.

In other good news, the Tokushima Hawks and the Naruto Ninjas, two baseball powerhouses, were pitted against each other. One major foe would be taken out in the first round. Furthermore, word had it that Seiko High School's baseball team had been hit with the flu. Seiko was another private school that drew players from all over the country. They usually made it to at least the quarterfinals, if not the semi-finals. One of their pitchers had gone on to play for the Seibu Lions, a contender in Japan's professional league.

So far, their team was pretty healthy, although Junji didn't show up for school the next day, and neither did Nana. Daisuke sent her a text message to see if she was okay: "Need help?"

"Taking a mental health day," she replied. Whatever that meant.

At lunchtime, since Nana wasn't around, Daisuke ate by himself.

Just as he was lifting the lid of his bento box, Shintaro came up behind him. Maybe he didn't have anyone to talk to since

Junji was out.

Up close, Daisuke noticed that he had a nasty bruise on his jaw, a Rorschach of pain.

"What happened to your face?"

"Walked into a door," Shintaro said quickly. "So where's your girlfriend today?"

Daisuke angled his body away. "Shut up. She's not my girlfriend. You don't know anything about her."

"Sure I do." Shintaro reached over Daisuke's shoulder and grabbed a wiener out of his lunch box. Before he could say anything, Shintaro popped it into his mouth. "Her mom's a *hostess* in my dad's nightclub. And my dad says that Nana can work there as soon as she's old enough. She's been doing a little moonlighting already."

A chill went down Daisuke's back. "You're lying," he said, although he knew that what he was saying must be true. At least in part. It would explain Shintaro's attitude towards her, and the rumors swirling around the school. He probably thought that Nana was beneath him because her mother worked for his dad. But no matter what Nana's mom did for a living, Shintaro had no right to talk trash about her.

"Just shut up and mind your own business, okay?" he said.

Shintaro reached over his shoulder again, but this time Daisuke slammed the lid on his bento box so he couldn't grab anything else. Part of him wanted to punch Shintaro in the face, add some more blues and blacks to that jaw, but that was a bad idea. Better to just walk away. He picked up his lunch and headed for the lawn outside. If they got into a fight, they could both be suspended from the team.

Nana finally showed up a week later for end-of-the-semester exams. Her hair was as shiny as always, but there were dark circles under her eyes. *Because she was working late in Nakamura's bar?* No, he wouldn't let himself even think that. She wasn't that kind of girl.

When she looked up, he caught her eyes. She nodded slightly, but there was no smile. And then he thought about all the phone calls and text messages that had gone unanswered. Maybe she just didn't want to hang out with him anymore. Or maybe her mom couldn't pay her phone bills. Maybe that would be just as well. Her life was a bit more complicated than he was used to. Forget about Nana, he told himself. What with studying and practice for the summer tournament, he didn't really have time for girls. At the moment, he needed to ace this exam. He braced himself for trick questions, but it was actually pretty easy, way easier than the Japanese kanji test would be. This one was multiple choice, so he didn't have to think too hard. He finished within thirty minutes then stretched out and looked around.

Junji's mouth was moving silently as he read over something on page two. Daisuke watched as he carefully marked an answer, then paused over the next question. Shintaro, on the other hand, was staring out the window, his face crumpled into a frown. He probably hadn't studied. Daisuke remembered how in elementary school he was always forgetting his homework. Well, that was his problem.

Nana was looking straight at him.

After class, she was waiting for Daisuke outside. He could feel Shintaro's eyes on him. He almost walked past her, but she grabbed his arm.

"Meet me at the shrine at three," she said in a low voice.

He nodded.

During exam week they didn't have baseball practice. They were supposed to spend the extra time cramming.

Daisuke went home and changed out of his school uniform, ate some lunch, and then hopped onto his bicycle and hightailed it to the shrine.

Nana was already there, sitting on the stone steps. She was wearing jeans and a black T-shirt.

"My mom can't pay my tuition anymore," she blurted out.

"I'm going to have to drop out of school."

"What?" This was the last thing he would have expected her to say. "Is your mom sick or something?"

Nana snorted. "Or something. She and her boyfriend broke up, and now she's lost her job."

"Oh." He shrugged, probably no big loss there.

"He's also her boss."

"But I thought she worked at Shintaro's dad's nightclub?"

"She does. Did."

He was too stunned to respond. Did Shintaro know about his dad and Nana's mom? Did Shintaro's mom know? Maybe she found out, and that's why his dad broke up with Nana's mom. This was all starting to seem like some sleazy TV drama.

Nana didn't seem to notice that she'd freaked him out. She just kept talking: "So my mother is a total mess. She won't get out of bed, and she's drinking way too much. We won't be able to pay our bills at the end of the month at this rate."

"How about your job at Lawson's?" he asked, trying to be helpful.

"Are you kidding me? I've been using that to cover school fees. I've been trying to save up a little for Takarazuka cram school, or music lessons, but there's never much left over," she said.

He thought of the money in his bank account. But even if he handed over his life savings, it would only hold them over for a month or two. It wouldn't be anywhere near enough to pay for tuition and cram school, Takarazuka, or otherwise.

"Last year I went into the club to get my mom to sign some paper for school. I was still wearing my school uniform—you know, with the sailor collar?—and there she was, chatting up some old geezer who runs a company. He said he wanted to take me out to dinner and he'd pay me ten thousand yen for my company." Her voice was cold and monotone. Dead.

Daisuke felt his insides freezing. He didn't want to hear the next words, but it was as if he were under a spell. He couldn't get away from her or stop her from speaking.

"So I went out with him." She looked up at him, defiance written all over her. "I hated it, though. Every minute. Every second. And I swore I would never do it again. But now ...."

Shintaro's version of Future Nana snuck into his head.

Nana propped her elbows on her knees and buried her face in her hands.

"Nana, you've got to get out of this town," Daisuke said. "Go to Hyogo. Now."

She held up her hands, her empty palms. "With what? And besides, who would take care of her?"

Daisuke paused. He knew how that was, having to take care of family. And speaking of family, shouldn't her dad be taking care of her?

"Do you know where your father is?"

She shrugged. "Matsuyama, last I heard. But we don't communicate. He doesn't want anything to do with me."

"That can't be true." If he knew she was a star student at a competitive high school, he'd be proud.

"Hey, what about your grandparents? Didn't you say that they still live around here?" He realized that he had never mentioned that Takai woman in his mother's French cooking class.

She looked at him. "They haven't had anything to do with my mother and me since my dad left."

"Well, you could write them a letter," he said. "It's worth a try, isn't it?" *Better than compensated dating.*

She looked at him for a moment, then put an arm over his shoulder and squeezed. "You're so sweet. Thanks for listening."

For just a second, he felt like a hero. But he knew that he wasn't.

Sure, he wanted to help Nana, but he didn't know what to do. All he knew was that he had to get his head in the game. With final exams out of the way and summer vacation stretching before him, it was time to concentrate on the summer baseball tournament. His team was strong, but they could use all the help they could get. On game day, he tucked a temple charm—a small, embroidered packet—into his back pocket. His grandmother had given it to him a long time ago, when he was still in elementary school, for good fortune on the field. He had it with him during every major game in Atlanta, including the one where his team became regional champs. As he mounted his bike, he smelled incense coming from the family shrine. He was pretty sure his grandmother was chanting sutras for him, praying for his team's victory.

Pumped up with adrenaline, he pedaled faster than usual, in a hurry to get on the bus bound for the stadium in Tokushima City. Now that the rain had lifted, the heat and humidity of summer had moved in. Even this early in the morning it felt as if a dragon was breathing down his back.

When he arrived at the school parking lot, he saw that about half the guys had already gathered. A limo bus, hired for the day, was waiting, its engine idling.

"*Osu!*" he said in greeting.

His teammates tipped their hats.

The brass band was there, grappling with their instruments. Some volunteer parents were loading coolers of ice and cold drinks onto the bus. Daisuke saw Junji across the tarmac and nodded. He nodded back, but he kept his distance. He was wearing his uniform, and his head was shaved in solidarity, but he and most of the rest of the first-year students would be in the cheering section of the bleachers today. They had little megaphones and banners to hold up at key moments. Tomomi and Maki were holding long, colorful chains of origami cranes which would be hung in the dugout.

"Okay, guys, time to board," Coach Yamada called out, motioning toward the bus.

Before getting on, Daisuke scanned the edge of the crowd one last time. There was no reason for Nana to be there at school, during summer vacation but he was still hoping to see her. He hadn't seen her or spoken to her since their meeting. His phone calls had gone unanswered. For all he knew, she'd already dropped out of school. But he couldn't think about all that right now. He needed to get into the zone. He needed to focus.

The stadium was about twenty minutes away, in a sports park at the base of Mt. Bizan. They stashed their gear in the locker room, and went out onto the field to warm up. Their game was the first of the day. Two more would follow.

He looked up into the stands. Some guy holding a camera with a long-lens was leaning over the fence: probably a reporter from the newspaper. He could see his mother, in a skirt, holding a parasol. His sister, Momoe was in the bleachers, sitting apart with a couple of friends. There were a bunch of girls from school, all in uniform, but none of them was Nana.

He picked out Shintaro's father, sitting just above the dugout, wearing sunglasses and working a toothpick in his mouth. He was with a couple of scary-looking guys with tattoos peeking out of their shirtsleeves.

"Uchida!"

"*Hai!*" He turned at the sound of his name and ran out into the outfield to shag some flies.

At exactly nine o'clock, a siren blared. The team ran onto the field and lined up. As the national anthem blared through the loudspeakers, Daisuke felt a spark of pride. He watched the flag rising up the pole, remembering how in Atlanta, he'd never sung along to the "Star Spangled Banner," mostly because he didn't know the words. But here, he sang. "*Kimi gayo...*" And then it was time for the game to begin.

His team was first up at bat.

Inoue hit the very first pitch and made it to first. A roar went up in the stands. Tanaka, the second batter, let the first strike go by, swung at an outside ball and missed, then wound up whiffing on the third. One out. And then Sagawa pounded a line drive into left field, and Inoue made it all the way to third.

The brass band struck up "Popeye, the Sailor Man." The cheering section began to chant: "*Gan-ba-re! Gan-ba-re!*"

Only minutes into the game, and already the opposing pitcher was looking flustered. He took a moment to calm himself. Daisuke watched his shoulders hitch up as he took a deep breath. Then he hurled the ball across the plate, and Noda, their clean up guy, popped it up into deep center field.

Inoue waited for the catch, tagged third, then dashed for home. He slid into the base, beating the ball. And they were ahead, 1 – 0.

By the time Daisuke's turn at bat came up, two innings later, they'd scored another run, and the other team was still at zero. Daisuke managed a two-base hit, and crossed the finish line two batters later when Tanaka was at the plate.

Ikeda changed pitchers in the fourth inning, which was never a good sign. And the game went on like that. By the seventh inning, they'd totally humiliated them. The game was called. Final score: 9-1.

The siren sounded again and both teams lined up to bow. The guys from Ikeda were wiping at their eyes and noses. Daisuke had almost forgotten about the crying. In America, if you cried after losing a game, you were a total wuss. In Japan, crying after a loss was almost required. If you didn't show some emotion, everyone would doubt your sincerity.

Their school song was broadcast over the loudspeaker, and they all sang along. And then they bowed to the friends and class-mates and family members in the stands who had come to watch them play. The captain from Ikeda's team presented Kikawa with the chain of origami cranes that had been made for their own team. These would be hung in their dugout at the next game, a week later.

They hung around to watch the following match-up to get a sense of the competition. The Naruto Ninjas, one of the strongest teams in the prefecture, was paired up with the Tokushima Hawks. Naruto had made it all the way to the semi-finals a couple of years ago, but today, they lost in the first round. And then, of course, they burst into tears.

After the game, Daisuke and his teammates took the bus back to school for a post-game debriefing.

"Let's go celebrate," Kikawa said, once the meeting was over and their gear was stowed. "Anyone up for some noodles?"

Daisuke's stomach grumbled at the mention of food. "I am!"

A few more guys chimed in, and they agreed to bike over to an udon restaurant near school.

At three in the afternoon, the restaurant was nearly empty. The boys quickly filled up the booths. Their voices and laughter drowned out the sound of the TV on the wall. A woman Daisuke's mom's age in a white apron and kerchief brought them cups of green tea and then went around with her pad, taking orders for noodles with seaweed, noodles with tempura, and noodles with fried tofu.

At that moment, with a two-base hit behind him, a steaming bowl of noodles in front of him, and his teammates all around, Daisuke couldn't think of anyplace he'd rather be. If he were in Atlanta right then, he wouldn't even be playing baseball. The season was over. Everyone was on summer vacation, looking ahead to football. But here, they were on the brink of something big. If they won the next two games, they'd be in the semifinal. And then they'd be one game away from the championship.

After finishing his noodles, Junji came up behind him and clapped a hand on his shoulder. "Nice hit," he said.

"Thanks." Maybe this was his way of apologizing for being a jerk. As long as he didn't mention Nana, Daisuke was ready to forgive him.

Daisuke was always the last to leave baseball practice. Whenever Coach was willing to stay late, he hung around for extra batting practice. He'd worked on his bunting until it felt as natural as sneezing. Sometimes it was just Coach, him, and maybe Golden Boy Kikawa out there under the klieg lights, but then one night he found himself alone with Coach Yamada. The bats were all tucked into the canvas bags, the balls piled into the plastic crate, the batting cage dismantled and stashed in the shed.

Daisuke felt a little shy at first, but Coach stepped over to the vending machine, dropped a couple of coins in, and reached down for two cans of Pocari Sweat. He handed one to Daisuke. They sat down on a bench and Coach started asking him about Atlanta. How many hours a day had the practice sessions been? (Two.) Had he ever visited the Coca Cola Museum? (Yes, with his mom and sister. They'd checked out all the key attractions while his father worked: the Margaret Mitchell House, MLK's birthplace, the field where cannons had been fired when Hank Aaron broke Babe Ruth's record for most career home runs.)

Thinking about Atlanta made him remember Lauren, the girl he did nothing about. Coach wouldn't have missed that opportunity. He'd know how to talk to Nana.

"Can I ask you something?"

"Sure. What?"

Daisuke paused, unsure. "How did you meet your wife?"

Coach looked off into the darkness at the edge of the baseball field, then took a big gulp from his can, and laughed: a rueful sound.

"She came to teach English at the school where I worked. She couldn't speak Japanese very well, and everyone knew that I was pretty good at English, so they kind of pushed us together. You know, so she'd have someone to talk to. I guess everybody else was scared to talk to a foreigner."

Daisuke nodded. He'd been scared, too, when he first arrived in America. He remembered how large Americans had seemed, their loose movements and lumbering bodies. Everything about them was big: their voices, their emotions. Before going to the States, he'd never seen a person with black skin, at least not live, in the flesh. But he'd heard all about gangs and drive-by shootings. Friends back in Japan had warned him of the dangers lurking on the other side of the world. And then there was that exchange student, Hattori, who'd been shot on Halloween just for stepping into the wrong yard. But the guy who'd fired the gun had been white.

Eventually, Daisuke had gotten used to Americans: blacks, whites, browns, all kinds. One of his best friends over there had been a kid named Jamal who was so tall that he could dunk a basketball without even really trying. And he'd fallen in love with a girl with hair the color of marigolds.

"Where'd you take your wife?" Daisuke asked. "The first time you went out?"

"We took the cable car to the top of Mt. Bizan. Have you been up there? You can see the whole city."

"Yeah." Daisuke had been to the top of the mountain lots of times, but he'd heard that it was bad luck to take a date there, unless you wanted to break up with her. It was a jinx for lovers.

Maybe Coach knew this, too. Maybe he felt sorry for bringing her up there now. His voice became softer, almost somber. "She was different from anyone I'd ever met. She didn't care about designer handbags or broken fingernails or the wind messing up her hair. She just wanted to go to some Third World country and help people."

"But she stayed in Japan."

"No," Coach said. "She went to Thailand for a few months to work with Cambodian refugees. But then she came back." And now she was gone again. "So why all these questions? Is there some girl on your mind?"

Daisuke looked away. "Yeah." He wasn't about to say her name. Coach knew her, after all. She was in his P.E. class.

"Well, have you talked to her?"

"Yeah. We've hung out a little."

"And?"

"She's kind of intense. And she has a lot going on in her life."

Coach gave him a big pat on the back. "Women. They're too much trouble. You might as well stick to baseball for now."

CHRISTINE

It's not a date, Christine told herself. And the only reason she'd lied to her parents, her kids, was to avoid confusion. They wouldn't understand why she'd want to have dinner with a man who was not her husband. She'd told them that she was meeting a friend from high school: true enough. But when her father had said, "You gals have a good time. Your mom and I will look after the kids," she hadn't bothered to correct him.

Koji frowned as she leaned down to kiss him. He stiffened in her embrace. Something was making him suspicious. Was it the blue silk dress? The lipstick? Or maybe that was paranoia. He hadn't liked it even when she'd taken a solo trip to Walmart the other day. Emma, on the other hand, hugged her knees, rubbed her face against Christine's legs and signed "Beautiful!"

"Behave, you two," she muttered under her breath. She tossed her head, as if she could shake off the sense of guilt already accumulating and grabbed the keys to her mother's car.

Andrew was waiting on the front steps of his house when she pulled up. He motioned for her to stay put and came to the car, opened the passenger door and climbed in. Christine was oddly disappointed. She'd hoped he'd invite her inside for just a minute, even. It felt as if he was denying her access, that he didn't want her to know too much about his life. It seemed unfair after she'd shared her children with him.

"Where to?" she asked, turning to him. He smelled of soap and toothpaste. His white shirt was freshly pressed, his khaki pants impeccably creased. Christine wondered if this attention to detail was something he'd picked up in the military.

He didn't answer at first. He looked her in the eye, then took in her mouth, the gold chain at her throat, the swell of her breasts. He took a deep breath, let it out in a long shuddering sigh, and angled away. "I made reservations at Dunwoody's. It's on the river. Go down Highway One."

"I know the place," Christine said, forcing her voice to be casual. "I've driven by there before."

Clearly, they were both nervous, she thought. And they were both attracted to each other. She fought the urge to reach for his hand.

This is what she wanted to ask him: What happened over there? Did you fire your weapon? Did you kill anyone? Soldiers? Insurgents? Women and children? How many? And afterward, how did you feel? Did it break your heart? Or were you so well trained that your emotions registered nothing? How did it feel to lose your comrades-in-arms, your friends? Did you share your grief? With your wife? And what happened when you were reunited with her? Did you dream of bullets and tanks rolling through dusty streets?

She'd never really known anyone who'd been in combat. She'd never seen the damage first-hand. In Thailand, at the Cambodian refugee camp, she'd seen men who'd stepped on landmines and those who bore the scars of torture, but she'd never met the ones who'd attacked them. She'd always thought of them as monsters, and yet at one time they'd been human, too: someone's son, someone's husband, someone's brother. Like Andrew. He'd been trained to kill, but also to protect.

There was something jumpy and strange about him that she found both frightening and alluring. Most of the time she felt ill at ease herself. She no longer fit in anywhere, no longer had a true place in the world. She could recognize this in Andrew as well. He'd been transformed by battle, and now, sitting here in this restaurant, he was acting out a charade. They both were. And beyond that, she perceived his loneliness, a great, gaping need that she was compelled to fill.

He picked up the bottle and refilled her glass.

"What's the story about your husband?"

Ah. The question. How could she answer that one, when she didn't know herself? Something was broken between her and Hideki and she didn't know how to fix it. Or maybe their cultural differences were irreconcilable. Maybe they should never have gotten married in the first place.

Christine shrugged. "He's a very busy man. I hardly ever see him."

He nodded.

The waitress brought their entrees: lobster tails for her, a glistening steak for him. They were silent for a moment.

"Marriage is different in Japan," Christine said, taking up her fork. She thought of Trina, separated from her husband for nearly two years while she worked on her master's degree. And her sister-in-law, who lived in Tokushima, while her husband lived and worked on the faraway island of Hokkaido. She only saw him a few times a year. Talk about a commuter marriage. "It's not unusual for couples to live apart for years, even."

"Sounds like the military," Andrew said, sawing at his meat.

"What about you? Any chance you'll get back together with your wife?"

"Ex-wife," he corrected. "And, nope."

"What happened? If you don't mind my asking."

He shrugged. "After I came back, we didn't have anything in common any more. She was afraid of me. I have dreams sometimes ...."

"At least you spoke the same language," she murmured. "At least you had similar backgrounds." Marriage, it seemed, was pretty much impossible.

He sighed. "I miss my girls."

They finished off the wine, then ordered a dessert to share.

"Do you remember dancing with me?" Christine took a bite of cheesecake.

"When was that?"

"At our five-year class reunion." He'd been wearing Polo cologne. The song had been something corny, Air Supply, maybe.

"Did I kiss you?"

"No. Of course not."

She thought about telling him then that she'd had a crush on him, but stopped herself. None of that mattered now. They were completely different people. He'd been shattered in the desert, and she'd spent all those nights in the hospital, watching over her sick daughter. Maybe mutual trauma wasn't such a great basis for a relationship.

Even so, she thought about touching him. When they got up from the table, he touched his palm to the small of her back and she felt a frisson. They were quiet in the car, a few murmurs about the food, the clarity of the stars, and then they were pulling up in front of Andrew's house.

"Wanna come in?" he asked. "Have a cup of coffee? I've got an espresso maker in there."

Christine hesitated for just a second before killing the engine. "Sure."

She stood waiting behind him while he fit the key into the lock and then waved her inside. He'd left a lamp on. Beyond the circle of light, she saw a low table, clear of any newspapers or magazines, and a couple of matching tweedy chairs.

She bent to look at the photos displayed on the end-table: his daughters in frilly Easter dresses, their school pictures, one of him and two other soldiers in uniform, backed by desert. She picked up the frame for a closer look. One private was black, one Hispanic. Christine guessed they were in their early twenties, if not younger, on their first adventure abroad. All three men were smiling.

Andrew stood on the other side of the room, watching her. "Those guys are dead," he said. His voice was flat.

"You know, if you ever want to talk about it, I'm here," she said quietly. "I'll listen."

He shrugged.

She thought of all that horror locked up inside him: the blood, the body parts, the bombed-out buildings. People screaming and crying and the ratchet of artillery. "Do you have some sort of group? A counselor?"

"I went to group therapy for a while at the V.A. hospital, but ...."

"Maybe if you wrote stuff down," she suggested. "It helped me, when I thought my daughter was going to die." She'd kept a journal while she was volunteering at the Cambodian refugee camp, too, but she didn't want to bring that up. He clearly didn't want to talk about amputees and war.

She put the picture back down on the table and went to him, touched his shoulder.

He turned and pulled her to him by the waist. His mouth came down on hers, his hands scooped her buttocks, pressing her pelvis against his. She felt him stir, felt the nearly unbearable flare of her own desire. And then he broke away and looked into her eyes for confirmation. She nodded, let him lead her by the hand to another darkened room, to a chenille-covered bed. He yanked back the covers and laid her against the sheets. His mouth was on her breasts, teasing through silk, gently biting her nipples, and his fingers were tunneling under her skirt, into her panties, seeking.

For a second, she flashed on Hideki, his hurt silence, but she quickly pushed the image away. She conjured a mysterious woman with a bottle of wine. And then she reached down to unbutton Andrew's chinos and take him into her hand. He groaned.

She smoothed her feet along his calves, one cold and stiff through the cloth. She couldn't help wondering about etiquette. Would it be kind to suggest that he remove his artificial leg? Would he be more comfortable that way? Or was it better to let him call the shots? Or maybe they should wait to make love until she knew the answer to these questions.

He eased off her just then and worked his pants down to his

knees, then rolled onto his back. "Climb on top of me," he rasped. She thought briefly about the softness at her middle before unzipping her dress. She hadn't let anyone see her naked in a long time, not even her husband. But all bodies were imperfect. Of all people, this man knew that. She tossed her pantyhose to the floor and straddled him. She rocked and rocked until waves of pleasure rippled through her. It was only later, when she'd collapsed against him, that she realized he was crying.

DAISUKE

Daisuke tried to call Nana on her landline, but he got this record-ing telling him that the number had been disconnected. If she wasn't going to bother to reply to his texts, he'd have to go see her in person. Well, she couldn't ignore him at work, especially if her manager was hovering nearby. He'd drop by on his way to batting practice.

"I'm going to Major Sports," he shouted out to his mother.

"Be home in time for dinner," she called back. "And pick up some milk on the way."

Milk, yes! That gave him the perfect excuse to pop into Lawson's.

He grabbed his favorite bat and balanced it on the handlebars of his bicycle, pedaling as slowly as he could. After all, he didn't want Nana to think that he was a sweaty pig. It was hot, though, so damp patches had already formed under his arms by the time he got to the store.

He glanced at his reflection in the window before shoving through the door. He was tanned and lean. His hair had grown out a little, but it still looked sporty. Hey, he thought he looked pretty good, except for the sweat stains. He pressed his arms against his sides and entered the store.

She wasn't there.

The manager, a thirtysomething guy with black-framed glasses, was straightening up the magazines on the rack.

"Hi there," Daisuke said. "Can you tell me if Nana Takai is coming in today?"

He scowled. "She doesn't work here anymore."

This guy was giving off a hostile vibe. Daisuke didn't think he'd be able to get more info out of him. The milk could wait. He'd go back outside and lean against the storefront for a minute.

What happened? Did she quit? Did she decide to take his advice and run off to Hyogo to be an actress? Or? He didn't even want to think of the alternatives, that she might have dropped out of school, or that she might be working illegally in a night club. Or worse.

He considered going straight to her house, but it was in the opposite direction. Better to wait till he'd finished practicing. Better to wait till he'd had a shower. He got back on his bike and headed over to the batting center.

When he got home, he took a quick shower, changed his clothes, and made his exit again. It was time to find out what was up with Nana.

"Where are you going?" his mother called from the side of the house. She was taking the laundry down from the metal pole where it had been hung to dry.

"Um, the milk?" He'd totally forgotten that he was supposed to pick some up. "And also, I'm going to make sure Nana's okay," he said really quickly, hoping she wouldn't quite catch his words.

"What?"

"I'll be back in time for dinner!"

She stood there, holding a pile of sun-dried towels as he zoomed off down the street.

When he got to Nana's house, he saw that her bike was parked in front. The curtains were drawn. He pounded on the door and waited. No one answered.

A window slid open a couple doors down. An elderly woman peeked out at him. Daisuke nodded to her and smiled. Finally, there was a flick of the curtains, footsteps from within, and the door opened.

"Hey, Nana." Daisuke couldn't help noticing that she looked sad. Even her clothes, a baggy, faded T-shirt and jeans with holes in the knees, seemed somehow gloomy. A few pounds had dropped from her frame.

"What do you want?" Her voice was flat.

"I just came to see how you were," he said. "I stopped by Lawson's ...."

"Yeah, I don't work there anymore."

He was waiting for her to invite him in, but she held the door open just wide enough to look out at him, ready to slam it in his face at any moment.

"So, uh, did you quit?"

"No. They fired me, okay? My mother went in there when she was drunk and made a scene. So now they think I'm bad news."

Oh, wow. Both Nana and her mom were out of work. Who was going to pay for school now? Would she have to drop out? Go on welfare? He almost wished she had run away, like he'd first thought. He didn't really know what to say. This was all way beyond him. But he wanted to do something to make her happy, so without thinking too much about it, he said. "Maybe I could help you get to Atlanta. We could go together."

The door opened wider. "Wanna come inside?"

The room was tidier than he'd ever seen it. The stench of booze was gone. Now it smelled like air freshener. The curtains were still drawn, though. That was weird.

"Where's your mom?" he asked, waving his arms around.

"In the hospital. Getting dried out." Nana flopped down on a cushion and motioned for him to do the same. She curled up into a ball, her hands around her knees.

"That's good news, right?" So why didn't she seem happier?

"It might take a while," she said, starting to rock. "And in the meantime, I need help."

"Name it." Here was his chance to be a real hero.

"The social worker is looking for me. I think she wants to send me to an orphanage."

"Seriously?" His stomach dropped like an elevator, almost as if he was the one about to be sent to some special facility. He'd never been inside an orphanage, but he'd seen them in movies: skinny kids with bowls of gruel, stern headmasters, quick with the whip. Surely it wasn't like that in real life, but even so, he'd do anything he could to keep Nana out of one. But what could he do? He wanted to be her knight in shining armor, but he wasn't sure how.

Maybe he could track down her dad, who would turn out to be a nice guy, after all. Or he could earn some money so she could go to Hyogo and become an actress/singer/dancer. Or ... wait a minute. Maybe she really could go to Atlanta. He bet Coach Harris knew someone who would be willing to take her in. She could babysit. A lot of Americans wanted their kids to learn foreign languages. Their neighbors in Atlanta had a Chinese nanny who spoke only Mandarin to the little white kids she was in charge of. For all he knew, that girl had moved on or gone back to Shanghai or wherever. Maybe those kids were ready to learn Japanese.

The following afternoon, they met up at the shrine.

Nana sat on the steps below him, using his legs as a backrest. Her skin was touching his skin. He could feel the heat of her seeping into his veins and spreading all through his body.

"How's your mom?"

He felt her shrug. "I'd rather talk about something else."

He looked up into the trees, searching for a safe topic. A few leaves fluttered down and landed just in front of them.

"Swallows or BlueWave?" Nana asked, rescuing him from awkwardness.

"That's easy. BlueWave."

She twisted her body so she could look at his face. She raised her eyebrows. "Because?"

"It was Ichiro's team. Before he went to the Majors."

She made a pouty mouth, as if she was not quite convinced. "How about you?"

"What?"

"Swallows or BlueWave?"

She pulled up her legs and belted her arms around her knees, leaning away from him. Her gaze drifted away, went off into the distance. "Swallows."

"Because?" He poked her in the side, expecting a smile, at least, but she didn't respond. She was still focused on the horizon, still pouting.

Finally, she turned to him and said, "Because then I could fly away from here."

Oh, okay. She'd gone all poetic on him. "If you were a wave, you could make it all the way to Hawaii or California."

"I thought we were going to Atlanta."

Now she was being serious?

"So," she said, "tell me about all the school we'll be going to in Atlanta. Are there gangs?"

"No, of course not," he said, though he wasn't completely sure. All they heard in Japan was how dangerous America was, how people killed each other daily, how everyone was packing a pistol, at least, and maybe even carrying around automatic weapons.

Rico had told him once that his dad had a gun in case of intruders, but he'd never laid eyes on it. He'd never seen a gun outside of Kmart. He didn't want to scare Nana out of going to Atlanta, so he decided not to mention anything about guns. America had a lot to offer.

"There's a huge shopping mall called Lenox Square," he told her. He figured most girls like shopping.

She rubbed her fingers together. "Yeah, but I don't have any money."

"You could get a job at the mall!" American teachers didn't care if students worked after school; not like Japan, where every minute you weren't studying was like a black mark against your future. Americans thought it was good to have a part-time job, and that it built character.

"Or you could be a babysitter," he said, remembering his

earlier idea. "You just play with kids while the parents go out to dinner or to a movie. I've heard of girls getting ten bucks an hour for that."

"Wow."

She was silent for a moment, as if taking this all in. "What about prom? Are there dances?"

"Sure." He laughed, surprised that she knew about prom. "There are dances all the time. Prom is just the biggest one, at the end of the school year."

"Will you take me in your limo?"

His dancing was about as good as his singing. And he didn't own a tux, though he guessed most guys rented them. And renting a limo was pretty expensive, he'd heard. He'd better start saving up. "Yeah, of course. And we'll go to dinner someplace fancy with tablecloths."

"Okay, then. I'll have to teach you how to do the tango." She twisted around and gave him her most mischievous smile.

In the afternoon, Nana tagged along with him to batting practice. She was actually pretty good at connecting with the ball. Maybe they should have her on their team.

After they'd used up their cards, they got cold drinks from the vending machine in the lobby and sat on a bench to drink them.

"Okay, now you have to go with me to karaoke," she said.

He groaned. "You know I can't sing."

"I'll do all the singing. You just sit there and listen."

Well, it's not like he had anything better to do. And listening to her belt out the theme from "Cats" wouldn't be so horrible. It would be pretty nice, in fact. "Deal," he said.

They finished their drinks, went back out into the heat, and biked to Amuse Palace.

"I need you to film me," Nana said, taking a video recorder out of her backpack. "I want to make a demo to send to producers and people like that."

Geez. Why hadn't they thought of this earlier? She could join one of those girl groups and make a ton of money. She wouldn't even need a high school diploma then.

She had this tough girl vibe, but every now and then a softer version shined through. He didn't know how to say all that without totally embarrassing himself, so he settled for, "Yeah, that's a great idea. You're, um, a really good singer."

He let her warm up through the first song, another one of Hikaru Utada's hits.

For her next number, Nana chose a ballad, this time in English. She started swaying with the music and closed her eyes. Daisuke could tell that she was really getting into the song. This might be it. He carefully raised the video camera and held it on her. Her voice curled around him, then climbed toward the ceiling, raising goosebumps on his arms. He did his best to hold the camera steady. Finally, when the music had faded, and her voice had spiraled down into silence, he turned off the camera. His hands smacked together in applause.

"Wow, it was like you were possessed."

"I've been practicing that one for years," she said, suddenly shy.

He imagined her becoming rich and famous. He imagined her family coming out of the woodwork, wanting to soak up some of the limelight, wanting to claim her at last. "Where did you say your dad was again?" he asked suddenly.

Nana shrugged. "Rumor has it he's in Matsuyama."

"That's not so far." At least it was on Shikoku, the same island where they were now. They could take a bus or a train, go there and back in a day.

"Have you ever thought about looking for him?"

A storm seemed to pass over her face. "I think the question should be has he ever tried to get in touch with me? And the answer is no."

"Maybe there's a reason for that. Maybe he really wants to see you, but he's afraid you won't want to see him."

"Or maybe he's moved on."

He could be unemployed and homeless. Or a gambler. Or a criminal. He might be in jail or dead, for all Daisuke knew. Or he might be loaded and living in a large, comfortable house with a Jacuzzi and a large-screen TV. He might have a spare room done up in pink and a hole in his heart. Wouldn't he be happy to see her either way? His own flesh and blood? Maybe she was a whiny, needy little kid when he left, but now she was something else: gorgeous, brainy, and talented. He would be proud of her.

"But what if he can help you?" Daisuke asked. "Your grandmother must know where her son lives. My mom has a cooking class with her. Maybe she can find out something." It could be that his mother knew already. Her son might have come up in conversation: a weekend trip, photos in her wallet, shared souvenir treats. Most people liked to talk about their children.

Even while the idea of solving this mystery was getting him all pumped up, he felt a squeeze around his heart at the thought of losing Nana to her father. What if he wanted her to stay in Matsuyama with him? And would she even be happy there? It was in the opposite direction of Hyogo and the Takarazuka Revue.

He had a vague memory of visiting there with his family when he was little. He remembered a green street car zipping through the town, spigots dispensing orange juice, and the bathhouse where a writer, the guy whose picture appeared on the thousand-yen bill, wrote a famous novel about a cat. He hadn't been back since.

Matsuyama didn't have a professional baseball team, but there was a semi-pro franchise. Maybe he and Nana could take in a game after they found her father. At any rate, they had to go. A trip across the island had more potential than the orphanage or working in a hostess bar. It might take some time for her to become a singer.

He couldn't think of a subtle way to bring up the issue of Nana's dad with his mother, so he just spit it out a couple days later when he found her at the ironing board. "Okaasan, Nana needs to find her father. Has her grandmother ever mentioned him?"

She gave him a suspicious look. "Is that any of your business? Maybe you should keep out of it."

"I'm trying to help."

She went back to her ironing, smoothing out a shirt front, maneuvering around buttons.

He waited.

Finally, she set the iron down upright and sighed. "No, she's never mentioned her son. She doesn't talk about her family."

"Could you maybe ask?"

"Being in America made you nosy," she scoffed. "You need to learn to respect other people's privacy."

He guessed that meant no. Next stop, the internet.

He spent a couple of hours searching the Web, finally printing out a list of possible suspects. Takai was a pretty common name in Japan.

When Nana dropped by later, she tossed a folded-up piece of paper on the table.

"What's this?"

"My father's address."

"You had it all along?"

She shrugged. "I looked him up on the internet. He wasn't that hard to find."

Obviously, she really hadn't been interested in contacting him before.

"Do you want to write him a letter first?" Daisuke hoped she'd say "no." He personally thought that showing up on his doorstep would have more impact. Plus, he was really starting to look forward to this road trip with Nana.

"I think it'd be fun to go to Matsuyama," she said. "There's this island full of bunnies that I've always wanted to go to. Do you know of it?"

Bunnies? Okay, sure. As long as they were real, not a bunch

of rabbit robots hopping all over. "No, I've never heard of it," Daisuke said. "Sounds cool."

She smiled for the first time in what seemed like a decade. "Let's just go see the bunnies, then. We can decide once we get there whether to visit my father or not."

Okaasan handed him a bento bundled in printed cloth. "I made lunch for you two," she said.

Nana bowed as if his mother had just saved her life or paid her way to college. Hadn't anyone ever made a boxed lunch for her before?

"Okay, we gotta go," Daisuke said. The plan was to ride their bikes to the nearest train station, go to Tokushima City, and then hop on the first bus bound for Matsuyama. It was a three-hour ride, so they could sleep on the way.

The ground was still dewy that early in the morning. It'd be another hour or so before the air became mushy and hot. There wasn't a lot of traffic, and not a lot of people on the streets, but they passed a group of elderly men playing gateball in a little park under the highway overpass. The tock of mallets on wooden balls punctuated the singsong of early birds. The men barely noticed as they pedaled past.

A woman in a nurse's uniform waited on the train platform. They were the only other passengers. They parked and locked their bikes, slid coins into the ticket dispensary, and lined up. Pretty soon, the one-man train came rattling down the tracks. They climbed aboard. Daisuke flopped onto the green-upholstered seat, but Nana remained standing, clinging to the pole, too keyed up to relax.

"Bunnies," Daisuke reminded her. "We're just going to see the cute little bunny rabbits."

The corners of her mouth twitched, but it wasn't quite a smile. "Yeah, I know."

Daisuke looked out the window as they crossed the Yoshino River. Off to the left, where the river poured into the inland sea, the sun was working its way over the horizon. A new day began. Tokushima City was coming to life. As they came out of the station, they saw people handing out packets of tissues. A couple of deaf guys leaned against the wall, talking to each other in sign language. The buses were lined up outside, some painted with manga characters or Sudachi-kun, the city mascot with a head made of citrus fruit.

"Over there," Nana said, indicating their ride.

Daisuke followed her across the street to the bus stop. The driver stood outside the door of the parked bus with a clipboard. He nodded to them as they handed over their tickets.

In Matsuyama, they hailed a cab and gave the driver an address. The taxi pulled up in front of a beige stucco house with a tiled roof.

"Here you go," the driver said over the noise of the radio. "That'll be eight hundred yen."

Daisuke was thinking that they should ask the guy to wait at the curb, just in case, but Nana tugged him out of the back seat, shoved a thousand-yen bill at the driver, and shooed him off. "Thanks! Keep the change!"

They watched as he rounded the corner, leaving them standing there, alone, at the gate of this strange house in a town far from home.

A big black sedan with white lace curtains across the back window crouched in the driveway. It looked like the car of an important man, or at least of a guy who had money to throw around.

Nana laid a finger on the buzzer.

A dog started barking inside the house. Daisuke imagined the two of them ripped to shreds by a Doberman or some other kind of guard dog.

"Yes?" A woman's voice, sweet as honey, came on over the intercom.

"We're here to see Mr. Takai," Nana said.

"May I ask who you are?"

Nana glanced at Daisuke.

He nodded and mouthed, "Go ahead."

"I'm Nana Takai. His daughter."

There was a click as the intercom was disconnected.

"Now what?" Daisuke asked.

Nana shrugged, but her eyes were on the house, shifting from window to window, as if she was trying to figure out how to break in. "We camp out all night if we have to," she said, crossing her arms.

After a few minutes, they heard the woman's voice, now as shrill as a whistling tea kettle, and the deeper rumble of a man. The dog joined in. It sounded even bigger and more vicious than before.

Daisuke pulled out his cell phone and made sure that it was charged. He tried to remember the phone number painted on the side of the taxi that had dropped them off.

Finally, the front door opened and a man with pomaded hair and Nana's nose came down the walkway. He opened the gate. "Since you're here, you may as well come on inside."

Daisuke was sure it wasn't the welcome she was hoping for, but Nana managed to keep her chin up as she followed him up the steps and into the house. Two pairs of slippers had already been laid out. They took off their shoes, slid their feet into the slippers, and followed Nana's father into a small room with a couple of sofas and a low table. He motioned for them to sit on one side of the table, and heaved himself into the seat across from them with a big sigh.

"Well. You've gotten big," he said, leering in a not quite-fatherly way.

She crossed her arms over her chest.

"What brings you to Matsuyama?"

Nana looked slowly around the room, taking in the golf trophies, the leather-bound books in the glassed-in bookcase, the gilded clock on the wall. It looked like he enjoyed fine things.

When she didn't say anything, he dropped his fake smile. "Did your mother send you here for money? She's always trying to get money out of me."

Nana snorted softly. "Maybe because she was raising your daughter? She worked her butt off for years just so I'd have something to eat."

He reached into his pocket and pulled out his wallet. "How much do you need?"

Nana shook her head, and now Daisuke could see that tears were pooling in her eyes. He wished he could reach over and take her hand.

"Mom's in the hospital. We're about to lose our house, and I'm about to be tossed into an orphanage."

This was the part where he should say, "I'm so sorry, my daughter. Why don't you stay here and live with me?" Daisuke would miss her like crazy, but at least she'd be living in a nice house. She wouldn't have to get a job. She could keep going to school.

Instead, the guy took three crisp bills out of his wallet—thirty thousand yen, about three hundred dollars—and laid them on the table in front of her. "This should be enough to get you back home," he said. "And tell your mother to come up with a better story next time." He leaned forward, as if he was about to stand.

"Wait." This was none of his business, he knew, but he had to do something. "Everything she said is true. She doesn't even want to live with you, if that's what you're worried about. She wants to go to Atlanta for foreign study."

"Atlanta?"

"Yes. She wants to be a professional entertainer. And I really think she has a chance. Here. Listen to this." He had brought along the camcorder. He fumbled with it, until he'd brought up the clip of Nana singing in English. As soon as the song started, he handed the camera over to Nana's dad.

Amazingly, he took it from him.

Okay, so the sound quality wasn't all that great, but any fool would be able to tell that she had a gift, one that needed to be nurtured. Real Nana, beside him, looked down at her lap while her voice seeped out of the camera. Her father put on a poker face. They were all still and quiet until the video ended. He handed back the camcorder with a grunt.

Daisuke could sense the slightest shift in his behavior, a softening. Maybe he wouldn't invite them to stay for dinner, but he seemed a tiny bit more relaxed. It didn't matter, though. Nana stood, grabbed his arm, and said, "Let's get out of here." She was through the door before he could make an argument to stay.

She stomped down the street, headed for the busier district a few blocks away where they'd probably be able to find a cab.

"What's your hurry?" he asked, coming up on her heels. "I think he was impressed. Maybe he would have offered more money. Or something."

"Forget it," she said. "Let's just go see the bunnies and go home."

Near the ferry port there was a grocery store. They popped inside to buy a head of cabbage and bag of carrots for the rabbits, and some rice balls for themselves.

The dock was overrun with little kids, most of them with colorful rucksacks strapped to their backs, and identical red caps on their heads. They were probably on a preschool outing. There were also a few young women in matching green polo shirts, keeping track of the kids, and a foreign couple. The guy's T-shirt said "University of South Carolina."

A few minutes later, the ferry came chugging up to the dock. After the boat was secured and moored, and the gangway laid out, the passengers started boarding. Nana and Daisuke got on last. They sat out on the deck, under the sun. The foreigners arranged themselves nearby. The air was cooler out on the water. A slight breeze dried the sweat on the back of Daisuke's neck.

As soon as the boat started to move, the foreign guy cracked a guidebook open and started to read out loud. "In 1926, chemical weapons were secretly produced on Okunoshima." He had an American accent.

"Geez, should we really be going there?" the woman asked, scratching at a mosquito bite on her shoulder. "Maybe there are still toxic fumes floating over the island."

The guy shrugged. "Says here that we can visit the Poison Gas Museum."

"Ugh. I'll pass. Hey, do you think that's why there are so many rabbits? Maybe they're from animal experiments or something. Maybe they're mutants."

"Naw, says here that some elementary school released their pet rabbits into the wild and they proliferated."

"Well, that's what they want you to believe ...."

Nana looked from the Americans to Daisuke. "Can you understand what they're saying?" she asked in Japanese.

"Um, yeah." He didn't really want to repeat it. Hearing about the Poison Gas Museum wouldn't cheer her up much. "They're just going on about the rabbits," he said.

She perked up. "I can't wait! I bet they're so cute, and fluffy!"

Although Daisuke usually found girls shrieking *"Kawaii!"* pretty annoying, it was kind of nice to see her like this. She was usually so serious. And if adorable bunny rabbits took her mind off what had happened earlier this morning, then he was all for cuteness. This morning had pretty much sucked.

The island was only a couple of miles away. They arrived after only twenty minutes of bouncing over the waves. At first it looked like nothing but a tree-covered hump, all lush and green. There was no sign of mad scientists, or bunny rabbits, for that matter.

Nana and Daisuke were closest to the exit, so they got off before the herd of little kids. The bag of vegetables bumped against his hip.

"Look!" Nana said, as soon as they stepped off the dock. A calico-coated rabbit was already hopping up to greet them. "Well, hell-o, there!" She squatted down and scrunched up her nose.

"We better get out of the way." Daisuke motioned to the wave of kindergarteners surging toward them.

"Yeah, okay."

They started walking down the street until they come to a grassy area where a bunch of white, brown, and black rabbits were hopping around. Some were lazing in holes which they must have dug themselves. They were supposedly wild, but they were completely fearless. A few came up to Daisuke and tried to nibble the hem of his jeans. They reminded him of the deer in Nara that had tried to eat his notebook during his fifth-grade school trip.

"Ready to make friends?" Nana asked with a sparkle in her eye.

"Yeah, sure."

She reached into the bag and peeled off a couple cabbage leaves. Immediately, about five rabbits rose up on their haunches, their little noses twitching. Nana ripped the leaves into tiny pieces and flung them like confetti. Suddenly, about fifty rabbits bounded toward them. The Americans' words came back to Daisuke. Were they about to face an attack of mutant bunnies?

Nana laughed, and tossed more cabbage. "*Kawaii!*"

He shook one off his leg and dug out a carrot. He looked around till he spotted a reddish-brown rabbit, craning its neck at the edge of the group. "Here you go, boy!" He broke off the end of the carrot and tossed it within a few inches of the rabbit. He snarfed it up.

"We should have brought your grandmother," Nana said.

"Yeah, maybe next time." The white rabbits did remind him of Mon-chan, but with more personality.

They were the kind of rabbits that magicians pulled out of hats. For some reason, Daisuke thought of this later, when Nana again disappeared, like a girl on a stage—there, and then, *poof*, gone.

CHRISTINE

What she felt upon waking the next morning was guilt. Not so much about having cheated on Hideki, although there was a twinge of remorse from that, but because she had diverted her attention from her children. She had wallowed in pure, physical pleasure. For entire minutes, she had been intent on nothing but the sensations of the body.

Meanwhile, back at home, her parents' house, things hadn't been going well. Emma hadn't made it to the toilet on time and her mother had left a bottle of Febreeze out on the table along with a terse note to Christine to inform her of the damage done to the carpet.

In the morning, Koji tearfully reported that Grandma had lost her temper at the dinner table. "She got mad when I started to sing," he whimpered.

Christine sighed. She remembered all the rules, of course—no singing during meals, clean everything off your plate or you don't get dessert, elbows off the table—but she didn't always enforce them at home. In Japan, you were supposed to lift bowls and make slurping sounds while eating noodles. And people were always talking with food in their mouths.

She wandered into the kitchen and found her mother there, vigorously swiping at the counter, a deep crease between her eyes. She was clearly in a bad mood. Christine couldn't help wondering if she suspected something. Was she grumpy due to the tolls of childcare, or did she suspect that her adult, married daughter had been screwing around?

In spite of the guilt, Christine couldn't stop herself from meeting Andrew again a few nights later. She returned home after midnight and tiptoed into the foyer.

"I hope you know what you're doing." Her mother flicked on the lamp, startling her.

Suddenly, Christine was sixteen again, and past her curfew. She couldn't meet her mother's eyes.

This was the third time she'd been "out to dinner with a friend." She promised herself every time that it would be the last, but as soon as she heard his voice on the phone, she turned into a junkie in need of a fix. She couldn't wait to feel his hot breath on her bare skin, to wrap her legs around his torso, to escape into pure feeling. And the way he looked at her, the worship in his fingers as he touched her, the gratitude in his eyes as he immersed himself in her. She deserved this, if only for a little while. Couldn't she have just this?

"Your husband called twice while you were out."

Twice? That was unusual. Maybe something had happened to his mother.

"Did he leave a message?"

"Nope. Just wondered where you were."

"What did you tell him?"

"I told him you were out with a friend."

Christine nodded. She hung near the doorway, afraid that her mother would smell something: the wine on her breath, or Andrew's aftershave.

Her mother hoisted herself off the sofa in that world-weary way she had when she was overwhelmed by the stupidity of others. "You're a married woman, Christine. You shouldn't be running around. I raised you better than that."

She started down the hallway to her room. Christine could hear her father's gentle snores when she opened the door. She wondered if they'd had a talk about their tramp of a daughter. Her body was rigid, awaiting release, but her mother paused, not yet through with her scolding. "You need to think about those precious babies in there," she said, nodding toward the closed door at the end of the hall.

As if she thought of anything else. Her shame faded into anger. What was that saying? Home was the place where they have to take you in? She was in exile, even here. And now she understood that there might never again be a place where she would feel secure. Love was, after all conditional. Sure, they'd read her emails, but they had no idea what she was up against in Japan. It was easy to be white and privileged and able-bodied. It was easy to judge. But she was tired and lonely, and she wanted things to be easier for her kids.

"We'll move out. As soon as I can find a place."

She'd invested in some mutual funds before the wedding, so she had some money saved up, her "divorce money," she'd some-times joked to her friends. She'd kept it as insurance that she would never stay married to Hideki for financial reasons. Hey, Japanese women did the same thing. They skimmed money from the household and called their secret stashes "heso-kuri." The money was enough to get them started. Of course, she'd have to find a job. Get a car. A computer, so she could hook up a webcam for the kids to talk to their dad. Furniture.

"Yes. Well. I think that would be best." Her mother disap-peared behind her bedroom door.

Christine slipped into the room where her children slept. She curled her body around Emma's. "We'll be fine," she whis-pered. "We'll be fine."

"I'm so tired of being judged," Christine said. She was sitting in Andrew's kitchen. He'd invited her over for lunch, and she'd lied once again to get her parents to look after the kids. They thought she was job-hunting.

Andrew reached across the table and took her hand. "No one's judging you here." He ran his thumb over her knuckles, brushing her wedding ring.

"I know. Thanks."

"Why don't you move in here for a while? I've got a spare bedroom." It was the room where his daughters slept when they visited. She'd peeked inside once and had seen the stuffed animals arrayed on the beds, a dress-up boa draped over a chair. She'd felt a pang of loneliness on his behalf.

"That would really go over well with my parents," she muttered. And my husband, she thought, but didn't say. But it was an idea, a possible temporary solution. Maybe she could help him in some way. She could cook and clean, drive him to those group therapy classes he'd been avoiding. Not only that, but she could chase away his demons for a while, get him out of his head. And the laughter of children was a balm at even the worst of times. Their presence would be like a gift.

"If we did, it'd be just for a couple of weeks," she added. "Until I find a place." An apartment on the first floor, with wheelchair accessibility. It would have to be in a safe neighborhood, reasonably priced, preferably near a playground or park. Was there such a thing?

"And you and I, we'd have to be," she paused, concentrating for a moment on the caress of his thumb on her wrist, "chaste."

He raised his eyebrows. "Chaste?"

"Well, we can't just shack up. It would be confusing for the children. You understand, don't you?"

Admittedly, it would be confusing for her, as well. Even now, as she sat at this table having sandwiches and coffee, she was torn between longing and shame. Until she decided what she was going to do about her marriage, she had no business sleeping under the same roof as this man. She shouldn't be here right now. She knew that soon, they would go into the next room, take off their clothes, and tear into each other. It would happen like this, again and again: raw, urgent need subsuming all else. Her body craved his, like nicotine, like heroin. It was all wrong.

She gently tugged her hand away from his. "Thanks for lunch," she said.

He became still and then, and in a sudden motion, swept

his arm across the table, sending the empty plates and cups crashing to the floor.

Christine heard the shatter of glass, the tinkle of porcelain, but she couldn't take her eyes off of his face. She wasn't scared. He didn't seem angry, so much as impassioned. He leaned across the table, his face directly in front of hers, as if he were about to devour her.

"Hop up on here," he said.

"Shouldn't we close the curtains?" she whispered. They were in broad daylight. What if someone came to the door?

"Nobody's going to judge you," he said. "Not here."

They made plans to go to the beach for a sort of a trial run. Christine didn't tell her parents that she was taking the kids to the coast with Andrew, but they knew anyway. From the window, her mother watched her load duffel bags and a cooler into the rental car, her lips pursed in disapproval. She came out to hug her grandchildren good-bye, then turned to Christine with arms crossed. "Have a good trip. Don't do anything stupid."

Christine glanced at the kids, buckled up and waiting. This was hardly the time for a scene. "Thanks, Mom."

She'd managed to find a rental house on the beach with wheelchair access. It had an elevator to the second floor, and a clear view of the Atlantic Ocean. They picked up Andrew in front of his house, then set out on the three-hour drive to Folly Beach. The kids were in the back with picture books and Nintendo games. Andrew did his best to engage them. "Llamas to the left," he said, indicating a pen of animals. From time to time, he pointed out roadside goats, or a field of cotton, but for long stretches, all they could see outside was row upon row of pine trees. By the time they got to Swansea, both kids, and Andrew, had nodded off.

This is enough, Christine thought, looking over at this man, asleep against the window. Just this: someone by her side, an adult, a companion with whom to share the small wonders of the day. She was so tired of being alone.

Andrew shifted in his seat. She glanced from the road to his sleep-softened face, the shock of white-blond hair. She reached over and drew a heart with her finger on his denim-covered thigh. This is what I want, she thought. What if she didn't go back to Japan? What if she stayed here with Andrew?

The rental house would eat a chunk of her savings, money better spent on Emma's therapy sessions. Soon, her little nest egg would be gone, and the wire transfers from Hideki would hardly be enough to cover rent and food, let alone T-ball and horseback riding. She'd have to give up tutoring and find more profitable employment. And even then, they'd probably be scrimping and saving, digging for coins in the sofa cushions. For one weekend, though, she wasn't going to think about all that. She'd allow herself to wallow in fantasy.

When they got to Charleston, they parked the car and wandered around the market. Andrew pushed Emma's wheelchair, while Koji trailed behind, brooding. Christine caught a few glances from the other tourists crowding the bazaar. What did they think? That the four of them were a family? Emma and Koji looked nothing like Andrew, and with their Asian features, they barely resembled Christine. People probably thought they were adopted. For a moment, Christine wished that Hideki were there instead so that strangers would be able to make the connection between her and her children.

When the kids started to get whiny, they headed for a supermarket, picked up a bag of charcoal briquets and groceries, and made their way to the beach.

Christine chopped up lettuce for the salad while Andrew fired up the grill. The kids were in the next room watching TV. They were wiped out from all that sun and surf. Maybe for once they'd sleep through the night, without calling for a drink of water or a monster check.

This fear thing was new. Emma had never been frightened

of anything before. In some ways, it was reassuring. Christine had been worried that she was missing out on some developmental stage. But now she was wondering how to convince Emma that the house wasn't haunted, that ghosts weren't hovering near the ceiling. And she couldn't help thinking that Emma felt more secure with her father. Maybe this new anxiety was because she had been uprooted, because her family was fractured.

Now the aroma of steak came wafting through the screen door. Christine thought of Andrew at the grill, of his muscled chest, his biceps, hard as apples. He could keep them safe, couldn't he?

"Almost ready," he called.

She diced up a cucumber and a tomato and tossed them into the salad, fluffing it up with a pair of tongs.

"Kids, dinner!" she called.

She waited for the stampede to the table, but all she could hear was the murmur of the TV. Maybe they'd conked out.

But no. They were both sitting there, rapt, watching a professional baseball game.

"I thought you were watching cartoons," she said. "Since when did you start watching baseball?"

Emma looked up at her. Her index finger grazed her cheek, then she held up her thumb. "Papa." Koji reached for Emma's other hand and held it for a moment, avoiding Christine's eyes. They missed him.

Regret surged inside of her. What was she doing to these kids? They weren't about to forget their father. They would never forgive her for this. She grabbed the remote control and clicked the TV off.

"Dinner's ready," she said. Her voice was harder than she intended, but Koji got up off the floor and went to wash his hands.

That night, Christine could hear Andrew moaning in the room across the hall. He was obviously having nightmares. But of what?

She lay there, listening to him, and the waves and the creaking of old wood, stricken with insomnia. She couldn't help thinking that the sleep of men was somehow fraught, especially for the ones who were conditioned to be stoic. Men like Hideki and Andrew. When she'd been at her most desperate, at night, after a visit to the ICU, tortured by her daughter's tenuous grip on life, she'd tossed and turned for hours. But when she'd finally dropped off, she'd slept soundly. A deep, dreamless sleep.

She slid out of bed and peeked into the room where Koji and Emma slept, their arms and legs splayed. Then she shut the door softly and crept into Andrew's room. His prosthesis was leaning against the wall near the outlet, hooked up to its recharger.

Andrew was thrashing, tangled up in the sheets. Sweat shone on his bare chest and forehead.

"Andrew," she said. "Wake up. You're having a bad dream."

She knelt by the side of the bed. "Andrew!"

He jolted awake, his eyes wild, and then suddenly, his hands were at her throat.

"Andrew!" She grabbed at his wrists.

He focused on her moonlit face and his hands fell away. "Sorry," he whispered. "Come here."

Curled up against him, she could feel the pounding of his heart. She smoothed her hands over his back, holding him close until his breathing became normal again.

"Where were you?" she asked.

"Fallujah." His thumbs circled her nipples.

"Do you want to talk about it?" She could feel his erection pressing against her stomach.

"Not really." He reached under her nightgown and pulled down her panties and strummed. She came almost immediately. She had to bite her fist to keep from crying out as he plunged into her. *This*, she thought. *I only want this.*

DAISUKE

In the next game, Daisuke hit a home run and they won with a score of 7-2. Then they took on Seiko, defeating them 5-4. Some of Seiko's players were still out with the flu, so it didn't seem entirely fair, but they celebrated anyhow. Their next game, the final, was against the Tokushima Hawks.

"There's no reason we can't beat them," Coach Yamada told them after Friday's practice. "You guys put up a fine performance in that practice game this past spring. You proved that you're just as good as they are."

That was the game where Shima broke his leg, the game that determined Daisuke's future.

They were all standing around the coach, their uniforms soaked with sweat. The screech of cicadas filled the air.

"They're just kids," Coach said. "They put their uniform pants on one leg after another, just like you and me."

There were a few chuckles.

"Go home, eat your dinner, and get a good night's sleep. I'll see you here tomorrow at seven a.m."

They doffed their caps, bowed, and scattered toward their bikes.

The next morning, when they ran onto the field for pre-game practice, Daisuke saw that the stadium bleachers were packed. He looked up into the crowd and picked out his mother, his grandmother, and his sister. His dad hadn't bothered to come. He saw lots of kids that he knew from school, and a guy who looked like the coach of his elementary school baseball team, but no Nana. He knew that he shouldn't be thinking about her right then. His mind should be laser-focused on the game, and nothing else, but he couldn't help it. He hadn't seen her since they'd gone to Matsuyama. A storm of questions was raging in his head. Was Nana okay? Was her mom out of the hospital? What could he do to help her get some money? What if she really did have to drop out of school?

They went through their usual drills, then Coach called them back to the bench. The dugout was now decorated with hundreds of origami cranes, the spoils of the last four teams they'd faced. They formed a ring around the coach.

"Now remember," he said. "Just relax and play like you always do. Try to enjoy the game."

They all nodded. "*Hai!*" But Daisuke could tell from the way that Sagawa was twitching, and from the wrinkles on Kikawa's forehead that they were nervous. They were all nervous. It felt like frogs were jumping around in his stomach.

"Okay, then," Coach said. "Go get 'em!"

The siren blared. They ran onto the field, fell into formation, and bowed. And then it was time to play.

Daisuke struck out his first time at bat. His second, he popped a fly to center. The game went back and forth, until they were down 7-6 with only two innings to go. At the top of the eighth, as Daisuke was on deck warming up, he glanced up at his mother and grandmother in the stands. He rested his bat on his shoulder and scanned the spectators again.

Wild applause broke out. The sound jerked his attention back to the game. Abe had managed to get onto first. So now they had the tying runner on base, with one out. A victory, a championship, and a trip to the all-Japan tournament at Koshien were within reach.

He took a deep breath, swung the bat a couple more times, tapped twice on his helmet for good luck, and stepped up to the plate. He glanced over at the dugout. Coach touched the bill of his cap, his chest, his left shoulder. He wanted him to bunt.

A sacrifice bunt would move the runner to second, and then, with luck, the next batter could send him home. It was a cautious move.

"Baseball is a game of probability," Coach always said. Probably the runner would make it to second if he bunted well. But if he swung, anything could happen.

He nodded, then waited for the pitch. It came flying, high and outside. He let it go. Ball one.

And then, he looked up to his left, and there she was. Nana. She was wearing a pink mini-dress and sunglasses, leaning over the rail as if she was trying to tell him something. He couldn't see her eyes, but he knew she was watching him, waiting for him to be a hero. He could hit the ball. He could do it for her.

When that ball came across the plate, he'd swing like Hank Aaron. Like Ichiro. He'd blast that ball into space. It'd be like the Bobcats vs. the Eagles all over again, this time on Japanese soil. He'd win this game and take them to the National Tournament. College coaches and pro scouts would come calling. His dad would be proud. And Nana would be amazed.

Daisuke looked into the pitcher's eyes, saw the determination there. They scowled at each other for a moment, and then he went into his wind-up.

The ball came shooting toward him. He swung.

CHRISTINE

The evening began like the one before, or the one before that: kids sprawled in front of the TV, Andrew nursing a beer on the deck, Christine rattling pans in the kitchen.

There was a pound of fresh shrimp stinking up the counter, waiting to be peeled and deveined. Christine was thinking of how she'd marinate it in vinegar and oil and herbs and thread it on skewers with onions and pepper. Then they'd toss it on the grill with corn on the cob.

The air was still, the waves only knee-high. Outside, a little further down the beach, a group of college kids were playing volleyball. Their shouts and laughter rang out. Seagulls circled and dipped. From time to time, they heard firecrackers, probably leftover from the Fourth of July.

Christine picked up the first shrimp, peeled it down to pink flesh. She picked up a knife and slid the blade along the black vein. In the next room, Emma cried out, a reaction to something on the TV.

She wondered if she should go check on the kids, make sure they weren't watching something disturbing, something violent, when the sliding glass door opened and Andrew stepped inside. She could tell right away that he was agitated. He held his shoulders back, tense like a cat, and his forehead was slick with sweat. His eyes flickered back and forth seeing ... what? The striped wallpaper? The linoleum squares? The mound of sea-smelling shrimp? The sands of a desert in Iraq?

Christine slowly moved the knife into the sink, out of view. She set a plate on top of it.

"Andrew," she said softly. "Andrew, it's me. Christine. We're at the beach."

He was muttering now, words she didn't understand, and she wondered if he was speaking Arabic or if those were Army words or something else. His hands clenched and flexed, clenched and flexed, and then he grabbed the glass vase on the table with both hands and smashed it to the floor.

Christine saw the pool of water, the scattered stems and blossoms, the shards of glass. She thought of her children's small, bare feet, those precious feet. For a moment she could think of nothing else.

And then, Koji's voice: "What happened?" His footsteps. His surprised face, in the doorway.

Andrew was grabbing at her arm now, pulling her toward him, and she could feel the glass stinging and shredding her feet, grinding into her soles.

"Koji, get Emma out!" she yelled. "Go, go!"

Andrew muzzled her with his palm, pulled his other arm against her throat.

Koji stood there, unmoving, his eyes full of fear.

"Go!" she tried to say. She told him with her eyes, but he stood there watching. For minutes, it seemed. Hours. Days. And then she was being thrown against the wall, slamming to the floor, her feet slippery with blood. Fists like baseballs pounding into her body.

She could hear her children crying. Both of them. The TV in the next room. The slam of the door. Andrew's heavy breathing. *Please don't hurt them. Please don't hurt them. Oh, God, don't let anything happen to them. I'll do anything you say.* A scream. Those college kids down the beach, laughing. Firecrackers. Seagulls.

HIDEKI

Daisuke didn't bunt.

Hideki had given the sign, knowing that the kid wasn't doing so well against this particular pitcher. Plus, he was nervous. Anyone would be, their first time in a tournament final. If Daisuke had obeyed the sign, they might have been able to get a runner on second, which would have put them in scoring position. Or they might have been able to at least stabilize the game until their ace slugger came up in the batting order again. They could have then tied the game, going into the ninth. But Daisuke didn't bunt. He swung. Hard. And he connected with the ball. It shot straight into the shortstop's mitt, and the shortstop had then fired the ball to first, and they'd tagged out the runner. Double play.

He betrayed me. That was his first thought. Then, *we are not going to Koshien.*

In spite of everything, they managed to hold off the other team in the bottom of the eighth inning and score one run in the ninth to bring the game into extra innings. But he'd had to change pitchers. Kikawa was showing signs of fatigue, and he didn't want to ruin the kid's arm. They lost for good in the twelfth. Everyone started crying: Daisuke, Kikawa, all the other players, the girls in the stands, parents, probably, as well. His own eyes burned with tears.

"It's just a game," Christine would have told him had she been there. It's what she always said.

But she didn't understand. Having lost the game, they had lost their future. Sure, they'd get jobs. Some of them would go to college, some would go to work in their families' fields, harvesting rice and sweet potatoes. A few of them might venture to the big city, but most would return home. They'd get married, have kids, go to work, drink beer, play mah johng, watch TV. They would be ordinary, and that shiny promise, that hint of greatness, would fade.

He felt like the Wizard of Oz. He'd promised to bestow great gifts—courage, heart, a straight path to glory—but in the end, he'd proven himself to be human, incapable. He was the wizened guy behind the screen. A failure.

For the rest of their lives, they would remember the arc of that ball, the glare of the sun, the soft thud as it hit the ground. The memory would stir up yearning and sorrow, and this moment would become a turning point, the very moment when all of their lives could have become different.

If they'd won that game, and made it to Koshien, Inoue would have been able to go to college in Osaka. Takata would have been able to get a job in the company of his choice. And if Kikawa had gone on to perform well in that fabled arena, he might have snared a contract. Koshien was where dreams came true. Ichiro Suzuki, Hideo Nomo, Hideki Irabu: they'd all first captured the nation's imagination in this sea-scented stadium amid the rush of trains.

He would be in mourning for the next couple of weeks. Then, he would buck up, put together a new team, and start thinking about the autumn tournament.

"Come on, Coach," Inoue's father said later, when they were packing up to go home. "Time to drown our sorrows."

He was so drunk when he got home, he could hardly make it through the door. The message light was blinking on the answering machine. Probably Christine. Most people he knew called him on his cell phone. In fact, he'd already fielded over a dozen calls from friends and colleagues offering their condolences. He pushed play. Some guy speaking English. Wait. It was his father-in-law. Something about the hospital. One of his kids? No, he'd mentioned Christine. Hideki gripped the table, then sank down in a chair. Had she been in some kind of accident? What was going on? The next message was from Koji, speaking in Japanese. "Mommy's friend beat her up. She's got broken bones." What? None of it made sense. He was too drunk to understand, and what time was it anyway on the East Coast of America? He put his head down just for a moment and passed out.

DAISUKE

When it was all over, when they were gathered back at school, ready for the post mortem, Coach Yamada bowed his head for a moment and said, "I know it hurts to lose, but you have nothing to be ashamed of." He looked his players in the eye, everyone but Daisuke, and said a few more words about their fighting spirit, the improvements they'd made over the season, good wishes for the future. The third-year students would have to wait until after graduation to play again, if then.

Coach Yamada wasn't the only one giving Daisuke the cold shoulder. His teammates evaded him as well. He knew that when they gathered later at a ramen shop to rehash the game, he wouldn't be among them. He wasn't invited. Only the catcher bothered to speak to him at all. "You messed up, bro," he said, chucking him on the shoulder. "It's gonna take a lot of laps around the field before Coach forgives you. *A lot* of laps." Then he took off on his bike, trailing behind the others.

Daisuke lingered, awash in shame and regret. He knew there was now little chance he'd be playing in the autumn tournament.

"Uchida!"

He turned at the sound of his name. Coach stood there, glowering. "Yes, sir?"

"Don't bother coming to practice next week. You'd better think long and hard about what you did today. If you don't want to follow my directions, then you might be better off starting your own team."

"Yes, sir."

The only thing that could save this day was seeing Nana.

Daisuke went to find her. Amazingly, it wasn't too hard. She was sitting on her doorstep, as if she expected him. "Tough luck, huh?" she said.

He didn't want to talk about the game. "Where have you been?" He hopped off his bicycle and sat down beside her, still wearing his dirt-stained uniform.

"I moved to Hyogo," she said, averting her eyes. "I'm going to a cram school for people who want to try out for the Takarazuka Revue."

He could tell that she was lying, but he didn't want to hear the truth. He knew that she'd dropped out of Tokushima Kita High School and she wasn't coming back. She would never sit in front of him in homeroom again. He felt a knot form in his throat and for just a moment, he imagined flinging himself against her and sobbing into her pink skirt. He'd lost the game, the girl, and the respect of his teammates. On top of that, his father hadn't bothered to show up. What else did he have to lose?

Nana laid her hand on his cheek. "Daisuke-kun," she whispered, the way that she now probably whispered to old men in some hostess bar. "Everything is going to be all right. *Ganbatte, ne*?"

CHRISTINE

Christine's eyelids flickered open. She saw the I.V. pole, the line snaking into her vein. Unfamiliar beige walls. She tried to move her hand, but it was too heavy. Her head was full of cotton. She was thirsty.

"*Mizu o kudasai*," she croaked.

"What did you say, honey?" Her mother's voice.

And then images seeped into her mind: Andrew's fists coming at her, Koji's frightened eyes. She tried to sit up. "Where's Emma? Where's Koji?"

Her mother leaned over her and gently pushed her shoulders down, against the bed. "Shh. They're fine. They're with your dad. We'll bring them in when you're feeling a little better."

"Water, please," she said, this time in English.

"Okay, honey. Let me just go tell the nurse you woke up."

She turned her head and caught a glimpse of her face in the chrome bar alongside the bed. Her eyes were masked in purple. A bandage striped her cheek. She ran her tongue over her teeth: they were all there.

Her mother came back with the nurse. "There's a gentleman here to see you," the woman said.

"Who?"

Before she could answer, a police officer entered the room. He was holding his cap under his arm. "Pardon me, ma'am. I know you're not feeling too well right now, but I'd like to ask you a few questions."

This was about Andrew, she realized. He must have been arrested, or they were thinking about arresting him. "Please," she said. "I don't want to press charges. Just get him some help."

The officer hovered, uncertainly. He'd probably heard battered women utter the same thing before. And then maybe he'd been called to their houses again six months letter to investigate a homicide. "Do you need a list of shelters?"

"No," she said. She wouldn't be seeing him again. Andrew wasn't a stalker, it wasn't like that. "He needs help. Get him a doctor."

"Well, okay, ma'am. If you need anything, here's my card." He put it on the bedside table and backed out the door. The nurse followed him.

Her mother cranked the bed into an incline and poured water from a plastic hospital issue pitcher into a cup. "Here you go."

"How long has it been?"

"A couple days," she said. "The doctors said you'll be all right. Your nose might be a little crooked, but there was no brain damage."

"Well, thank God for that." But there would be other kinds of damage, she knew. Her children, for example. They must have been scared to death. They'd need therapy. And Hideki. He'd find out about her affair. There's no way that she could lie about a thing like this. There were witnesses. Koji would talk.

"My husband ...."

"Oh, he'll be here later. Your dad's going to pick him up at the airport tonight."

"That's not possible," she said. It was the middle of the summer tournament. He would never leave his team during such a crucial time. He'd probably lose his job or be demoted.

"You'll see him soon. Now, I think you should rest."

HIDEKI

Standing in the doorway of her hospital room, Hideki remembered how surprised and grateful he'd felt when Christine had returned to Japan. They'd gone out for a drink and she'd talked about Thailand, but he'd hardly heard a word. She came back for me, he'd thought, staring at her white hands as they fluttered like doves. Not long after, he'd written a letter to her parents declaring his intentions.

"I promise I will do my best to take care of your daughter," he'd written. "I will make her happy."

He sometimes imagined what their lives would be like if Christine had continued on her world tour. If, after the Cambodian refugee camp, she'd gone on to India as planned, and then worked her way through Africa, on up to Europe, before flying back to America. Maybe she would have met some other guy, a charming Parisian or a fellow backpacker from the States. Maybe he would have gone along with his mother's matchmaking efforts. He might have married someone like Daisuke's mother, a woman who smiled and bowed and kept whatever discontent she felt locked away.

But he hadn't. He had married Christine, and they'd had two children, and he'd left her all alone. He'd failed to make her happy. He'd broken his promises.

In the spring, he would be transferred to another school. A few months later, he would drive his daughter from Tokushima to Fukuoka, a seven-hour journey by car, to meet with the famous orthopedic surgeon he had seen on TV. The doctor would tell him that Emma was not a candidate for surgery. Emma, the famous doctor said, would never walk unassisted. On that same day, the baseball team that Hideki had coached until April would win the prefectural championship, and a ticket to Koshien, under their new coach. Hideki would come to understand that there was no such thing as pure joy, that even the greatest happiness was tarnished somehow, temporary, but worth striving for all the same.

He didn't know any of this as he stood over his wife's hospital bed, staring down at her purple, swollen face. She didn't look like the woman he had fallen in love with, a principled woman who would never have cheated on her husband.

Her eyes were closed, and he considered stepping away from her, undetected. He could take his children back to Japan or leave them behind and start a new life.

Christine's eyelids fluttered open. "You're here."

He nodded.

"The kids?"

"They're fine. I saw them earlier."

She reached out to him. He hesitated for a moment before clasping her hand between his two.

"I'm sorry," she said. Tears slid from the corners of her eyes.

She had so many things to be sorry for that he wasn't sure what she was apologizing about. He didn't want to hear the details. Maybe if he wasn't forced to imagine her betrayal, all that had happened that summer, he would be able to forgive her.

"I'm sorry, too," he said. "Hey, you know, Koji was your hero. He dragged Emma out of that beach house and ran for help."

"He's so timid." Her voice was barely a whisper.

"Not as timid as we thought. He's actually very brave."

Emma and Koji hadn't been in to see her yet. Christine's parents thought that the sight of her would frighten them. They were probably right, but those kids had been through worse. They were tough. He'd bring them in the next day.

He tugged a tissue from the box beside Christine's bed and dabbed at her tears. "Come home, okay? Please come home."

END

ACKNOWLEDGEMENTS

Back in 2008, Ira Wood, the editor and publisher of my first novel said, "Why don't you write a novel about Japanese baseball?" Thus, the idea for this book came about. *The Baseball Widow* was over ten years in the making, and at many times I thought it would never see the light of day. However, after an encouraging word from here and there, and due to my own attraction to the story, I kept returning to it. Some of the earliest readers of this novel may not even remember having read it, but I would like to thank them anyway, especially Louise Nakanishi-Lind, Katherine Barrett, Helene Dunbar, Caron Knauer, and Leza Lowitz. I'm also grateful for feedback from my cohort in the University of British Columbia's Optional Residency MFA Program, where I shared some chapters, and to my instructors Nancy Lee and Annabel Lyon. A big thanks to Wendy Jones Nakanishi, Karen McGee, Trevor Raichura of *Hanshin Tigers English News*, Kevin Chong, and Eric Madeen for their additional input and support.

Parts of this novel were previously published in somewhat different form in magazines and journals, and in my short story collection *The Beautiful One Has Come*. I am grateful to the editors of *Literary Mama, Ars Medica, Wingspan, Tales from a Small Planet, Anak Sastra, The Font, MiNUS TiDES International, Wordgathering,* and *The Best Asian Short Stories 2017,* where those sections first appeared.

My baseball coach husband responded good-naturedly to endless queries about Japanese high school baseball, as did my son. For research, I watched the excellent documentary *Kokoyaku: High School Baseball* by Kenneth Eng, and read books and articles by Robert Whiting, including *You Gotta Have Wa* and *The Meaning of Ichiro*, both of which I highly recommend, and of course I spent many hours watching the National High School Baseball Tournament at Koshien on TV. My late mother-in-law shared her parasol with me when we sat in the stands watching local teams play.

Finally, I am deeply grateful to my intrepid publisher Nancy Cleary and her team, who bring passion and enthusiasm to every project. Thanks for making this dream come true.

PRAISE FOR SUZANNE KAMATA

On *Squeaky Wheels: Travels with my Daughter by Train, Plane, Metro, Tuk-tuk and Wheelchair*

"*Squeaky Wheels* is a thoroughly enjoyable, frank mother and daughter tale of self-discovery that dishes up plenty of captivating travel inspiration along the way." —*Pink Pangea*

"By the end of the book, a fresh addition to expat Asian memoirs, the trip becomes more than just about art, travel, and independence, but also about how Kamata sees her daughter grow and become an independent young woman with friends, interests, and travels of her own." —*Asian Review of Books*

"It's a book that reaffirmed my faith in humanity. Kamata manages to remain profoundly human and avoids the dreaded 'inspirational' story, yet still crafts characters we care deeply about." —*Mom Egg Review*

"*Squeaky Wheels* ... vividly immersed me in Japanese daily life (education, social mores, food, high and low culture, parenting) from the perspective of an American mother raising a biracial child in Tokushima."
—**Claire Fontaine**, Co-author of *Come Back: A Mother and Daughter's Journey Through Hell and Back* and *Have Mother, Will Travel: A Mother and Daughter Discover Themselves, Each Other, and the World*

"*Squeaky Wheels* is a beautiful record of a mother's journey with her wheelchair-using daughter around the world. You'll love travelling with Suzanne and Lilia in Japan, America, France and beyond, exploring art, culture, food and life. More than a travelogue, however, it's a moving odyssey of a mother's determination to give her daughter room to dream, create, and be herself without barriers of any kind. With honesty, humour, insight and courage, *Squeaky Wheels* shows us that the best part of travel is always coming home to ourselves."

—**Leza Lowitz**, Author of *In Search of the Sun: One Woman's Quest to Find Family in Japan*

"Thoroughly engaging, with much to say about what it means to parent fearlessly. Life presents obstacles, but you don't know which can be overcome without taking risks, and the fine balance between toughing it out and learning to accept help can't be learned until you're out there, pushing the limits. Bravo to Suzanne."

— **Jane Bernstein**, Author of *Rachel in the World: A Memoir* and *The Face Tells the Secret*

"Kamata's vivid descriptions, razor-sharp sense of humor and willingness to open her heart and innermost thoughts to us makes this a delightful read from beginning to end."

— *Tokyo Weekender*

On *The Mermaids of Lake Michigan*

"In this intricately woven coming-of-age tale, Kamata explores destiny and regret...with tantalizing glimpses of a scandalous shipwreck-diving great-grandmother."

—*Publishers Weekly*

"Kamata's coming-of-age story mixes bits of magical realism with the trials of growing up in the 1970s suburban Midwest...this quick read may interest fans of Jodi Picoult or Kazuo Ishiguro."

—*Library Journal*

"A water-loving girl struggles to find her place on land in this novel. A lyrical, compelling coming-of-age story with magical elements."

—*Kirkus Reviews*

On *The Beautiful One Has Come: Stories*

"It's clear that Kamata deeply understands the questions her characters grapple with emotionally, as well as the intimate details of day-to-day life in Japan" —*ForeWord Reviews*

"Kamata provides a refreshing alternative, one that focuses on female protagonists, but which also looks at daily lives, both the mundane and the spectacular." —*Asian Review of Books*

"The stories...have a universal appeal but will strike a familiar note in particular with those who have spent considerable time outside their comfort zones." —**Sharona Moskowitz**, *JQ Magazine*

"[Kamata] uses finely honed powers of observation and a mastery of narrative techniques to avoid the pitfalls of pathos which might trap a less talented author."

—*Pacific Rim Review of Books*

"*The Beautiful One Has Come* poignantly shows the pains and the pleasures of living in a culture that is not your own. Kamata also illuminates the modern struggles of everyday people, showing us that perhaps foreigners are not the only ones searching for belonging in this traditional society."

—**Margaret Dilloway**, Author of *How to Be an American Housewife*

"With evocative grace, and the authority of real experience, Kamata takes us on a tour through a garden of lives which touch Japan. Each story wanders as delicately as a small stream, with jewel-like descriptions and plot points waiting to be discovered around every corner."

—**Rebecca Otowa**, Author of *At Home in Japan: A Foreign Woman's Journey of Discovery*

On *Losing Kei*

"Very affecting...The American woman in Kamata's very interesting novel runs into a number of problems once she is married into a rural Japanese family... It is a text for all of us."
—**Donald Richie, *The Japan Times***

"[Kamata] manages to move the action rapidly along without revealing too much or disclosing too little, and to keep the reader anticipating the next unexpected turn of events."
—***The Pacific Rim Review of Books***

"...an effective portrait of the agonies of mothering a child in absentia, but fortunately for Jill, its ending contains a tender affirmation of the effectiveness of hope."   —***Brain, Child***

"A gripping, entertaining yarn and a no-nonsense depiction of motherhood, expat life, and family turmoil in an eternally stranger-than-fiction land, *Losing Kei* is a formidable novel by any measure."   —***Kansai Time Out***

"Vivid atmosphere and characterization."   —***Publishers Weekly***

"An intriguing look into one woman's experience with a culture very different from her own."   —***Booklist***

CPSIA information can be obtained
at www.ICGtesting.com
Printed in the USA
BVHW072332310821
615746BV00002B/104